THE HIGHLANDER'S BRIDAL BID

Nicole Locke

MILLS & BOON

First published in Great Britain 2022
by Mills & Boon, an imprint of HarperCollins*Publishers* Ltd,
1 London Bridge Street, London, SE1 9GF

www.harpercollins.co.uk

HarperCollins*Publishers*
1st Floor, Watermarque Building,
Ringsend Road, Dublin 4, Ireland

The Highlander's Bridal Bid © 2022 Nicole Locke

ISBN: 978-0-263-30203-5

11/22

This book is produced from independently certified FSC™ paper
to ensure responsible forest management.
For more information visit: www.harpercollins.co.uk/green.

Printed and Bound in Spain using 100% Renewable Electricity
at CPI Black Print, Barcelona

I share many things with my family, DNA being the most obvious. But not so obvious is the love of reading romances, HEAs and humour. Loads of humour.

I think of all the years dressing up, of Thanksgiving dinners, and the competitive games we played. Of growing older yet, and sharing conversations and life, tears and laughter.

This book is for Diana and Michelle. It has been a gift to share not only genes, but love, and decades of time as well.

Chapter One

April 1297, Graham clan land

'It's late,' Camron of Clan Graham slurred. 'We should go to bed.'

'No,' Hamilton, his brother, mumbled. 'It's early—see how the sun is about to rise?'

Camron lifted his head from his brother's shoulder and looked to where Hamilton weakly pointed. 'It's just another campfire that hasn't died yet.'

'Ours has.' Hamilton kicked out in front of them, and Camron almost fell forward until his brother settled so he could slouch securely again.

He could feel the cold April night upon them. It was that reason why three additional fires with logs and benches were set up outside the village where Clan Graham could congregate and celebrate the return of him, his brother and others, and bid goodbye to the ones, the scouts, who would take their place on the outer reaches of their land.

He couldn't hear voices now. Did they leave hours ago or was it early like Hamilton thought?

Their fire was out. And out of all the revellers, only he and his brother sat on this log slumped against each other, holding the other up, side to side.

'We need to get to bed,' he said again.

'Not sure I have the use of my legs,' Hamilton replied.

Camron knew he didn't have use of his legs, but everyone else was gone. If he intended to leave, they needed to work. 'How much ale did we drink?'

'We're the last Graham standing,' his brother said.

They weren't standing, but he was too tired to point that fact out.

'Never bet against a Graham on drinking—you will always lose,' Hamilton continued.

'I *am* a Graham.' Camron felt like he'd heard Hamilton say such a thing before.

Maybe it had been last night. After all, that was how it started, and how most of their competitions, challenges and bets began. Since the moment they realised they looked the same, exactly the same from height to colouring to their toes, they were constantly trying to outdo each other to prove their differences.

Not to themselves, but to the clan. For himself he always felt different than Hamilton. On top of that, it was obvious…he was more reserved, whilst his brother liked to boast he was brave or bold or some other such ridiculous word. What he truly was, was a troublemaker.

When the betting happened it was usually Hamilton who started it. Camron tried to rub his forehead and missed.

'Ow,' Hamilton said. 'Why did you poke me in the eye?'

'Nothing less than you deserve,' Camron said.

'Maybe you shouldn't have drunk so much mead.'

He did? That's why his head pounded. He had drunk Seoc's mead. The man was as large as an oak and just as thick. He made the mead so that he could get drunk. It wasn't meant to be drunk by anyone else in any quantity.

'I thought we were drinking ale?'

'We were. Apparently, you wanted a headache in the morning.' Hamilton rested his head on Camron's shoulder. 'I need to sleep.'

Camron did as well. Instead, they sat on a hollow log with the mist dampening their clothes.

He didn't feel altogether cold, but he didn't know if that was because the fire that used to be at their feet recently died, if the mead coursing through him kept him numb or the heavy lump of his brother leaning against him blocked the wind.

He crossed his arms around himself. If it was cold, he'd get up. But since it wasn't…

'It's good to be back home,' Hamilton said, his voice low.

Camron startled awake—had he been asleep? Hamilton let out a snore. His own voice or his brother's, it didn't matter…the words were exactly how Camron felt.

Over the last years, the peaceful existence his clan enjoyed had been difficult to maintain.

It wasn't only because of the tensions between England and Scotland or because of King Edward and last March's Battle of Dunbar when Sir Patrick of Graham had died.

In that battle he and Hamilton had fled to the forest whilst dragging their friend Seoc behind them. Seoc had received a chest wound that had brought on a terrible fever, and almost took his life.

Peace was also interrupted by the clans around them. Most of the clans had always had some friendly rivalry. Some, like the Buchanan and the Colquhoun clans, weren't so amicable. Lately between those two there was increasing tension that not even a marriage between them had eased.

He and Hamilton had celebrated that wedding with them all, but the celebration was filled with some heavy foreboding Clan Graham didn't want anything to do with, and fortunately, he and Hamilton hadn't got involved.

The mounting strife between England and Scotland was enough to keep them occupied. Since Dunbar, regular patrols and messages to exchange information between clans were necessary if not vital to save lives.

He wondered if it was doing any good. Even now, William Wallace was intending some strike against the English. It may be in Stirling, but no battle was far enough away for anyone to be safe.

He and his brother were unmarried and well trained with the sword. As a consequence, they were the ones often sent out to communicate with other clans or to do patrols. This was the first night they, and many of their friends, were home. Hence the celebratory drinking.

And now came the almost desperate despondency he always felt. He loved being home, but there was torment here as well. A constant malady that had nothing to do with wars between countries, and everything to do with Anna, a woman he fell in love with when he was but ten.

'You sighed heavily again, brother.' Hamilton's head lifted, then resettled on his shoulder. 'You thinking about her already? We haven't even been here one full day.'

Did it matter if they were here an hour, or had been several years away? His thoughts always returned to her.

'I'll be seeing her today. Best to think about her and be prepared than round some corner and be surprised.'

'Thought I'd got you drunk enough to make it through the night,' Hamilton said with a sigh.

'Is that why you challenged us to drink so much ale?'

Hamilton sat straighter, adjusted his seat, then slumped back against him. The feeling he was just getting back in his arm numbed again.

His brother was a heavy man. Of course, the same could be said about him. Identical brown hair, identical brown eyes. Not as tall as some of their clansmen, but reported twice as strong. Not even their parents could tell them apart all the time. A fact they had often taken advantage of.

When he thought about their appearance, he never saw himself when he looked at his brother. If anything, he felt he was looking at the opposite of himself.

The exception was Anna, who always knew

who he was. Of course, that could be because he'd been staring at her since he was a child and couldn't ever seem to look away.

'I didn't start the ale challenge,' Hamilton said.

Hamilton always started the challenges between them…or almost always. 'How can you remember with the pounding in your head?' Camron said.

'Your head's pounding, mine's just tired.'

His whole body was tired and filled with a familiar circumspect expectancy. 'I'll see her today,' he said again.

A long pause. 'We won't be back as long as last time.'

That was why he worried. After wanting her for ever, would there ever be a point he'd have her?

He still couldn't remember why at aged ten he was out that evening so long ago. It was one of those nights where the air was thick with water, but hot. He remembered the clan had all been asleep, but the dark sky was lit with a full moon.

Wearing a short tunic, he'd got out of bed, and held out his hands to feel the moisture and see the moonbeams reflected in the beads. Fascinated by some sort of enchantment, he hadn't realised how far he'd travelled carrying the water and moonbeams until he was through a small copse of trees along the river's edge.

That's when he saw her. Alone, sitting on boulder and half turned so he could only see her profile.

Anna of Clan Graham was five years older than him, and though young, there were several potential suitors waiting. Something adults talked of but he'd never bothered to understand.

Perhaps it was the hour or the enchantment he'd carried from his bed. Maybe it was the silence broken by the gentle lapping of the water or the bright moonlight which broke over all the water until it looked like jewels scattered at her feet.

But nothing was as beautiful as the young girl-woman who was running a comb through her wet hair. With her arms uplifted, her white chemise clung to the damp curve of her back and hid the feet she'd tucked underneath her. He always thought her blue eyes were striking, but that beauty was shared by that sheet of black silken strands which rivalled any unlit night.

'You asleep again?' Hamilton said.

'I'm drunk,' Camron confessed. Hamilton already knew the story of Anna and that night so long ago. His brother wouldn't appreciate the re-telling.

'I can feel my legs now,' Hamilton said.

'You want to get up?' His brother would have to get up in order for Camron to have any chance of moving from this log they sat on.

'No,' Hamilton said.

That was…surprising. Not the answer, but the way he said it. His brother sounded reflective. His brother never reflected.

'So we stay here,' Camron answered.

'We'll be leaving again soon for the outer boundaries.'

Not even a day returned, and their thoughts continually strayed to the trials ahead. Their time here was short, but it seemed even that peace, too, would be marred with the strife elsewhere. King Edward's demands were unwanted, and seemingly unending.

'Murdag's a bold lass, isn't she?' Hamilton said. 'I'm looking forward to the next few days, I'm telling you.'

Murdag, a childhood friend, was their age and Anna's younger sister. As twins, they'd given as good as anyone when it came to games and trouble, but Murdag always had more tricks to show them. The years hadn't tamed her.

'She's the one who started the counting cups bet last night,' he groaned.

Hamilton chuckled. 'She did.'

There was admiration in his brother's voice.

That was new and needed understanding. As close as all of them were, it bore thought that none of them were yet betrothed or had families.

'She's comely,' he offered, testing his brother if his thoughts went that way. He couldn't see it, as Murdag was practically a sister to him. But then…he was never Hamilton.

Hamilton snorted. 'Especially when she brandished her goblet our way.'

Last night, Murdag was standing on a boulder, her legs apart, the fire behind her. Her challenge to them wasn't the only surprise.

'You didn't look away,' Camron admonished.

'Not a chance when she wore such a thin gown and was challenging us to a drinking duel.'

The womanly curves of Anna's younger sister were there for all to see. No doubt every man did. Except for him, as he'd been looking around for Anna, who had never shown.

'I'm in lust,' Hamilton sighed.

That wouldn't be a first.

'Let's not go there,' Camron warned. Except the look on his brother's face last night was as if he was seeing Murdag anew. He was already besotted.

'Not go there? We're there, brother. She's our age, and we've returned in time since she's unclaimed. I'm a fortunate man, I am.'

The probable reason Murdag wasn't betrothed was that there wasn't a man brave enough to tame her. The very reason Hamilton had no wife was because there was no one to tame him.

The two were far too alike; she was practically a sister, and he had to be imagining Hamilton's interest. He must be joking.

His stomach roiled. 'Why did we drink mead?'

'Because we were both still standing?' Hamilton said.

'Did Murdag drink with us?'

'She was long gone by the time you poured the sweet nectar.' Hamilton snorted. 'Seoc was still here... I think.'

He'd better have been. 'We need to get to our beds so we can sleep.'

'Too late for that. The sun rises.'

Camron peeled open his heavy lids. The darkness of night was a grey now. He'd be cursed to a day of churning bile, constant thirst and exhaustion. Maybe that would be enough distraction to avoid Anna for another day.

The pang in his chest at that thought was evidence enough his intention wouldn't hold. It was an ache to avoid her, but even more to see her and not have her.

With a slap to his thighs, Hamilton stood. 'Well, I'll call it a draw on who won, but be warned, brother, I won't back down or draw on the challenge we set for ourselves today.'

Arm tingling, his entire body protesting, Camron pushed off the log.

'Was it a bet that we can stand?' Camron said. 'Because I'll declare you the winner so I can lie down until I'm dragged out of bed by whomever dares interrupt my sleep.'

'Fine idea for you to sleep,' Hamilton said with too much glee. A sure sign he didn't drink as much of Seoc's mead as Camron had. But also a certainty that he was up something.

Camron stumbled to the nearest tree, unlaced his breeches and quickly relieved himself. 'Why the glee about when I sleep? Did you put thistles in my bed?'

With that pressing concern out of the way, he turned to his brother, who was lacing up his own breeches.

Hamilton always did that differently than him. How could no one tell them apart?

'Because whilst you sleep,' Hamilton said, 'I'll have a head start on wooing the woman I love.'

The woman he loved. Now he knew his brother jested about Murdag.

'Have a fine time,' he said, knowing he'd be better off sleeping.

'Time doesn't matter...except for you,' Hamilton said. 'Don't you believe you've waited long enough?'

There was that reflective tone again.

'What are you talking about?'

Hamilton's grin turned crooked. 'Oh, come now, you won't get out of the bet by forgetting about it. Not this one, not now. I have finally pushed you into a corner to do something, and after seeing her in that thin chemise, I'll have to be more persistent in my wooing of Murdag, too. I couldn't be the only one to notice those hips in the firelight. This is just what we need to begin.'

Did his brother want to pursue Anna's sister in truth? Something clanged inside Camron. Some warning, like a sword slap to the gut, or a fist to his temple. Hard. Jarring. Dangerous to health and well-being.

'What exactly do we need to begin?'

Hamilton grin turned to laughter before he winced. Camron felt satisfaction at that. Maybe his brother had drunk as much as him after all.

'You truly forgot about the bet?' Hamilton said. 'Oh, this is good. Far too good.'

'Tell me what bet.' He had no patience for his brother's games today when he intended to lie in his bed until evening's meal.

Hamilton wagged his finger. 'You're not getting out of it. Not this time, 'cause if you do, I'll...

tell *her* of all the maudlin years you've wished for her. No! I'll tell her we made the bet. Then she'll not want anything to do with you.'

There was only ever one *her*. 'What is it you've done?'

'Not me. You wanted this. You made the challenge,' Hamilton said.

He never made challenges…or almost always never. And he couldn't back down when his brother was this deadly serious. Though Hamilton's eyes shone with some tricks, that reflective tone was still there underneath the challenge.

'Brother…'

'Swear an oath.' Hamilton's eyes narrowed, all humour gone. 'Tell me you swear to uphold the bet. Tell me or I will ruin any chance you have with her. It's been long enough. There is no more time. You heard the council—you know what comes our way, what comes every Highlander's way.'

'Tell. Me. About. The. Bet.'

'You bet that you'd marry before me.'

'Marry before you?' Camron said. 'What are you…? Who are you to marry?'

'Murdag. I'll marry Murdag.' Hamilton gave a swift grin. 'Which is perfect, since you swore before we left again to marry her sister—'

'Anna,' Camron said.

Chapter Two

'Swing me, swing me!' Lachie exclaimed, tugging on Murdag's hand.

Her sister groaned.

'You shouldn't have drunk so much last night.' Anna of Clan Graham grabbed their younger brother's other hand, and Lachie immediately started peddling his feet, causing her sister to stumble.

When Lachie began to fall, Anna immediately reached out to help him. Only for her hand to be grabbed by her sister, who gave her a warning look.

Anna straightened and looked away. Lachie, unaware, rolled to his stomach, propped himself up and pushed himself to standing. Grinning wildly, Lachie grabbed their hands again to swing. This time Murdag widened her stance.

Lachie, Lachlan, was much younger than both

of them. Ten years to her twenty-six, and Murdag in the middle at twenty-one. Lachie was their mother's last child, and all the more precious because she'd died in birthing him.

They never knew if their mother noticed her son's crooked left foot. Something they'd bound with linen and whittled branches. It got better, but never fully straightened like his other foot.

It didn't slow down his spirit, however. No, the only thing that did that was acknowledging his foot and helping him. Something some of her clan still did, despite the private conversations and the begging to do otherwise.

Run, swing. Run, swing. Lachie was getting too big and heavy for this game, but as long as he asked, Anna and her sister would do it.

'How's the head doing?' she teased.

'Better than my stomach.' Murdag released her hand, shook it and grabbed Lachie's once again. 'You should have been there last night. They set up three bonfires and most of our friends had returned. Seoc, the twins…'

'I'd rather stay home.' Anna looked pointedly down at their brother.

The last time barrels of ale were opened, and additional fires were set, Lachie had tripped and fallen. His burns since then had turned to scars. Ever since, she intended to keep him away until his growing exuberance matched some caution. Unfortunately, she feared his caution was as finite as Murdag's.

'Father came home early,' Anna said.

'I came—' Murdag said. 'Wait, there was something he told me to tell you.'

'What was it?' Anna waited, but when Murdag shrugged, unable to recall, she added, 'Apparently, you didn't come home early enough.'

Murdag scoffed. 'I was home before the others…'

'Stumbled home, you mean,' Anna bit out and realised her tone of voice sounded bitter.

Murdag stopped swinging, and Anna stopped walking. Lachie tugged at them both, but they didn't move, and he didn't let go.

Instead, secured again, he leaned forward, then back.

Anna glanced at her sister, who eyed her carefully. An apology was needed. She didn't resent staying home with Lachie; she enjoyed time with her brother very much. When she was being honest with herself, she knew she used him as an excuse to stay away from the rest of the clan. She didn't feel comfortable in those situations any more. Not like she did when she was younger.

'I hope it was fun,' she said, trying to soften her last comment. 'It's just that I worry about you.'

Murdag shook off Lachie's hand. 'Brother, you must do something else before my arm falls off.'

Lachie clenched her hand even more until Murdag gently punched him in the arm.

'Ow!' Lachie laughed.

'You want more?' Murdag said. 'Or will you run?'

Shaking off Anna's hand, Lachie unevenly ran away.

Anna's heart broke when he ran in the opposite direction of the other boys playing with sticks and rocks.

When he was younger, they all played together. But as they grew the other boys could do more, and Lachie couldn't keep up with them. Now her brother was mostly ignored. She feared about taunting too, but Lachie never confessed to it. His expressions, however, weren't as frequently happy as they had once been.

'Well?' Murdag said. 'Do you want to talk about it…again?'

She knew what Murdag referred to, or rather, *who* she talked of: Alan of Clan Maclean. A man befriended by their friend Seoc years ago and who came for a visit three years ago. Handsome, charming, he'd swept through their Graham clan like a comet. She fell in love. Fully. Utterly. She couldn't talk about anything else. But for a little over a year now, she never wanted to talk about him again.

'I only meant that if you were drunk, and the men who were newly home took advantage—'

Anna knew she'd made a mistake when Murdag's cautionary look turned dark, but she wouldn't apologise. She had learnt a lesson with Alan, and it was one she'd try to prevent her sister from ever experiencing.

'What you mean is to warn off every man who looks my way,' Murdag said coolly.

'Is that such a terrible warning?' she said. 'I could have used that warning myself.'

'Perhaps not if it's a stranger.' Murdag clenched her jaw. 'But who, exactly, do you mistrust in Graham clan, Anna? And why do you keep hovering around Lachie? You know he wants to keep his pride and not let his foot hold him back.'

There wasn't anyone on Graham land she didn't trust; it was the Maclean who'd betrayed her and her clan. As for Lachie… 'I'm not letting his foot hold him—'

Murdag pointed. 'You're doing exactly that, and have been for too long now. When's it going to stop?'

'Maybe if I, instead of June, had been watching him by the fire that time, he wouldn't have fallen, burned himself and been scarred!'

'That was years ago. He's more sure-footed now.'

'Is he?' Anna said. 'Because I think I just saw him fall. Maybe if—'

'Maybe if, maybe if?' Murdag said, looking pained. 'This isn't about Lachie and his abilities, and you know it. We even tried to teach him to swim. When am I going to get my sister back? Yes, Alan of Clan Maclean lied to you...lied to all of us. But you keep holding on to it and wield it like a weapon at the rest of us. There are days I wonder who you are any more, and you keep pushing Lachie further away.'

They had tried to teach Lachie to swim, but she had been too scared for him and ruined it. She'd vowed not to do that again, but then she'd fallen for Alan, and his charms. It'd been so easy to fall in love with him. He was a friend of the clan, he was handsome, he'd seemed like everything she wanted. Except he was nothing but a liar. Now... everything was ruined.

She knew all this when she was feeling logical, but when she wasn't... She was all emotions, and not necessarily the right ones.

She didn't want to fight with her sister. For the last year, it seemed to be all they did. Anna knew it was her fault; she just couldn't seem to help it. There was something inside her that wouldn't let what happened to her go.

'Murdag, you know—'

'There you are!' a male voice called out.

Anna looked over her shoulder. Beileag, their friend who was closer to Murdag's age, walked quickly, her long legs taking half the time as anyone else's. Hamilton and Camron, who were flanking her, kept up well enough.

Seeing Beileag with the twins wasn't common. Alone, or with her and Murdag, Beileag was quite forceful. However, around anyone else, her friend was reserved, all because of her own mother. But that was something that could never be resolved. Not as long as Beileag's father never stood up for his daughter.

It was good to see Beileag be a bit freer, so when Hamilton waved, Anna waved and smiled back.

She already knew it was Hamilton who'd called out. Not only from the voice, which was almost identical to Camron's, but because Camron, the other twin, was the reserved one. They were closer to Murdag's age of twenty-one, younger than her twenty-six, but they were handsome in their way. It was a wonder he, or Hamilton for that matter, hadn't been betrothed yet.

Maybe they would be good for her sister or Beileag? Neither of them were for her, and that had to do with more than the fact she'd found another grey hair today.

Her father said his mother's hair had turned grey early, but that didn't matter. It was only a reminder her time was past. Though after her experience with the man she refused to think of today, she had no intention of betrothals or kisses from other men. But for Beileag…

She eyed how close Camron walked to Beileag. Was there interest there, was that why they walked with their friend? Their height was almost the same, Beileag tall and willowy, Camron striding with an easy grace that always surprised her for a man of his strength.

Something scraped across her heart at seeing these two together. Most likely a reminder of her argument just now with Murdag about how much she'd changed in the last year. Whatever she did, she wouldn't let the past ruin her friendships.

Hamilton sidled up to Murdag. 'How are you feeling today, Murdag?'

'Better than you, no doubt,' Murdag said.

When her sister gave her a quick look, Anna knew the rest of their discussion was over for now.

Hamilton gave her a winning grin. 'Oh, you

sound like you want me to be less than my fine self, lass, but alas, I am as braw as I ever was.'

'He's not,' Camron said. 'And has been blaming you all morning.'

'Me?' Murdag put her hand on her chest. 'You both accepted.'

'Accepted?' Anna said.

Murdag pursed her lips as if in jest, though her eyes were dimmer as they looked at her. 'I may have challenged the twins to a drinking game.'

'She climbed that large boulder, and everything.' Beileag clenched her hands.

The boulder would have required someone to lift her up there, or for her to have her rear in the air before she made it to the top. 'You climbed that boulder?' Anna said.

'How else was I to be heard?' Murdag protested.

Anna wanted to argue, but not in front of everyone. Still. Her sister would always be bold and take risks, but the twins were famous for their challenges, bets and out-drinking their entire clan. 'No one beats them when they drink ale.'

'No one beats *me*,' Camron said.

'I think you mean me,' Hamilton chuckled.

Camron rolled his eyes, but along the way, they snagged over hers.

If she imagined they held a little longer, it

was only that…in her thoughts. When he'd been a child Camron had stared at her and everyone talked of it. She'd thought it rather sweet, though she didn't understand it. But as he got older she caught him at it less and less, and during her time with Alan it had stopped completely.

So her thinking he was looking at her now couldn't be true, unless he noticed her grey hair like she did.

'They've been gone for months and months,' Murdag said. 'I was hoping to catch up.'

'Not a chance,' Hamilton said. 'But it was entertaining you tried.'

'Entertaining?' Murdag said. 'I kept up with you until Camron suggested mead.'

Camron made some choked sound. '*I* suggested Seoc's mead?'

Anna was as shocked as he was. Camron, with his steady watchful brown eyes, increasing the challenge? He was the one who usually helped in the aftermath of Hamilton's jests.

Hamilton elbowed him in the ribs. 'Everyone was going to sleep, we were still up, and you thought the mead would settle the bet.'

'Never again,' Camron said fervently.

'That's what you say now.' Hamilton laughed.

Everyone had an easy camaraderie, a shared memory of last night. There was a pang in her heart which Anna tried to dismiss. It was only her raised emotions because of her argument with her sister.

She'd missed their welcome home. The old Anna would have been right there with her sister—granted, probably right there telling her not to do it, but she would have been around other people.

But she wasn't the old Anna; she was the older and wiser Anna, the one who wouldn't get fooled by anyone again. And wouldn't put herself at the mercy of rowdy crowds with knowing smirks and pitying eyes.

It was past her time for all that as well. Her friends, her sister, were all younger than her and should be betrothed by now. She would take care of their father as he aged, and Lachie until he grew up, and it would all be as it should. She just needed this uneasiness of the past year to be gone.

'Oh!' Murdag placed her hand on Anna's shoulder. 'I remembered what father wanted.'

'What's Padrig up to now?' Hamilton said.

Were his eyes lingering on her sister? Murdag glanced at him and then back to her. But Hamilton's gaze stayed on Murdag, and Camron was still standing near Beileag.

The twins had travelled much over the past years with training, learning the land, negotiations and relations with surrounding clans. Every time they returned they were a bit different. Now they were here, and maybe matters were about to change even more than she thought. She couldn't see Hamilton and Murdag together, they were too much the same, but that didn't mean they wouldn't.

And Beileag's and Camron's arms were at their sides, but if one looked closely it appeared the backs of their hands were almost touching. Maybe there was interest there too.

Again that restlessness reared up again. Again she squashed it down.

'Are you listening?' Murdag said in exasperation.

Shaking her thoughts, and glad Murdag was talking to her at all, Anna said, 'I'm right here.'

'Cousin Ailis is about to have another baby. Father said that our mother, if she were here, would have our heads if we hadn't seen to her niece by now. And so will Aunt Blair.'

Anna winced. Ailis of Clan Colquhoun's mother was their aunt, and she was every bit as fierce as their mother had been. She should have thought of this before now.

'I'll go with you,' Hamilton said. 'Bit of a long ride, and you'll need an escort.'

Hamilton kept glancing at Murdag as if she'd

agree at any moment. All the while Beileag looked like she was both disturbed and about to laugh, and Camron looked…cross.

Murdag just looked confused. 'Ailis is going to want Anna and her parsley broth, as well as all those other things she does when we're feeling poorly. It's why Father told me to tell her, but I forgot. I'm not the one going.'

A long pause occurred as Anna expected Hamilton to laugh and make the offer to her instead. It was the polite thing to do, but he didn't.

Well then. At least she knew how she fit into this group of friends. It was for the best, she reminded herself. She was older, she was tainted by a scandal, and maybe she should just go. In fact, with all the apparent discontent between her and everyone else, it would be best if she left.

'If one of us doesn't go, Aunt Blair will indeed be annoyed,' she said. 'I should get my preparations done then.'

'I'll go,' Camron said.

She pointed to the garden. 'I'm merely walking over there to see what—'

'I'll go with you to Colquhoun land, Anna,' Camron explained.

Of course Camron would make the offer to go after his brother had made a mess of things again.

But she could do this on her own. She wasn't someone's mess to clear up.

'It's not that far. And it's travelling on our land and then theirs. There's hardly any—'

'I'll go,' Camron reiterated, using a firm tone she'd never heard before. 'It's long enough; you don't know what you'll come across.'

That was…too much. Too awkward. She couldn't imagine travelling with the boy who'd once stared at her when she was young, and who possibly now liked her friend. Did he think to question her on Beileag's interest in him? Just the thought of such a conversation made her want to find a horse and begin the trip right then.

'I want to go tomorrow,' she said. Surely, he wouldn't be able to go that soon for reasons that didn't benefit the clan. She wasn't in on the council hut conversations, but that didn't mean she didn't know they occurred.

'Then we'll go tomorrow morning,' he replied in that even calm voice which was the antithesis to his brother's more outgoing one. But again there was an implacable tone in his voice that couldn't be denied, or crossed.

She blinked, waiting for something more familiar about him to come about. This was Camron, the younger man who stepped in whenever his brother's jests went wrong, the boy who'd once got caught with frogs in his braies, and so he felt obligated to make the offer. Or maybe he wanted to ask her about Beileag.

But… But he wasn't looking at his brother or Beileag, he was staring at her. His light brown eyes having a depth about them she'd never noticed before. A warmth that only increased the longer she stared right back.

It was too warm, too… Oh, this was not good.

Looking away, she let out the breath she held. It was all nonsense. This was the same Camron she'd known all her life, the one who'd watched her as a child as if at any moment she'd perform some miracle. And who, after Alan, didn't watch her at all.

'Yes, all right,' she agreed. 'Perhaps after first light. There's still much to do in the morning, but I would like to get started early.'

He curved his lips as if he was satisfied that she'd agreed. It suddenly made his features quite…pleasing, and she grabbed her skirts to leave.

'I'll prepare the horses, and food?' Camron said.

Since when did the men take care of the food? She felt as if he was trying to keep her there. All too aware of their audience, who were utterly attentive, she said gruffly, 'I'll do the food.'

Hamilton looked entirely content, Beileag curious. Murdag… If Murdag wasn't taking her horse and roaming the outer fields, hunting or doing something to put herself in danger, her sister was often bored. But though her sister still looked a bit peaked from last night's mead, she was as rapt as the other two.

As far as Anna was concerned there wasn't anything to be rapt about. Were they pitying her, or having a private jest behind her back? She didn't know why, but she wasn't going to stay and find out.

Running her hands down her skirts, Anna said, 'Well then, we'll meet tomorrow at my home in the morning. I'll pack what we need, stay a night, maybe two, and return.'

'I'm looking forward to it,' he said.

She swore Hamilton laughed, but he hid it in a cough. Without bidding any of them goodbye or waiting one more moment for any further words, Anna pivoted and left them behind her.

Chapter Three

$\sim\!\!\!\infty\!\!\!\sim$

Camron shook his hair as he strode out of the icy water. The sun barely shed its light across the misty grass.

This time of year, he'd prefer to bathe later in the day or at least in the rippling river; it wouldn't be as cold as this pond which still had frost clinging to the edges. But he needed a quick clean with no interruptions. After all, this morning, his Anna wanted to travel to Colquhoun land to visit her cousin and he didn't want to be late.

He was so cold his body was shaking, but merely the thought of Anna, who had been more than irritated at him for insisting on accompanying her, swept heat through him.

Oh, she was a strong woman, and her not so subtle protest on his going was only a bit of that fire that that bastard she'd fallen for had almost doused, but it was there. He should know, he'd seen it enough over the years.

Shaking himself again, he kicked off his sopping wet breeches and braies and flung them on the branch over his head. Filled with restlessness or anticipation, probably both, he needed to hurry and dress. Soon, he'd have the time needed to woo the woman he'd wanted for longer than any man should.

He'd made a bet to marry Anna?

The moment Hamilton's words had registered he'd swung at his brother's smirk. Unfortunately for them both, his coordination was off, and he'd missed. Whilst his brother was still surprised, he'd stormed off.

A few hours of reprieve before his brother was at it again, following Beileag and asking where she was going, following along until there was Murdag. By the time he saw Anna, there was no changing his direction either.

He'd made a bet to marry Anna.

Was he more surprised by himself for making the bet or…the fact he'd waited so long to claim the woman he'd always respected and admired?

He could believe the bet had happened, but did he actually make it or did Hamilton? With the night a blank, anything could be true. He wouldn't put it past his brother to have made it all up as another game or jest. Did it actually matter if the bet happened or who made it? Hamilton threatened he'd confess to Anna there was one, and if he did…any chance Camron had with Anna would be gone.

He was many things, but a coward wasn't one of them, and when it came to her he didn't want to be a coward any more.

A little over five years between them, but it might as well have been centuries. Too young when he'd first noticed her, then too unsure to pursue her. Then when that Maclean came, and he saw the joy in Anna's eyes, he'd—

But there was no Maclean any more, only him. And no more waiting.

How many times had he said that to himself? Too many moments, too many years. He'd step up, attempting to gain her notice of his intentions, but there were always interruptions, or it simply wasn't the right time. More years passing, until Dunbar, until now when there were still more battles to fight, more blood to be shed.

He'd wasted so much time; had he run out completely?

He'd made a bet to marry Anna.

Nigh on shivering, he resolved that it was time to woo her. He was here now, and over the next few days, he'd have her almost to himself. It was enough.

Ripping off his wet tunic, he slapped the linen up with the rest.

'You have to see now,' a tiny voice called out.

'There's no time. I'm leaving this morning and I have to—'

Suddenly in front of him, Lachie skidded to a halt, his balance off so he hit the tree. Without touching him, Camron reached out to make certain the boy didn't fall when Anna, the possessor of the other voice, skidded around the other tree, and then stopped.

Truly stopped, one hand braced on the trunk, one foot in front of the other.

Body utterly still, but not her arrested expression. Brows high, a warm flush starting softly on her cheeks, but turning redder as it continued down her throat.

Just stood there, as her expression went from some soft bafflement to something infinitely more lively until there was a bright sheen to her eyes.

When had he last seen her look so…alive? So here? When had she ever looked at him like that? Never.

She didn't release him from those eyes of hers,

and he wasn't looking away. He wasn't capable of it.

His thoughts had all been on her, and suddenly here she was. Her hair was one long plait today that swung over her shoulder, her gown well worn and thin in places, outlining the plumpness of her breasts, that fascinating curve of her thighs.

Her lips parted, a slight pant, and he swore he saw the tip of her tongue just there, but those lips closed again before he could be certain… When they parted once more he knew she wanted to say something to him.

He wanted, no needed, to hear it.

'You're…here,' she gasped, her gaze dropping. Instantly, released from that startled brightness, that bewitching blue spark, Camron felt a light go out.

Felt…a cool breeze where there shouldn't be.

He was naked!

Stumbling over, he snatched up his clean, dry braies he'd brought to change into and shoved them in front of him.

'What…what are you…?' she stuttered.

'Merely waking up before we go,' he said.

'You've got to see this, Anna! You've got to see!' Lachie swerved around them and ran to the pond's edge.

Lachie's childish glee skipped across the tension between them like a rock slicing on water.

'What is it I have to see?' Anna called out, not taking her eyes from Camron.

He liked that very much, as well as the slight hesitating crack in her lovely voice. Anna didn't usually lose her composure, and the fact it may be unravelling because she'd spotted more of him than expected was heartening.

Very heartening.

'I can't show you there, you have to come here!' The boy laughed.

That would prove troubling. Camron couldn't completely dress without revealing more of himself, and she couldn't move forward...without seeing more of him. They were at a standstill.

He knew, instinctually, she'd have to break it for he couldn't straighten his thoughts. Plagued with the bet and his brother's words, he couldn't quite quell the truth that she was here in front of him and looking at him.

She was...looking at him. And she wasn't stopping.

Those eyes, still wide, didn't close. She didn't pivot away. Instead, they flickered from his slicked-back hair, over his bunched muscled arms still clenching the scrap of linen to his front. Running her gaze down his legs like the small rivulets of water.

She looked to his very toes, then back up again. He felt that look in the back of his *heels*...and other places.

More dangerous places.

'Can you turn around, please,' she said at last. Her voice lost any of that hesitancy, and part of him wanted to acknowledge the bit of strength she had there.

But she was still looking at him. Looking as a woman would at a man, and something inside him eased.

All his life, he had danced around this woman. When he was too young, he'd simply watched her from afar, felt some sort of loss when she didn't join with his friends, but instead associated with others her age.

Others who'd mostly turned away when her heart was broken, and his clansmen had whispered behind her back or pitied her. This last year, since Alan left, he'd watched her retreat, then lash out at anyone who tried to help until he'd stepped further into the shadows so she wouldn't lump him in with the rest of the crowd.

And in all those months of being reserved around her, being oh, so attentive to show her he was different than that brash cur she'd given her heart to…she'd never, not once, noticed him. Not as he needed her to.

He needed her to look at him *this* way.

Lachie was shuffling along the rocks by the pond's edge behind him, and Camron knew it would be reasonable, sensible, to hide behind a tree and dress. But he wouldn't do that. He wasn't going to make it that easy for her to go back to ignoring him.

'You turn around,' he said.

'What?'

'You turn around,' he repeated. 'I was here first. Bathing, minding my own, when you burst in here.'

'It's morning,' she said. 'The whole clan is up and about doing their chores. Children are doing theirs.'

True. Never had he bathed at this spot at this particular moment of the day. There were days and times customary for all of that. But they were leaving shortly, and he'd had trouble waking up at this hour after a late night in the outer fields with Seoc and Hamilton last night. Since returning they'd all had trouble sleeping.

But Anna was before him and none of that mattered. 'The whole clan isn't here. Only you and Lachie. He doesn't care about my state, but you seem to.' And because that restlessness—or perhaps it was anticipation from the bet and Hamilton's taunt about telling her that still beat through him—he added, 'Why is it you care so much?'

She sputtered. 'Can you put some clothes on!'

All she had to do was turn around, and she wasn't.

Goose pimples raced across his skin, and he was losing the feeling in his toes that were flexing on the sandy dirt. His body was one shudder away from showing Anna his weaknesses, but there was no way whilst he was in a standoff like this that he was backing down.

'You appear to care overly much, but still you don't turn.' He dropped his voice low. 'Is there something you see that you like, my Anna?'

There, her eyes were darkening just that bit, and he felt a flash of lust hardening his flesh underneath his hands which were still clenching the inadequate bit of linen. Fully intent on talking to her more, he took a step forward toward the woman he adored—until a deep splash stopped him.

Eyes widening for altogether different reasons, Anna lifted up her skirt and raced past him.

Camron threw on his clean tunic and ran after her. The pond was small, but the benefit of it was that it was deep. Deep enough to bath a full-grown man, deep enough for a boy who couldn't swim to drown.

Anna was at the edge, her terrified eyes watching Lachlan floundering in the middle. Her movements clumsy as she tried to undo her boots.

'What are you doing!' She clenched Camron's arm, dug her fingernails in deep and yanked him toward the water. One foot in the icy water, he frowned and stopped.

Tossing her boot, she shoved him on. 'What are you waiting for?'

He was waiting for signs that Lachie was struggling, but the child had a huge grin upon his face. Was he actually attempting to swim? The boy was going about it all wrong, then... More frantic words from Anna, more struggling to get her other laces off.

He'd never seen her like this. Her hand gripping his arm for balance, her head bowed, her arse in the air. Did she even realise she used him as a tree to balance herself upon?

'Anna,' he said, and when that didn't work, he grabbed her arm and repeated her name.

But even that didn't work because she took that as extra support and her boot was almost all off.

'You fine, Lachie?' he called out.

'Yes! Is she watching yet?' The boy flopped about. He had strength, but that would wane.

Something had to be done, but for now his lass was crying and cursing him.

That wouldn't do. Oh, so carefully, he cupped her face. Her skin was soft, warm against his icy cold hands. Attempting to stop her frantic words, he pulled her upwards. She yanked his arm, but he wouldn't let go until she looked at him again.

'He's good, lass.' He dropped his hands to her shoulders. 'Look. He's swimming for you.'

She jerked out of his hold to watch her brother.

'She's looking, lad, now stop your flopping and lie on your back!'

'I'm swimming, not sleeping!' the boy protested.

'He gets that cheek from you.' Camron tilted his head to her, but kept his eyes on Lachie.

Anna grabbed his hand.

His heart stopped at the sudden unexpected touch.

'You won't be sleeping; you'll be floating,' he said. 'Now on your back, arms out, legs out.'

A squeeze to his hand as Lachie went under. 'Stay.' He shifted closer to her. Felt the edges of her skirts wrap around her bare legs.

Up popped Lachlan.

'Kick with your legs, no arms, just your legs— now flop on your back,' Camron encouraged.

Down went Lachlan again, and again he bobbed back up.

'He's going to drown,' Anna whispered.

'No, he won't. He'll get this.' Anna was leaning into him, her eyes intent, but he took no pleasure in her touch because she was clearly worried.

She worried for everyone, and he loved that protective side of her, though many argued with him otherwise. And in truth over the last year he had seen and been told how her protective side had—

'I'm going after him.'

'Still your legs. Now do your arms like this!' he called out to the boy.

'What are you doing?' she asked. 'He's not even looking this way.'

'He can hear me,' he said. 'His head's above water. Give him a chance.'

'I wanted to show you that I could swim before you go,' Lachie cried out, his little body bobbing, his eyes staring straight at the spring sky.

'Ach, that you have, lad,' Camron said. 'And a fine way of doing it, with a great big splash.'

Lachie laughed.

'Not so funny when you worry your sister,' Camron added. Anna's hand trembled in his, and he knew it wasn't from the cold. Lachie needed to prove himself to his sister, and soon.

Lachie stopped his gentle kicking, sank and sputtered up again. 'Sorry!'

'Face and toes up. Lie still on top!' he instructed.

Lachie sank again.

Anna's beseeching eyes swung to Camron.

'I'll get to him,' he told her. 'But have some heart, woman. That water is cold, and I just got out.'

It seemed as if his words had dunked him and Anna in that ice cold pond. For she stiffened and snapped herself away. He didn't only lose the warmth of her hand, but her leaning ever so sweetly against his side. Two more steps away, and her eyes swept over him with an irritated disdain.

'You're still not dressed?'

'I'm dressed.' He crossed his arms, aware of the slight hitch in her breath as his sole piece of clothing, one short tunic, rode up.

It was cold, and men were usually known to lose a bit of their heft. But she'd leaned against him and he had waited too long to claim this woman. And that little bit of flustered irritation, and pointed gaze, was sealing the fact no cold could affect him. In truth…there might be an increasing complication for her if she intended not to see anything more of him.

As if sensing the growing issue, Anna huffed, and turned markedly away from him. 'Lachie, come back here.'

'How am I to do that when I'm sleeping on water?' he asked.

'Use your arms!' she said.

Lachie immediately lost his coordination and sank again.

Rounding on him, Anna pointed. 'I'm in my gown, you're not fully dressed—why aren't you out there?'

'I'm not getting back in that water,' Camron said. 'He's got this.'

'I'm good!' Lachie was still staying afloat, his legs doing that slight fluttering.

'See?' Camron said.

There was a look in her eyes, something that eased just behind her worry and irritation. No time to find out what it was.

'It's cold!' the boy exclaimed.

'Just now noticing that?' Camron laughed. 'My balls fell off the moment I hit that water; yours must be made of iron.'

'Are they still in here with me!' Lachie's eyes were wide even from that distance. 'Am I swimming over them?'

'Truly!' Anna hissed. 'Do you have to?'

Camron winked. 'It's what men do, lass.'

Again that look, before she swung her gaze away. He wanted to hold her face in his hands again, peer deeply in those blue depths until he found out what that look was. After all these years of watching her, of their few smatterings of conversation he almost had memorised, of listening to her talk with others, how could she have any secrets?

'Reach one arm above your head,' Camron said. 'Now the other. You got it?'

'I do!'

'He's struggling.' She stepped closer to him.

Not touching, but he liked that she sought him for support. Though everything in him wanted to touch her, he held still. 'It's all right. We'll get him here.'

'Move your hands a little in the direction you want to go, kick along with it and you'll turn yourself towards us.'

Lachie went under again.

'I can't do this!' Anna cried out, and she marched fully clothed into the pond.

'Anna!' he called out, but it was too late; she'd reached her brother.

Lachie laughing stopped.

'Grab on to me,' she said.

'I don't want to.' Lachie punched his sister's billowing gown, then went under again.

She grabbed his arm, and the boy fought her, swallowing water.

'No! Why do you have to be so mean?' Lachie coughed. 'I'm swimming.'

'You're not, you're drowning, and I don't have time for it this morning.'

Lachie clenched Anna's shoulder. 'You ruined it!'

The happy, proud moment was gone, and now Camron faced a worried Anna and an embarrassed boy.

How could he have not seen how much she worried? Because he was expecting the Anna he still remembered, the Anna who was protective and encouraging. But that encouraging bit was missing right now. Anna was missing much of her fire since the Maclean was run off.

As Anna treaded water, and Lachie held on to her arm, Camron gave an encouraging smile to the boy, whose own expression was sullen and angry.

When they got to the edge, he held out his arms and pulled them out of the heavy water. 'That was a fine showing this morning, lad, and when I get back, we'll give it another go,' Camron said.

'Do you mean it?' Lachie stood there, his expression as sodden as his clothing.

Anna panted beside him. Drenched, she was

still impossibly beautiful to him, except for her frown…which had only increased, and that wariness and worry in those blue eyes of hers.

'Of course!' Camron said. 'You floated well, and that was your first go!'

'See, Anna! I did good! I'm going to tell Raibert!' Grabbing his clothes, Lachie hobbled off.

'I think we're done here for today.' Anna flipped her hair out of her face, and begun to wring out her skirt.

'I'd say we've caused enough damage,' he said. 'I'll get the horses ready whilst you change. We'll leave as soon as you are ready.'

'Leave?'

'To see your cousin, Ailis,' he reminded her.

One hand gripped her skirts even tighter. 'What?'

'We're still leaving this morning, aren't we?' he said. 'We're not that far behind.'

'We're not leaving together now.' Anna backed up one step, two. 'You're not… You're not safe!'

'What?'

Releasing her skirts, she said, 'I mean, this wasn't safe for him.'

He pointed off where Lachie had run. 'But he's not going with us.'

'I mean, now he thinks you'll be swimming together when you get back,' she said. 'When my mother died, I promised to my father I'd take care of him.'

Ah. He'd been young when Anna's mother had died in childbirth with Lachie, but he remembered his own family talking of it, watching Anna's family grieve and then change. Especially her.

'I know.'

'You need to let me take care of him.'

'You are.'

She pointed to the pond. 'That wasn't me taking care of him. That was you interfering and encouraging him to swim, and then you promised him you'd do it again?'

They were Grahams and they helped each other. Anna couldn't be in all places all the time, and eventually he'd be sent out again. Lachie needed to be able to swim.

'He's going to try again. You know that.'

She lifted her chin. 'So I'll teach him to swim properly. But that will be up to me. As will this journey to Colquhoun land. You just…leave me alone to get on with it.'

This went beyond her worry for her brother which they would still need to discuss. She was throwing excuses at him to stop him travelling with her. 'Not a chance. I told you I would ride with you.'

'But I don't think it's a good idea,' she said.

It had been fine yesterday, and it was a better decision today. Despite this delay it was still early enough to go. But her eyes…she was trying to get out of it, and he wanted to know the reason because if he had to guess…it was that she saw him naked. That she *saw* him. Finally.

'I already told everyone else I was taking you, too,' he said. 'Do you want to tell them why you won't travel with me? Would it be because I am not adequate company or protection?'

He watched a thousand emotions cross her beautiful face. He ached to unwrap all of them, but he'd pushed hard already, and knew she'd back away if he did it again.

In truth, if she truly didn't want him to go, didn't care at all for him in any way, she could have her say, and he'd walk away. Bet or no bet, and his long desires be damned. If she didn't want him, there was nothing more he could do.

She looked to him, to where Lachie had run off. 'I simply don't want to continue discussing Lachie with you whilst we travel, agreed? He's my responsibility, not yours.'

Her brother was growing quickly, and if Lachie asked him for help, and if Camron wanted to be part of her life, he'd eagerly take some of that responsibility as well. They could, however, figure out how to do that later.

'We won't talk of Lachie for now, then.'

Her eyes narrowed at his qualification. 'And I don't need protection.'

'No protection,' he agreed, 'only company.'

She huffed. 'You need clothes still.'

'I wasn't intending to ride naked,' he said, not hiding the relief in his tone now she was agreeing again. 'And you need clothes too. Unless you prefer we both ride without?'

When she merely gaped at him, he couldn't hold back his laugh. Ah, it would be a good day if she was still ruffled at catching him unawares whilst bathing.

'If you're still capable, I prefer clothed. Very clothed,' she bit out. Then chin firmly out, she turned and strode away. He watched her run back through the small copse of trees towards the village.

A few steps and he grabbed his clean, dry braies he'd dropped, then his fresh breeches.

He was looking forward to this journey. Only the second day of the bet, and he already had Anna all to himself.

Chapter Four

'Maybe we should have left earlier.' Anna looked up at the dark clouds threatening towards the west. This time of year, dark clouds weren't cause for concern, but the increasing wind was.

If she had sensed any storm threatening before, she would have called off the travel for another day. Perhaps even begged Murdag to go in her stead. However, when they left Graham land, it had been light grey sky, and still early enough in the morning.

It hadn't taken any time for Camron to prepare the horses with their satchels and for her to get a promise from Lachie to not swim whilst she was gone. Strangely, her father, her sister and all their friends were there to wish them a safe journey as well.

She couldn't shake the feeling they had other motives for seeing her and Camron off.

'We've made good time these last hours,' Camron said. 'And leaving when we did was worth it, no?'

Had she sounded ungrateful? In truth, she was humbled by Camron's care of Lachie this morning. Although, if she thought of it, she wasn't surprised. He was one of the few who had always been aware of her brother's pride, and his struggle with his footing.

'More than worth it,' she said. 'But when we're soaked through and die from coughing, I want it noted that I mentioned leaving earlier.'

He gave her a wide grin, and her heart flipped. When he smiled like that, it transformed his features in a way that was simply noticeable. More than noticeable. So heart-stoppingly handsome that she gaped at him until she wrenched her gaze to a spot just over his shoulder.

His very broad shoulder. One she knew had a smattering of freckles on top as if there'd been times he'd taken off his tunic and run around bare-chested...

'It's well noted, if we should die,' Camron said. 'I'll etch out some letters in the dirt so everyone knows.'

'And I'll etch out how helpful you were to Lachie,' she said.

His eyes widened, and then softened. It affected her as much as his grin did. She felt *warm*. Was there a flush to her face now? He couldn't be affecting her so.

It was Camron. Simply Camron, who looked just like his brother. Except Camron had never looked like Hamilton. To her, Hamilton wasn't even attractive. There was nothing wrong with him, but his personality was far too brash. Too much of a reminder of— No, she wouldn't think about the Maclean.

Camron also had a pleasing timbre to his voice and absorbing observant eyes. Eyes she currently felt on her. When she looked at him again, his brow grew quizzical.

'Good to see the lad grow up, is all.'

That wasn't all. 'You've been good with him.'

For a moment, she almost felt like apologising for her shortness earlier on. But she knew that only came about because of her sister arguing with her about her overprotectiveness, and the fact Lachie had yelled at her for ruining everything.

Neither of them understood she was only trying to protect them from hurt. She knew what she felt wasn't wrong. Still, Camron didn't know what was happening with Lachie or her sister or why. And in truth, he hadn't been around most of the time Alan was with her. This day would be long enough if there wasn't some ease between them as they rode to Colquhoun land.

'It's easy to do,' Camron said.

Not for everyone, and Camron deserved to know why she was concerned. 'He can't keep up, and the boys are treating him differently now.'

He huffed. 'They're good friends; they'll grow out of it.'

She had hoped so too. 'There are even adults who ignore him now. He's not a helpless infant or young and endearing any more, so—'

'Who?' Camron interrupted.

His voice had gone low, determined. It was that voice he used when he said he'd be coming with her on this trip.

'Who treats him this way?' he said again.

If she told him, would he protect her brother? She knew the answer to that, for how many times over the years had he protected his own brother?

Camron was loyal, and for one bright moment she actually wanted to tell him. To give the responsibility over to him. Camron was well respected in the clan, and they'd listen to him.

As fast as hope and relief threaded through her, so, too, did unease. Since when did she give up responsibility for anything to anyone? When did she last place her trust in someone other than her father and sister? It had been with Alan for two years, and for the last year she'd been paying a heavy price for her lack of judgement.

What could Camron do for her or her family? Nothing. She needed to remember that. What occurred this morning was a reminder of that.

'Doesn't matter,' she said dismissively.

Brows lowered, he looked to protest. When he didn't, she was surprised. Over the last year, people had had many opinions and suggestions.

Except since he didn't protest or offer anything, she didn't know what else to say, and that odd tension between them, the one she couldn't shake, increased until she felt as if she could physically feel it between them.

What was this?

She should have felt nothing as he rode at her side. Pace after pace he matched her silently until she couldn't stand it. He said nothing, didn't look her way, and yet still she felt his presence, his unspoken questions.

'I'll take care of it, Camron,' she said finally, glancing over at him until he looked her way, and his gaze did that roving thing from her covered head to her hands on the reins.

'I know you will,' he said. 'But if I'm there, and they say something about Lachie, you can't expect me to sit idly by.'

Couldn't she? How many others had, or made it worse by whispering behind Lachie's back? And yet, how many times had she seen Camron care for his brother? Maybe he understood her concerns more than others. How did she feel about that?

Too many questions!

'It won't come to that,' she said with as much conviction as she could. Maybe Camron would respect her opinions. Regardless that she'd be accompanied by him for several days, she needed to put some emotional distance between them. Even if he was protective of his brother, it didn't mean he understood how she acted with Lachie…or her sister or anyone else for that matter.

This connection or tension or whatever it was between them since this morning, or perhaps yesterday when his eyes locked with hers, shouldn't exist.

'Remember how you and Hamilton used to trip each other up to see who fell the farthest?' she said suddenly.

His brows drew in, his expression turned to a wary curiosity. He couldn't guess what she was doing, could he?

She tried to laugh. 'You two used to get into the oddest fights…but that time you tripped Hamilton into the mud and he grabbed your ankle to pull you in as well is something Murdag still laughs about!'

Camron's eyes... Half amused, half something else. Wounded, maybe? Like she'd hurt him. How could she hurt him if they were only recalling memories?

'That was long ago; we were seven then, I believe,' he said carefully.

'You were so covered in it, and I remember most of your clothing dragging—' She stopped. Had to stop. Because their clothing had been so saturated in mud the twins couldn't stand up, or maybe they were still fighting, but whatever it was, two mud-covered twin boys, without clothing, had eventually emerged from the well of mud. At the time, it had been funny. Except now—

'So you've seen me naked twice now?' Camron gave a bit of a smirk.

Her cheeks flushed. Partly because of the words, mostly because Camron's smug half-smile should have annoyed her, but instead it made that heat flare inside her.

Foolish! She should have remembered more of that day. Now all she could do was make comparisons, and since this morning was fresh in her mind and that mud incident truly was long ago, her mind simply wanted to stay on the present...

and how very naked, and very much *there*, Camron of Clan Graham had appeared to her.

Was it only this morning when she'd chased Lachie to the pond only to observe this man instead?

It was as if their roles were reversed when she couldn't keep her eyes still on merely one part of him. His dripping deep brown hair plastered against the lines of his jaw, curling around the shell of an ear. The water beading at his throat.

She'd kept staring as he'd stood there, so utterly still. As he took a great breath, his chest expanded, and upon his release those defined muscles along his stomach and hips contracted. Flexed. Inviting her eyes to continue to see all the other minute detail lower down.

He'd been wet, all over, rivulets coursing through the various defined muscled lines, and that trail of hair arrowing down.

The way her heart stopped, and her eyes registered before the rest of her what she was seeing. Skittering her gaze quickly across the full resting length of him, which should have been better or at least somewhat decent of her.

But wasn't any better because his hands had clenched and unclenched against the sides of his thighs.

His hands…those fingers! His right hand tapping out a rhythm on his bared thigh. The corded muscles engaged, solid there as if he could walk for days, or take the two strides towards her in a heartbeat.

She, who couldn't move at all, not whilst those fingers tapped against his own skin as if he played some instrument, as if he drummed out some secret message.

It was a gesture she'd seen him make all his life. It wasn't a nervous twitch—the man was the epitome of calm. It was…it was like he was counting something…but what? Over the years certainly she'd wondered, but right then? What had he needed to count then?

Because he'd stood naked in front of her. Bemusement and something like wonder in his expression. When it was her who felt those emotions. It was like she had never seen a naked man before.

She had never seen *him* naked before. And everything…everything about him wasn't expected.

It wasn't just the male definition of him; it was the texture of his skin, the freckles on the tops of his shoulders, the way the water darkened the smattering of hair on his chest, the goose pimples she could see along his arms making her wonder about the feel of them. Was he cold, but he'd looked so warm, so—

Rain hit her hands.

Flinching Anna looked around. The day had turned even darker.

Camron cursed. 'It's coming in fast and hard.'

There was nothing but wide-open fields before them. 'There's no shelter around here. The trees are too far spaced.'

'There's shelter, but it's a good way off.' The wind whipped his hair across his cheek. 'We'll need to hurry.'

Leaning forward, she urged her horse to catch up with his. They couldn't outrun this storm. This time of year, spring always clashed with winter. Now they seemed caught in some battle as the temperature dropped further and the rain slashed hard against them. Beneath her the horse shivered, and she slowed down. It wouldn't do for it to get overheated. Camron looked behind him, slowed down as well and pulled beside her. Lightning cracked across the sky.

Shouting out, Camron yanked his horse to the far right. In all the years she'd travelled to Colquhoun land, she'd never gone this way, but she had to trust that Camron, with his years of scouting, would know better.

On and on they went until she didn't know

whose land they were on any more, but the terrain changed from rolling hills to rocks, and the horses were practically crawling from low visibility by the time they reached one peak. Camron dismounted and came over to help her. Fisting her heavy sodden skirts, she fell into his arms, and he lowered her to the ground.

Quick, efficient, his hands pressing more water against her side, she felt his strength and his warmth, and shivered when he let her go.

He took the reins of both horses whilst she gathered her dress, tucking the bottom up into part of her belt. It wasn't proper, but the wool dragged heavily otherwise. When she straightened, Camron was already ahead, and when she caught up, she saw the cave he headed towards.

Entering it she expected to see no more than a temporary shelter, but there were chests along the side and firewood, with large logs for seating.

'Do you see any creatures?'

She shook her head, whilst Camron strode boldly to the back where she could barely see him, and returned to the horses.

'Seems empty,' he said. 'We'll have to watch the entrance tonight. Though the fire and our presence should be a deterrent.'

'What is this place?' she said.

'It's a cave that many Colquhouns, Buchanans and Grahams use,' Camron said.

'When they're getting along?' She tried to take in everything here; it was like a haven in the middle of a storm…literally.

'This isn't the only spot we use—' he snapped his head to the side and sneezed '—but it's the best and the closest.'

'What can I do?'

He indicated with his chin. 'Get the fire started? I'll take care of the horses.'

The horses were at the entrance of the cave where there were large logs which she guessed were for the saddles.

She headed to the back. Though the mouth of the cave was large, the day was dark, making the back of the cave dim, but she could just see a shallow pit with ash and kindling with flint to the side. Everything was dry, unlike her.

Starting the fire was quick, but it wasn't simply for them, so as it grew in strength, she added more logs.

'Thanks for throwing more on there,' Camron said. 'The horses won't come closer, but they'll need to dry out. They'll be standing a while at that entrance, and the last thing we need is any hoof care. We'll have to replace the firewood when we leave. The logs will be wet, but we can spread them out to dry.'

The rain was like a wall of water behind him. 'We'll be here a while?'

'Most likely.' He spread the horses' blankets on a long branch that was balanced near the fire. Now that there was light, she could see a mixture of crude and finer amenities. Someone had built the wooden racks for clothes or blankets, but chests meant true supplies were brought here to leave. Camron moved efficiently amongst all of it.

'You've been here before.'

He gave a curt nod. 'I've stolen enough bowls and knives from my family in the hope of making decent contributions to these chests. A time or two, bastards have stolen them. Now I check we have any before I make soup.'

He had a whole other life out here, one where he knew people she didn't. Who stole bowls and other supplies, and who made Camron laugh even when he was visibly shivering.

'It's strange…' she began.

He raised his brow and waited.

'You were here, whilst I was…' What was she saying? Something that seemed too personal, and yet was a truth. Just mentioning it, however, didn't feel like mere information. It felt like a confession or a wish.

And the way Camron stilled, he didn't take it as something idle either. 'Not so far away,' he finished for her.

Abruptly standing, she wrapped her arms around her middle. 'I can't believe this is here.'

Camron strode to the chests, swung one open. Then another. When he got to the third, he dug around, and cursed.

'No bowls?' she teased.

'No clothes. There's some braies in here, but no tunics.' He pulled out a blanket and handed it to her. 'You'll need to put this on.'

She took it. 'Put it on?'

He pointed. 'Those bare racks will hold our clothes while they dry.'

Gooseflesh rose on the back of her neck and down her arms. It was practical they changed, and yet…how many times did she catch him looking her way since the pond and feel how his gaze was almost tangible?

'I promise to look,' Camron said.

'What?'

'You're wondering whether I'll peek. All I will tell you is it's only fair.'

The word *peek* made her want to laugh, especially when Camron looked expectant.

'I came across you in the pond by accident!' she said.

He grabbed his wet tunic and pulled it off. 'I'll go first.'

She'd never seen this teasing side of Camron before. Camron was usually quiet compared to his brother, but then how would she know how he was when he was alone? This was the first time they'd been together like this.

The fire blazed, arcing warm light all throughout the cave, but it wasn't their surroundings fascinating her, it was him. It seemed as if he was teasing or tempting her as he took whatever linen was in the chest, maybe the clean braies, and swiped at his hair, his back and shoulders. All the while the yellow flames highlighted and shadowed his masculine form.

She...liked how he looked. Liked him in ways that weren't because he'd once been a boy, or a friend and neighbour. Whatever this was...desire, lust, need, want. She felt it. For him.

Outside the rain howled; the horses at the entrance pawed and snorted. She should be comforting them, and yet, she was incapable of walking away from the sight of him.

Leaning down, he pulled off his boots and set them by the fire before he unlaced his breeches and hooked his thumbs in the fabric. Only then did he snap his head up, and smirk.

Glaring at him, Anna turned around. Behind

her, Camron made some sound between laughter or disappointment, she didn't know.

'It was an accident last time I saw you,' she said.

'So you say,' he said. 'But you still didn't turn around.'

'You didn't ask, nor turn around yourself.'

A chuckle. 'No, I didn't, and so what does that say about us?'

Everything. Nothing. This time there was a reason for them to be bared before each other, and they had ample opportunity to give each other privacy. And yet…

'I'm done, your turn.'

When she turned back she didn't know what to expect. A blanket around him, certainly, but not…

'There's not a larger one?' she said through a dry throat.

'That's yours, this was the only other one left.'

Why did all these moments where he was naked feel stretched out to her? Why couldn't she move, when there were tasks to be done, horses to comfort?

His brows drew in. 'Anna, you've got to change out of those wet clothes.'

'I know.' Her body gave great wracking shakes, and she didn't know if it was entirely from the cold. She wanted him as a woman did a man, wanted him in a way she'd never felt for Alan.

His expression turned grave, and she knew that because she was still taking him in. Shouldn't his legs look comical under that little blanket, his knees knobbly? But all she could see were strong masculine thighs, the brown hair covering his legs and the thought of what that would feel like when they were against her own.

'Even if the rain let up within an hour, we won't make it to any homes whilst there's still light,' he said. 'We're here for the night.'

This was merely Camron, whom she'd known his whole life, and yet he wasn't. She couldn't make him into that boy any more; she wasn't certain she wanted to. Not when he kept his gaze steady on hers all the while his hands clutched the blanket as if he wanted to help her...or drop the blanket.

'Anna,' he growled.

She took it for the warning it was. 'I'll change.'

On a rough exhale, Camron turned his back to her.

It took her a few more moments to catch her own breath before she knew what needed to be done. Take off her sodden clothes, cover herself in an expansive blanket, sit by the fire almost naked with this Highlander. She could do it... even though her hands were trembling and she'd forgotten how to undress.

'I don't hear you,' he said.

'The laces are stuck.'

A deep pause before he said, 'I could help.'

'No, I've got it.' Almost.

He stayed turned around, but whilst she struggled with one lace, then another, she quickly learnt it didn't matter that he had his back to her because she practically felt him standing there. Saw the way his shoulders rose and fell with his breath. Saw him shift his feet, as if impatient to turn.

Once the laces were free, her gown and chemise simply plopped to the ground, and she swore he tipped back his head and groaned.

Cool air on her skin, but she felt immediately warmer, and strange simply standing naked near a man who couldn't see her. When she threw her sodden clothes over the long wood framing to dry, she thought his body shuddered.

'I'm hurrying.'

'Not fast enough.'

She almost felt like taking longer. It wasn't her fault her clothing had more lacing than his. She swiped up the slightly damp braies he'd used to dry his own skin to do her own. Then she wrapped it around her hair to wring it dry.

'Move to the other side of the fire. Please, woman, have some mercy. And put the blanket on.'

'I'm almost there.' She didn't know why he was in such a rush other than this strange tension, but that had to be because they were undressing. But between that and his teasing, it made her want to ask him about when he was a child watching her. Which was foolish because he hadn't done that in years.

There was no need for a man, for he was a man, in all ways she could see that now, to want to see her when she was older than him and it showed.

'Are you almost done?' he said. 'Now put some distance between us.'

He had kept his back to her all the time. 'How would you know I'm almost done?'

He growled. 'Shadows.'

Oh, my word. Anna gaped at the cave's wall. There, as perfect as could be, were complete outlines of horses, fire flames, great grey blobs of hanging clothes. And one man…and one woman.

'Oh!'

'Yes, oh, now can you put the damn blanket on?'

But she liked the shadowed rendition of herself. Tall, thin…no grey hair to be seen. Just her.

She couldn't explain what she did next to anyone, but her arms went up over her head, and she rolled her wrists and arms like some dancer from old.

She was taller, thinner, with extra-long limbs, but every swirl of her wrists, flutter from her fingers and rock of her hips was apparent on the wall.

When Camron spun round, his blanket flared out to show all the cave inhabitants exactly what was underneath. She shrieked and grabbed the blanket at her feet.

Chapter Five

'Too late to be hiding anything from you,' Camron said. But his Anna was doing the best she could with a half-folded blanket in front of her, covering herself.

Unfortunately, despite his words to her, she had grabbed that blanket quicker than he'd hoped. Except for one stiff rose-coloured peak of her breast for the barest of moments, he was denied everything else.

'Are you going to be dropping that now?' Holding his own blanket, he pointed at hers.

'Turn back around,' she ordered.

'I gave you enough time and warnings.' More than his heart or body had wanted to give. He knew everything she'd done was innocent, that she'd had no idea that with every twist of her body he could catch glimpses of her limbs, her hips, that dip of her waist.

When she'd grasped the linen of the braies in each hand, stretched it behind her to dry her back with one stroke and another, her breasts had swung. Each curve and tip revealed and then hidden again in shadow, revealed and hidden to the point he'd had to widen his stance and beg his body to think of anything else.

'Teased me enough, you did.'

'Teased you? It shouldn't have mattered if some—' She opened her mouth, closed it. 'You shouldn't have looked.'

'Every man would look when a woman arches her back and raises her arms above her head like that.'

He expected another retort or demand. Instead, he got an Anna who was clearly second-guessing herself as she gingerly unfurled the rough wool blanket in front of her. One who also kept her words to herself, leaving him with silence.

If he could have words with the Maclean, and dole out some violence, he would. He'd damaged this brave woman's heart. At least he was here now to make certain she raised her arms above her head as much as she wanted.

But flirting with her wasn't the way to erase her uneasiness. Though the spirit that she'd shown him, however inadvertently, was heartening. As was her flash of shyness when she realised they would both be barely covered and alone in a cave all night.

And now he was thinking too much on that.

He needed more than distractions to coax her out from whatever she hid behind when it came to him. A shield? No…something much more permanent. A castle, with a great big door and gates and ramparts. That's what his Anna had done to herself over the last year since Alan Maclean had shown his true colours.

'Hungry?' he said. 'I'm starving.'

She took a few steps back, looked to the horses. 'Should I get—?'

'I put the satchels over here.' Tightening his hold on his blanket more against the cold than decency, he strode towards the satchels. Grabbing the straps, he brought them in front of her. Keeping his body angled, he knelt and grabbed two brooches from his supplies.

'Here.' He held one up for her. 'It's not ideal, but they might keep the blankets on us whilst we eat.'

When she took it, her fingers brushed with his. Those same fingers she'd spiralled to make a pretty picture against the wall. How easy would it be to clasp that hand to tug her onto his lap?

'You're still cold,' he said. 'Go nearer to the fire, and I'll pull what we need from these.'

'I'm hardly incapable of—' She stopped.

Perhaps because he'd turned and wasn't as careful with his angles, or because she could see in his gaze how he hungered for her rather than the food he searched for, she simply gave a brief nod, and walked the few steps to the firepit where she adjusted her blanket and worked on her own brooch.

When he was done, he handed her an array of what they'd both brought, and then went to work on his own blanket, which was too short to be used as any kind of cape, so he wrapped it around his middle and pinned it. He was warmed up enough. Some more adjustment of the clothing on the wooden racks and they should be dried before they slept.

He hoped. For to remain around this woman half dressed would likely kill him. Fascinated with her colouring since he was a child, he'd watched her body change from a young woman into every fantasy he could ever think or dream of.

He pointed to the log at the top of the pit. 'Should we sit?'

Looking behind her, she stepped back and sat, adjusting the blanket one way, then the next. That blanket. As much as it covered her from neck to feet, as thick and woolly and scratchy as it probably was, it did nothing to stop his imagination.

Not when the reality was Anna's dark hair was wet and unbound to dry by the firelight, when the flames caressed across her cheeks and the hands clutched around her raston. When the long lines of her neck and the tips of her toes were visible.

Not when the bulk of the wool didn't hide the curve of her hip, or the bump of her lush bottom.

And made all the worse because to avoid the smoke of the pit, he had to sit on the same log as her. Something she'd realised before him because she had already slid to one end and arranged the food on the ground halfway between them.

'This will work, won't it?' she said.

'It's perfect.'

'It's what we brought, so it'll have to be.' She gave a soft laugh. 'For what it is.'

What it was, was perfect torture. Aware of her eyes on him, he carefully adjusted the blanket around his waist before he sat on the same log. There was plenty of space between him and the fire, and more than ample space to move freely as they bent for the food.

'You think the horses will be fine?'

The horses needed a bit more care than he'd given them. Once he had freed them of their saddles, they had both shaken the water off them… and onto him. He was actually grateful for the musty blankets to make him smell less like a stable.

'The land's dry beneath their hooves,' he said. 'We can check on them after we eat.'

Nodding, she pinched a chunk of his cheese. 'I can't believe I've lived near here for years and never knew of these caves.'

'The elders of the clans have kept the cave's location a secret on purpose,' he said. 'It's used for mostly clan business.'

She frowned. 'So not until you are…what then?'

'Not until you're old enough to hold a secret, which I can understand. I know if Hamilton or I knew of this in our youth we would have used it for other reasons.'

At the blush of her cheeks, he realised how his words had come across. What other reasons would a young man need use of a cave for other than seduction, away from prying eyes?

'So now you're telling me clan secrets?' she said after a pause.

'Suppose we're old enough to keep a secret, aren't we?' Camron coughed when he realised the ramifications of that. It was one matter to take a day journey, but their being alone together like this overnight would need to be a secret of sorts.

Yet he hadn't even thought twice about bringing her here.

'So you say. My sister would kill me if I didn't tell her about this,' she said. 'Father once helped with the birthing of a horse, and though I knew, I forgot to tell her about it. She was as understanding as could be to my face, but every morning for two weeks, I'd find one of my shoes in the stables. One. So in order to be ready for the day, I had to hop to the stable to put on the remaining shoe.'

He smiled. 'How'd you reconcile?'

'Fortunately, because I was early to the stables to finish getting clothed, I was witness to another birth and able to tell her about it.'

Camron laughed. 'She could have done far worse to you.'

'I know,' she said.

'She's older now, so maybe holding secrets wouldn't end in such vengeance.'

'That was six months ago.'

He laughed. 'Well, it'll be certain death if you don't tell her of this.'

She arched her brow. 'Especially since she could have a good ride before she got here. Secrets and horses are her favourite things. I must tell her.'

Visions of Murdag hiding Anna's clothing in the stables and a bare Anna with unbound hair

with just a blanket around her filled his mind…
and other parts of his body as well.

'Well, there's nothing for it, then.' He cleared
his throat. 'As long as she brings—'

'Bowls?' Anna quipped.

'Certainly that, as well as blankets, firewood—' he plucked at his blanket '—and clothes
with her, she's welcome.'

Her eyes went to his fingers pinching his blanket and held a bit longer. Did she want the blankets gone as much as he did?

Taking a quick bite of her bread and swallowing, she said, 'If you think any of that is a deterrent, you don't know how much my sister loves
her challenges.'

He did know. Which was why he knew, and
maybe unfairly, that she wasn't a good match for
Hamilton. His brother also liked his challenges,
maybe too much. If he and Murdag wed, who
would bring them balance? Or maybe he was
wrong on that and a relationship didn't need balance. How was he to know when the only woman
he'd ever truly wanted he'd never even kissed?
Of course, he'd made that bet to do just that, but
he didn't want to think of the bet now. What he
and Anna had, or could have, had nothing to do
with that bet.

How easily he was affected by her! He tried

to eat as she so easily did, but the food kept getting caught in his throat. The fire, food and their sitting positions were natural distractions so he shouldn't have been so aware of Anna in the cave with him, but nothing could compare to her.

Every time she bent for food or drink, a tendril of hair would fall over her shoulder, or the fire would highlight the shell of her ear or the tapering of her fine fingers. He was in agony, but it was the sweetest kind. For once he had her all to himself.

'So besides surviving your sister's revenge, what else were you up to while I was gone?'

'You know of my sister's revenge—tell me about you and your brother instead.'

His chest warmed at that. 'It'd be a tiresome conversation if I shared all the tales of Hamilton's jests, or his ideas of justice against me when he thought he was being bested.'

She brushed her hair over her shoulder. 'Can't imagine that conversation ever being dull.'

From her open expression, he knew his Anna truly wanted to know…but he wanted to kiss her. Giving up on trying to sit next to her and eat, he set his cup of ale down and stood.

'It'd certainly be a long one,' he said gruffly. 'What about you and your sister?'

'What of us?'

'You seemed to be arguing when Hamilton and I last approached you both.'

He didn't need to be looking at Anna to know she didn't want to talk of it. So he was surprised when she admitted, 'We've been doing that a lot lately.'

It was her use of the word *lately* which gave him a clue as to perhaps what they'd been arguing about. The Maclean. He hadn't been home much in the last three years, so he hadn't been around a lot when Alan was there, or for much of the aftermath, but he was there enough, had heard enough. What he didn't want was to talk of the Maclean just now.

'That's a rite of passage between siblings, isn't it? They know you best, can love and frustrate you like no other.'

Her gentle relieved smile was all he needed for now. 'No sibling talk, then,' she said. 'Then tell me of... Seoc.'

Walking to the horses, he glanced over his shoulder. 'That's not what I thought you'd talk of instead.'

'Were we to have an itinerary planned for a conversation in case a rainstorm forced us to seek shelter in a cave?'

He liked this Anna with her retorts. Maybe he was fortunate, and he didn't have to wait any longer to talk freely with this woman. Maybe they simply had to have this moment.

'I've stared at you most of my life, Anna, and yet, you're the only one who's never asked me why.'

Over the flank of his horse, he could see her bite the corner of her lip. When she turned to him again, he raised his brow.

Hers only lowered. 'You don't do it any more, so…why should that matter now?'

She didn't see him or perhaps she didn't want to talk of it. His Anna seemed to have many topics that he wasn't to address. Still…there was time.

He patted down his horse, to check if it was dry and if there were any injuries or had taken any harm in their rush to be here.

'How's your brother?' she asked.

Another question he wasn't expecting. 'I can't remember him staring at you as a child, but he did tell me a time or two to look away. And I thought we weren't to talk of siblings?'

Anna went quiet again, and Camron spared her another glance. Now she was looking at the fire, the light flickering across her long limbs. Her hair seemed to be drying, and a few tendrils floated around her face.

He wanted to tell her why he'd watched her, but then it would be so easy to move that conversation to why he watched her now…and what else he wanted from her.

Yet she looked contemplative. 'What is it you want to ask?' he said. 'We're here, alone—it could be anything.'

'Seoc.' She bit her lower lip. 'He seems much changed.'

He was, but he was also quiet about it. 'He's still making terrible drinks.'

The smile she gave didn't reach her eyes. 'They are terrible, but he won't stop if everyone still drinks them.'

'True,' he said.

'I don't want… I'm not entitled to any of your confidences.' She tucked her hair behind her ear. 'But is there anything I can do to make it better?'

How to answer? He ran his hands down her horse. Maybe he was a bit rougher than intended because the mare stomped, so he let up on the brush. The rest of him, however, was tight. He'd come over here to care for the horses, to provide himself with a distraction, but it wasn't working. His Anna, who'd suffered much, had a generous heart.

She was worried for their friend. They all were. But for her to care so deeply felt overwhelming in the intimacy of the cave. He was already wound tight from simply being near her.

'I think time will help.'

After a moment she nodded, but it wasn't decisive.

'You don't think so?' He slapped his hands against the blanket around his waist. Watched how her gaze slipped to there and, almost against her will, stayed.

His Anna was definitely attracted to him. But now wasn't the time for rushing matters. Not when the opportunity had come up to discuss other obstacles between them. And that was Maclean's ghost.

'It's nothing,' she said slowly. 'You're right, time does help.'

She said that, but clearly didn't believe it. The fact she thought time didn't heal meant she was resigned to stay this way for the rest of her life? Suspicious of people, mistrusting, alone?

He wouldn't have it.

And her feelings weren't nothing. Not when Anna avoided looking at him as she tied up the rest of the food and put it back in the satchels. Then avoided him further yet when she stood and brushed crumbs off her blanket over and over.

'Maclean was more of a bastard in every way.'

Her breath hitched. 'Why would you suddenly bring him up?'

'Anna, you're the most intelligent person I

know. We can't pretend that when you doubt time heals matters he isn't the cause of your thinking.'

She snapped her head up. 'I don't think you have a say in that, do you?'

Even thinking of that man sent him into a rage, and it wasn't jealousy, though that had been there in the beginning. It was something closer to a vengeful fury. 'I can't account for your feelings on that matter, but for mine, he was a coward, a fool and a thousand other insults I'd rather not say.'

Something crossed his Anna's eyes when he showed her some of his anger for what the Maclean had done to her. But whatever it was, she added, 'I may feel you're right about a few of those insults.'

He couldn't help the grin he flashed. Especially not when her expression became less guarded.

'Still,' she said. 'I do tend to argue with my sister more often since he was found to have made promises to me, and to other women too.'

He...didn't expect her to be free with her words when it came to Alan and his betrayal. He, along with every other Graham, had watched those two fall in love, the absolute utter joy on Anna's face every time she ran across the field to greet Alan when he came riding in to see her.

That joy, that love, had shredded Camron's

heart to watch, and yet because he loved her, he wanted her to be happy.

And when he was being truthful to himself, he admitted Alan had been likeable, and had seemed to fit into the clan very well. But when all his lies finally unravelled and Seoc had discovered the other women Alan was courting at the same time as Anna, the clan had run him off, but it was too late to save Anna's heart.

Only a little over five years separated he and Anna. When he'd become entranced with the fairy in the moonlight, he was ten and she fifteen. That difference in their ages had felt like centuries. But when Alan came... Camron was just eighteen. He'd felt so close to being the man for her. But she was twenty-three and not looking at him in any way like a woman did a man. Not the way she looked at the Maclean.

Not the way she'd looked at him ever since she'd seen him bathing in the pond. He'd have a harder time wooing Anna now that she mistrusted men, but he knew she was worth it. As for her arguing with her sister... That was easy to dismiss.

'You're only arguing more because you're being protective.'

'I'm what?'

'You've always been—'

'I think you should be quiet now.'

Just like that, Anna was in her cold castle, and behind the gates again. Those soft looks, that almost gratefulness when he'd told her he despised Alan as much as she did, was gone.

Yet he knew he'd said the right words, that they were the truth. Anna did need to let go of her family. Lachie was growing up so quickly, and Murdag should be free to be wooed, even if it was by his brother. But he'd said them in the wrong way, and there was no way he couldn't rephrase them and not sound false. But he wasn't going to simply let everything go. He just needed to choose his moment.

'Our clothes are probably dry now,' he said instead.

She strode over to them and tested the cloth herself. 'Turn around.'

He did. It was going to be a long night of want and regrets, but Camron couldn't lose hope. Not completely. After all, she was nearby, and it was more than he'd had ever before.

Chapter Six

'It's so good to see you, Anna,' Ailis said. 'But when will you tell me why you're truly here?'

It been over two years since she'd visited her mother's sister and, Ailis, her cousin.

They'd been close when they were younger; when her mother was still alive, they were side by side almost every day. But since Lachie…and then Alan, she'd let their closeness go.

However, when she and Camron arrived early yesterday, it seemed like no time at all had passed. Ailis's little home was a bit more crowded, and a lot more chaotic, but that was because of her three growing children, who had all taken an interest in rocks and had brought them into the house. Ailis hoped it was simply a phase.

'Why I'm here?' Anna strode across the small bedroom and sat on the edge of Ailis's bed where she lay. 'Aren't the copious amounts of tinctures I've offered you reason enough?'

Ailis grimaced. 'I'm still burping up mint, so for me that is an argument for why you shouldn't be here.'

'I'd be offended—if it was my idea to be here,' she smirked, but then realised how her jest might sound. 'Not that I didn't want to be here.'

'I know what you meant.' Ailis patted her hand.

Anna sighed. 'Father mentioned me coming and that you might have use of my paltry skills.'

'Don't you mean parsley skills?'

Anna rolled her eyes. 'Oh, that's a terrible jest.'

Ailis squeezed her hand before letting go. 'I'm pregnant; there are times I can barely remember my name. You should be grateful I can make a jest at all.'

Ailis had always been a kind spirit, but this generosity went right through that strange restlessness she'd been fighting for days now. Anna knew she'd just confessed she wouldn't have come at all unless her father had made her. When did she turn so cruel?

'I didn't mean to stay away for so long.'

'I know,' Ailis said. 'Remember, I could have come to you.'

'You have three children, one on the way and a husband. I, on the other hand, am just me.'

For some reason that sounded worse, and by Ailis's softening gaze, she knew it.

Ailis tsked. 'You'll make a good mother.'

'I'm too old!' Anna said.

'You're the same age as me.' Ailis raised her brow. 'Are you saying I'm too old?'

'Your body knows what's it's doing.' Anna chuckled. 'I think mine would be…surprised.'

'Unless you got a husband, I think we'd all be surprised.'

Anna couldn't hold her smile. She was supposed to have had a husband. Alan had made many promises to her, but apparently, he'd made the same promises to several other women as well.

Ailis exhaled roughly. 'He wasn't right for you.'

Anna appreciated Ailis not mentioning the bastard's name. 'Now you tell me.'

Ailis smirked. 'If you would have come and seen me—'

Anna blamed her sudden sob on Ailis's gentle jesting. Covering her mouth, and blinking away threatening tears, Anna said, 'I'm sorry, I don't even know what just overcame me. You'd think I was pregnant.'

'Now, I'm insulted,' Ailis said. 'But if you need to cry…'

'I refuse to do so.' Anna shook her head and placed her hands in her lap. 'Honestly, I am well.'

Ailis looked to the door, her expression turning calculated. 'I think I know why you're emotional.'

'I already had that time this month.'

Ailis shook her head. 'Tell me about that Highlander you travelled here with.'

'Highlander?' Anna said, stalling. Did Ailis think her sudden display of emotion had to do with Camron, and if so, how? Because she was barely able to tell herself she had emotions when it came to him. Attraction certainly. It was so acute she couldn't ignore it. But other emotions? That seemed…dangerous.

'Don't pretend you don't know who I'm talking of,' Ailis said.

'Did the mint help your stomach?' she asked instead.

'Anna…' Ailis warned.

'I'll tell you, if you tell me.'

'Must be important, then,' Ailis said.

After the pond, after the cave, she was beginning to believe it was because when had she last been so attracted to a man? Even with Alan it had been different. Not so intense. At the cave, she couldn't stop staring at him. The way the too small blanket hugged his waist. The way he'd handled the horses…and took care of the food and clothes.

Until he'd made those foolish comments, she'd almost thought he respected and liked her. She'd thought he wanted to kiss her. But obviously that was her own imagination.

Now, after her temper had cooled, she couldn't quite shake the feeling of how he'd looked in the fire's light. Or when they'd sat on the log, how everything he'd said held a more intimate meaning.

'Perhaps.'

'It did help,' Ailis blurted.

'Good, I can give you more.' Anna walked over to the table and crushed more mint leaves.

'I'm going to hate the smell of that when you're gone,' Ailis warned.

Anna turned and faced her cousin. Again, she was reminded of how gentle and forgiving Ailis was, how understanding. She couldn't imagine confessing anything to Murdag, not because they weren't close. But mostly they argued, and Murdag never had any softness for understanding. She cared, loved, but then moved on.

'I think he's handsome,' she said finally.

Ailis snorted. 'That's all? You made me confess to the mint working and you're going to simply state what we all know?'

'More handsome than his brother.'

Ailis gave a smile. 'Ah, that's more like it. You know he stares at you when you're not looking.'

'He always used to do that,' she said.

Ailis bracketed her arms and pushed herself up. 'No, I mean since you've been here.'

Anna shook her head. 'He's been too busy with his friends.'

'Apparently, you've been watching him as well.'

Anna took in a breath and held it. She wasn't going to run away from a bed-bound pregnant woman. 'I don't want him. We argued on the way here.'

'We're arguing now,' Ailis pointed out.

Were they? Maybe she was a bit fractious with her cousin. But with Camron her body and emotions stayed in knots, even when they'd got dressed again last night and lay down to sleep. The mild weather the next day had helped relieve the tension a little, but it seemed they both wanted to race to get to Colquhoun land the next morning. The entire time, they'd shared only a few words.

'He basically said I was too protective, and that the… Maclean made it worse.'

Ailis raised her brow. 'And you're not?'

She wasn't expecting that.

Ailis sighed. 'I don't want to hurt you. I'm not

saying you being protective is bad. It shows you care, Anna. Did Camron say it was bad?'

He'd seemed very at ease when he'd mentioned it, as if it was an easy answer for him. Simply a truth of who she was. There had been nothing in his tone nor expression that belittled it either. In fact, she had stopped him from saying anything more on it.

'I took it that way because Murdag and I are always arguing about it.'

'Maybe talk to her instead of arguing?' Ailis frowned when she didn't answer. 'Then what about Camron? You don't argue with him every time you talk, do you?'

Anna shook her head.

'But there's something there, isn't there? He travelled with you here.' Ailis folded her hands over her stomach. 'It's me, Anna. If you can't tell me, who else can you?'

'I have to ignore whatever is between us,' Anna said uncomfortably. 'It's too soon.'

'It's been over a year since—'

'I still can't trust him,' she blurted. Five simple words, hard won for her to admit.

'Ah. And you won't...until you do.'

'That makes no sense.'

'You have to learn to trust...in order to trust.'

'Pregnancy doesn't give you a right to be so vague.'

'Pregnancy makes me break wind.'

'Well, I can't say your remarks aren't the same.

Laughing, wincing, Ailis rubbed her belly.

Anna grabbed the cup on the table by her and held it up to Ailis. 'You should drink this.'

'More mint water?'

'Of course it is,' Anna said.

Ailis grimaced. 'There's not a chance of that making it down my throat and staying there.'

Setting the cup down, Anna softened her expression. 'It's coming soon, then. I can't believe you're having another.'

'Not soon enough. I swear each child gives me more grey hair,' Ailis said.

'You haven't one grey hair on your head,' Anna said. 'Unlike me.'

'So like your mother, going grey early,' Ailis mused. 'But I remember big sweeps of it, or am I wrong?'

'No, she did have a lot. I swear it was all Murdag's fault.'

Ailis laughed, then breathed in sharply. 'Kicking today!'

Anna looked to the door and outside. It was just now dark. 'Your mother will be back soon.'

'She needs more rest than I do.' Ailis grinned.

Ailis glowed, and it wasn't only the pregnancy. She was simply happy.

Whilst Anna was more miserable. She'd always wanted children and now she didn't feel as if that would ever be possible. And she was realising maybe it wasn't simply a physical issue, but in her heart as well.

The chasm in her heart wouldn't ease. Why didn't it go away? Alan had taken two years of her life, but it had been over a year since then. Why wasn't she over him…? No, she was over him; she simply wasn't over the mistrust.

How could she fully trust a man like that ever again?

Ailis tilted her head. 'You know I've missed you and have always felt sorry we lost touch.'

Aware Ailis watched her, Anna cleared her throat and forced her thoughts away. 'I could have been much better myself. And I promise with this baby, I'll be here as often as you need me…that is if you want me to.'

'Always!' Ailis laid her hand on Anna's arm. 'I do so wish I'd been there for you when you needed it.'

Anna wasn't prepared for Ailis's unwelcome comment. Oh, she wasn't surprised that Ailis knew what Alan had done; everyone did. But as usual he was the last person she wanted to speak of.

Stepping back, forcing Ailis to take her gentle hand away, Anna answered, 'I was blind to friends and family when the Maclean was around, and not nice to people after he left. It's probably for the best you weren't there.'

Ailis curtly shook her head. 'I didn't mean what that braggart did to you—we've talked enough about him. I meant when your mother died.'

That was…unexpected.

'We were only children ourselves, remember?' Anna said.

'I still felt like I could have done something more.'

She remembered that time all too well. Lachie having to nurse with Beileag's mother. Her father grieving. Murdag too young to fully understand the loss.

For a fortnight, Ailis's mother had been there, but then she'd left, taking Ailis with her. Ailis, who was the only one her age who understood the lack of a parent since her father was dead.

Clenching Ailis's hand in hers, she said, 'We'll make up the time now.'

'Until tomorrow when you leave.'

'Lachie—' she said. It still made her uneasy

to leave him for so long. It wasn't that Murdag or her father couldn't cope, but she preferred to be there.

'I know,' Ailis said. 'But he's better now?'

He was getting better. Camron had helped him swim in the pond, and maybe he could learn more, as well as new skills when they returned. What was she to make of that?

So many years she'd lost; she now knew it wasn't simply from Alan's treatment of her, but that she'd changed after her mother's death. Grief for one reason, and Lachie's care on her shoulders another.

She'd forgotten how hard it had been. How worried she always was. Her father had depended upon her to take on her mother's chores, but she'd adopted her mother's role in the household too.

How had she forgotten?

Maybe that's why it had been so easy for Alan to come charming his way into her life. She'd clutched onto him as if he were the last ray of sunshine. When his lies were revealed, she'd been swept away to somewhere dark again. Is that why she looked to Camron now? To bring back the sunshine?

'That's it, isn't it?' Ailis gasped.

'That's what?' Had Ailis been talking to her? She picked up the bucket of wash water.

'Have you given your heart again?'

Anna spilled some of the wash water on the floor before she set the bucket down and turned. She didn't have a heart to give. It'd been severed from her very soul. 'I need to see to this.'

'Anna, please,' Ailis said.

A pregnant woman, her friend, her family, shouldn't have to beg. Anna turned fully to look at her cousin, whose expression was soft, but along the edges she could see pity there. She held firm against it.

'He's just returned, so it can hardly be anything more than…interest. And if it is, it's only on my part.'

'Even after he had words with Ewan last night?' Ailis said.

If the whispers were true, Camron had firmly discouraged Ewan of Clan Colquhoun from having any interest in her. If true, it suited her fine. She didn't want Ewan, and after what he'd said in the cave, she shouldn't want Camron either.

That might take some doing, however.

'I saw none of that, so who's to say it's true? I only talked briefly with Ewan yesterday,' Anna said. 'And even if it is true, Camron's made no declaration to me. Not that he should.'

She caught Ailis yawning. She made a terrible cousin. Here she was gossiping when Ailis needed to rest.

'Get some sleep for now. I'll go, and I'll come and say goodbye in the morning before we leave.'

'You'd best.'

Anna laughed. 'So demanding.'

'So wanting not to be in bed, like you wouldn't!' Ailis laughed, then waved her on. 'Go, before I start drooling and snoring all over you.'

Chapter Seven

'Anyone feeling we should let the fire die?' Seoc threw on another log, squatted next to his bench and poked the fire with the thick branch.

'Feels good,' Hamilton said.

Sitting on another bench with his brother, Camron knew all three of them weren't ready to retire yet. The night was crisp, clear, and the sky was lit by uncountable stars. It was time, but they wouldn't be falling asleep soon.

Since he'd returned from Colquhoun land almost a week ago, he'd been getting even less sleep. Mostly because a certain black-haired woman had been ignoring him.

He knew he'd spoken too early on her care of her family, and friends. She loved them. As long as he'd known her, she'd always been protective of them…to the detriment of herself. How many times had he seen her with dark circles under her eyes, and her shoulders drooping? How many times had he watched Murdag attempt some independence only to be kept close?

But he'd not been home long, and there were still lots of matters between him and Anna to work through if he was to build a relationship with her. Patience hadn't been his friend so far, but he had to continue to use it because of their age. Perhaps, in certain matters, he should display more?

He didn't know. There wasn't that much time left for them. War was looming, and in one drunken moment he'd made a bet which shouldn't count, but…there was a truth to it even so.

'What feels good is not drinking your mead.' Camron stretched out his feet and rolled his shoulders.

'It was your idea,' Hamilton snorted.

Seoc chuckled, winced, then rubbed his chest. He'd done that often since they'd returned from Dunbar last March. Camron thought it was the scar that pulled at him, but Seoc never said anything, and neither he nor Hamilton dared ask.

The truth of that day, and the months afterwards, were still too prominent in their memory. The battle was hard enough when they had to flee, but losing their laird, Sir Patrick, was a harsh reminder that though their hearts were strong, they were still only men.

Men who knew that the world outside their home was changing…and it was causing them to change as well.

Used to being on the road and keeping watch, none of them could sleep through a full night. So though there were other Highlanders now in the outer reaches of Graham lands ensuring the safety of all, his friend and brother often came to this lone spot to while away a few extra hours before sleep claimed them.

Being here with them felt more like home now than sleeping in the bed he'd had since he was a child.

'So, Camron, when are you going to tell us what happened on your travels with Anna?' Seoc sat back on his own bench.

Never. 'Not much to tell.'

Hamilton stretched his hands to the fire and clapped them. 'I've been trying for days to get him to confess.'

'And he's stayed silent?' Seoc said.

Hamilton nodded. 'A certainty something happened.'

'Ah, maybe he had to fight for her hand whilst she was with those Colquhouns,' Seoc teased. 'You know how they are.'

'Persuasive red-haired devils.' Hamilton turned to him. 'So was that it? Did someone there notice Anna's beauty?'

He still seethed from watching Ewan's easy ways with Anna. About the fact he'd had to declare his intentions regarding Anna in private to Ewan, although the facts came out anyway. He regretted it only because he was certain it had made Anna retreat further into her castle where he couldn't reach her.

If he'd only stated his intentions towards her in the cave before they'd talked of her family.

Laughing, Hamilton's thumb pointed at him. 'See, this is how he's been. Especially as Anna's been avoiding him since they returned.'

'You going to ask me whether she's worth it? Aren't you going to say I told you so? It's not like I wasted years thinking of only her. There were other matters keeping us occupied.'

'Dunbar, Seoc,' Hamilton said. 'Losing our Patrick. Endless scouting, and nights sleeping in the rain.'

'Those odd goings-on with our Colquhoun cousins.'

Hamilton rolled his eyes. 'The wedding games were good though…'

There were so many regrets, matters he couldn't repair. 'I didn't stay faithful to Anna.'

'You weren't meant to. She wasn't yours. She had that Maclean,' Hamilton said. 'And none of the other women were her, we knew that. I stopped questioning your feelings for her years ago. Certainly, I teased you about it when you were so obsessed with her before our balls had even dropped…made sense though after they did.'

'Careful.'

Hamilton rolled his shoulders. 'How could I doubt how you felt about her when you saw her happy with Maclean and you stepped back?'

'When we *thought* she was happy,' Camron growled.

'Face the truth, brother, that man did make her happy.'

Jealousy burned, but it was the truth. Another regret. 'I wanted that for her; I wanted her to be happy. Damn him.'

'I know. And that's when I knew whatever it was you had felt for her was true. I could never do such a selfless act. I can't remember the last time I didn't do anything that didn't serve me.'

Camron glanced at his brother.

'Stop looking at me like that. I can have these thoughts.'

His brother never had those thoughts, and he'd

never sounded so conflicted or bitter about them. Hamilton wasn't patient, and liked to get his way.

Maybe they were more alike as twins than he'd thought, because when it came to Anna, he was starting to feel the same way.

'Don't think of these things,' Hamilton advised. 'There were other women for you, Camron, because you thought, as we all did, that Anna would marry Alan. You were trying to forget her.'

'How did you get so wise?'

'I'm good with games and distractions.'

Hamilton *was* good with games, but…were they a distraction too?

'Maybe now there will be no distractions. And Anna hasn't been avoiding me.' Camron pulled his feet in.

Hamilton snorted.

Anna had been avoiding him; all the ride home they'd spoken but a few words only. Unfortunately, the weather hadn't cooperated with another storm to stop their speedy return to Graham land.

'I have been occupied teaching her brother to swim,' he added.

'Thinking to gain her heart by befriending her brother?' Hamilton said. 'That's clever.'

Something close to anger seared through him. Were Seoc and Hamilton two of those clansmen Anna had warned him about? Did they dismiss

Lachlan as unimportant because he had an oddly shaped foot? 'Lachie's a fine boy, and even better company. I'm honoured to teach him to swim. He's fast, quick to learn—'

'He's well fair gone,' Seoc said.

'See I told you,' Hamilton replied with satisfaction.

It took Camron a moment to realise they were talking of him, not of Lachie…and that they had planned this conversation. He just didn't know why.

'What's going on here?'

'We know you love the boy, just as much as you love his sister,' Seoc said.

It was hardly a secret.

'With that display, I think it's fair to say your feelings for Anna have only deepened,' Hamilton added.

All because he'd defended, vehemently, Anna's brother. They had laid a trap for him, and he'd fallen for it. But his brother was wrong. Whatever he'd felt for Anna had changed over the years, but the depth remained the same. If Eve had taken ribs from Adam, Anna had possession of his entire soul, and always had. 'My feelings for her are the same.'

'Oh, but her feelings for you are different?'

Hamilton said with some pleased tone in his voice that made Camron curl his fingers.

'If you could see your expression, as we do, my friend,' Seoc said. 'You would know we don't need the details to wish you congratulations.'

There was a change between them, but unless he could get Anna to take another trip, he didn't know how to keep her in one place long enough to have the time alone with her again. Clan business kept him busy as well. But he'd find the time, so those half-moments he'd shared with her would become something more.

'I bet he hasn't kissed her yet,' Hamilton remarked. 'There's too much tension in him.'

'Agreed,' Seoc said.

Camron rubbed his face. It would be a long night ahead if he was to be interrogated all night. 'Don't you have any of that mead?'

Seoc raised a brow. 'Haven't learnt your lesson? Maybe you should try my new spiced ale. I've done—'

'You poisoned us with the last ale you spiced,' Hamilton interrupted.

'I've perfected my recipe,' Seoc grumbled.

'Like you perfected that grass water concoction?' Hamilton quipped.

Camron laughed. Since they were children, Seoc was constantly having them try new drinks.

The grass and water 'ale' was something he'd made when they were children and Hamilton had never let him forget about it.

'You didn't have to drink that, just like you didn't have to drink my mead,' Seoc said.

Hamilton groaned. 'It's been less than a fortnight, and my head still hurts. Why didn't anyone stop us?'

'I couldn't get you to stop drinking the grass water either,' Seoc guffawed.

- 'That's because there was a bet made,' Camron said.

Hamilton rubbed his stomach in memory. 'Only made us stronger.'

Camron slipped his hand to his side and tapped his fingers there. Would this bet to marry make them stronger? The thought of that first night pulled him in too many directions. Contentment for returning, revelry with friends he hadn't seen for months, the roiling of his stomach content the next day, the bet…and Anna.

Always Anna. That day at the pond, her gaze on him so real; the heat of it was constantly there as they'd travelled to Colquhoun land, as he'd met with friends. Ones who teased him just as Hamilton and Seoc were doing now.

He wanted more than her gaze. Being so near her in the cave that night, her body trembling from the cold, from the unspoken desire between them, wasn't nearly enough.

'You two could always stop making bets.' Seoc stood, stomped out his large feet and then sat again. They were all restless, and tired.

'Then where would you get your amusement at our expense?' Hamilton said.

'True!' Seoc laughed through his words.

It was good to see his friend laugh. Good to be here with them all. Not good to be reminded of the bet, which meant nothing to him because it wasn't important.

Hamilton's eyes locked with his. Oh, his brother was thinking on it as well.

'How's Murdag, Hamilton?' he asked.

Hamilton looked away. 'Better than ever.'

'Murdag?' Seoc coughed, then rubbed his chest again. 'Don't you mean Beileag?'

Camron wanted the attention off him, and back where it needed to be, on his brother. 'Last I knew my brother liked a certain woman with a thin chemise who stood on a boulder.'

'How did I miss Murdag wearing a thin chemise?' Seoc said.

'You were probably behaving honourably and not looking as she stood on the boulder in front of the fire.'

'You all made me pour the ale that night; I

missed it,' Seoc said. 'Just as well if you have your eye on her, Hamilton.'

Hamilton nodded as if he appreciated Seoc's comment. Except…his brother didn't act like he cared if Seoc saw Murdag's figure in the firelight or not.

'What?' Hamilton said.

Camron shrugged.

'You have a strange way of wooing Murdag by hanging around her friend so often,' Seoc said.

Camron thought so as well, but more than that, he knew if Anna had stood on a boulder like that, she wouldn't have been up there long enough for anyone to see her.

'I agree with Seoc. If you like Murdag,' Camron said, 'I'd stop hanging around her friend.'

Hamilton nudged him with his shoulder. 'Doesn't matter. I'm going to win.'

'Win what?' Seoc leaned forward.

'Brother,' Camron warned.

'Ach, come on, he's got to know sometime. He'll find out when it comes to the happy moment anyway.'

He didn't want to talk about any of this. The bet had meant nothing to him when it was made. A drunken wish at the most.

'What did you do now, Hamilton?' Seoc yawned.

'It wasn't me,' Hamilton said. 'Odd, I know, but this was, and has always been, Camron's idea.'

That was a strange way of starting the conversation. Always been? What did his brother mean by that?

'Now you have to tell me,' Seoc insisted. 'Is this another challenge or a jest on someone, and why would your twin, Lord of the Calm and Reasonable Manor, suggest something that even has you filling with mirth?'

Camron scowled. Even if Hamilton won the bet, he didn't want anyone to know he'd done such a selfish, immature deed. As if a wager could win the woman he loved? Foolish!

More fool himself, because he'd actually been trying to win her since they'd returned from Colquhoun land. Day after day he went to her, prepared with words and deed, and then it was as if her brother had always been waiting for him.

No matter where he intended to approach Anna, out popped Lachie. He couldn't say no to the boy. Those big hazel-blue eyes, and the youthful jubilant pride in his accomplishments, did much to mollify his frustration. Even so, days had gone by. How could he win her hand if they didn't talk?

Yet, Hamilton boasted he was to win Murdag?

He should have punched his brother that day. It didn't do to have this restlessness, and it wouldn't do if Hamilton won Murdag because he'd been too busy teaching their brother to swim to pursue Anna.

'Not a chance,' Camron said to his brother.

'Not a chance for what?' Seoc said. 'Equal frowns on your faces, and it's like I've been hit on the head. I'm seeing double, and seeing double of you doesn't do it for me.'

'Seeing double of Una's treasures likely would,' Hamilton said, referring to a particularly voluptuous widow of the clan.

'Another truth from you, my friend.' Seoc chuckled.

He needed to win Anna. His brother and Murdag didn't matter. He needed her more than ever. He wanted to feel those eyes, her touch, on him. He was burning with it.

Stretching his arms over his head, Seoc asked, 'I'm getting weary. Will you two tell me what's going on?'

Hamilton was right: if they married, this might all come out anyway.

'We made a wager to marry before we leave again,' Hamilton said.

Seoc looked baffled as he eyed them both.

Did his friend believe they were to marry each other? 'The less bright one with sentences is attempting to marry Murdag, and I'm to try and marry Anna.'

Seoc's great arms plopped on his lap.

Hamilton raised his hands almost apologetically. 'It was Camron's wager. Thus I'll win this one.'

Never. Anna was his. 'When have you ever won a wager from me?'

Hamilton scoffed. 'We'd be here all day if I regaled all my winnings, brother.'

'Are you sure this is not a jest?' Seoc said, pointing at one and then the other of them. 'Because I've had to bear enough of both your jests and your bets all my life.'

Camron raised a brow. 'Bear the brunt of our jests?'

'I must have been hit on my head. Or…have you put something in my drink?' Bafflement etched across every bit of his expression, Seoc stared at Camron as if wanting him to give a different answer. Seoc also looked uncomfortable and cross. On a man of his size all these emotions weren't unnoticeable. Camron simply looked back. He was the one who'd made the bet, so he had to own up to it.

'Your head's fine, our friend.' Hamilton chuckled. 'This may be the most awe-inspiring wager yet!'

Camron frowned at Hamilton's too bright words, and wide smile. Did his brother believe this to be a jest? He was in earnest. That would have to be remedied. It was bad enough they'd made the bet in the first place. Didn't do to make it into some farce. This wasn't a drinking game or a chance at knucklebones. Women's lives…their lives…were at stake.

Seoc stood to his full height and glared at Camron. 'This is true? You offered to travel with her…to be alone with her…so you could try and win a bet?'

What could he say? The existence of the bet and his feelings for her were both the truth, though they weren't related. Camron nodded.

'You fools!' Seoc stormed off.

He'd never seen his friend so angry or lose his temper with them like that, but he couldn't blame him.

Hamilton's wide smile was gone as if it had never been. 'That wasn't the response I expected.'

'What else did you expect? It's a foolish thing to bet on.'

Hamilton's brows drew in. He looked like he

wanted to say something, but he sighed and stared at the fire.

'Is it true you've become close with Beileag?'

Hamilton looked down at his feet and nodded. 'I could see I wasn't wooing Murdag properly and asked her to help.'

'She knows of the bet?' Did the whole clan know?

'Don't worry, brother, she thinks I made it.'

That didn't lessen his fear. Tapping on his leg, ignoring his brother, Camron turned his attention to the fire.

He didn't care if Hamilton won Murdag's hand before him or if Beileag knew about it. He cared if Anna discovered his bet. With more people knowing about it, the chances of that happening only increased.

Tomorrow, no matter what, even if he had twenty ten-year-old boys hanging off his arms or gripping his hands, he'd just grip Anna's too and tug her along with them.

He needed to know what that look in her eyes at the cave meant, the secrets she held. He needed her to fall in love with him before she found out how foolish he'd been.

Chapter Eight

'Well, Anna, I'm off to the fields.' Padrig of Clan Graham slapped their kitchen table.

Anna gave her father a pointed look. 'Where else would you be going if not the fields?'

'Probably a little here, a little there.' Her father slouched farther back into his chair.

They both knew full well her father would be off gallivanting a little here, and a little more there. If he got going, he could walk clear to the ends of the earth. She was always grateful he'd stuck around.

It had been especially difficult after their mother died. Lachie being born was one of the great joys of their little family, but there was always this shared grief her mother wasn't here to see him grow.

Something had died inside all of them that day, but her father had changed the most. His usual wandering, dreamy spirit became more grounded, but also more burdened. Whilst Anna appreciated his help, she'd felt like they'd lost an essential part of her father too.

'What's happening in the field today?' she said.

'Sheep, sheep and some cattle,' he said.

'Sounds exciting.' Anna smiled.

'It is for the sheep,' he said. 'Now I truly must be off.'

Her father was barely dressed, hadn't broken his fast and his boots were still by his bed.

'How about I be off first?' she suggested.

Her father took another sip of ale. 'What are you up to?'

Anna smirked, loving this game they played. 'Laundry, gardening, gardening or laundry.'

'Sounds exciting,' he said gravely.

'It is, for the…mint,' she huffed, knowing she'd already used mint as an example recently. Every day she needed to think of something else. Socks, boots, braies. Anything. But as the years went on, it got too difficult for her unimaginative soul.

'Got to be quicker than that, Anna my dear,' he chirped.

'I'll never be quicker than you,' she said fondly.

'That's likely true, but at least your day is certain to be better than mine.' Her father emphasised every word in a long lament.

'No doubt.'

They often joked on how terrible their chores were. Though in truth, she suspected her father loved to roam with the livestock and ensure no beast was left behind. She also suspected he liked doing so because many of the other clansmen his age were out roaming about as well and they could all regale each other with stories and shared woes.

Her father tilted his shaggy-haired head. 'What's bothering you?'

She should have left already. Her father loved to talk, but he was an even better observer.

Too much was bothering her this morning and none of it she wanted to think of. She'd been fine all these years. Perfectly fine.

But she was inexplicably attracted to Camron of Clan Graham and no matter how many days passed where she ignored him, the feeling didn't go away. But being attracted to him didn't mean she trusted him, and he was going again soon anyway. After Dunbar most of the men rotated duties. She simply needed to last a bit longer and she'd be safe once more.

'You need me to cut your hair,' she said.

'For what? I'll pull it back.'

'That's what you said before.'

'Are you distracting me?' Her father lowered his cup. 'What has Murdag done now?'

She was trying to evade his keen eye on her own problems, but she was happy to talk of her sister's. 'Nothing yet, but you know she will.'

'I hope so.' At her raised brow, he added, 'If she's not causing trouble, then you would, and I'm not certain you're up to making a good job of it.'

Maybe she could have caused more trouble like her sister if she hadn't taken on the role of their mother—no, that wasn't fair. She'd done that because she liked to care for others.

And certainly, she felt like she could give Murdag a run for her money at making mischief lately. Her sister hadn't ever run into a naked man—twice—that she knew of.

Her father's eyes narrowed on her, and she knew she needed to leave immediately. 'I'm off!'

'Not so fast!' her father said.

On a sigh, Anna turned.

Her father raised a brow. 'When are you going to talk to your sister?'

'We've been talking.'

Her father shook his head. 'Words on the weather and food do not count. I thought you going to see Ailis would help with whatever is between you two.'

'I've only been back a few days.'

'Almost a week.' Her father pointed out.

And in that time, she'd not only been avoiding her sister, Beileag and Camron, she'd been thinking on Ailis's words as well. Except... Ailis hadn't given her any advice on how not to overly protect her family...only suggesting that she should learn how to trust in order to be able to trust.

Not very helpful when Murdag kept giving her the cold shoulder, or pointedly asking her if she had any restrictions she'd like to add to the list.

'Sort it out, would you,' her father said, 'because I'm not getting any younger.'

Anna crossed her arms. 'So you'll die if I don't mend things with Murdag?'

'You admit you've fallen out, then!' With a grin, her father pointed in the air.

Releasing her arms, Anna sighed. She wasn't going to win at word games or discussions with her father today. 'I'll talk to her.'

When Padrig smiled and waved her off, Anna took her leave as quick as she could. Emerging from her home, wrapping her arms around her middle merely to stave off the mist, Anna almost walked into the two figures in front of her.

One was her brother, all bright-eyed and fidgeting. Attached to his hand was Camron, sleepy-eyed, frowning, wearing wrinkled clothes and displaying his hair half sticking out on the side.

Perhaps he had been lounging in his bed longer than her father. Still, he gently pulled Lachie forward.

She hoped whatever they wanted from her was brief. Days of ignoring him, and it was as if they were back in the cave and he was admitting to watching her make shadows. But it was worse today.

The little bit of sleeping masculine vulnerability Camron displayed was doing something to her. Like making her want to put her arms around him, to see if he looked as warm and soft as he appeared. Then kissing him on the jaw until that little bit of grumpiness faded.

'Can you come with us this morning, Anna?' Lachie asked.

His little voice sounded so formal.

Anna glanced at Camron, whose expression hadn't changed. In fact, she wasn't altogether certain he wasn't still asleep.

'Aren't we already here?'

'He wants to take you somewhere, Anna,' Camron said.

The rumbling roughness of his voice rolled over somewhere near Anna's heart. There should have been nothing near Anna's heart that felt anything at all. They'd talked in the cave, but then he'd brought up how protective she was and…

she realised she'd never asked him what he actually meant.

Afraid of his answer, and her attraction to him, she'd been avoiding him on purpose.

But she couldn't ignore what he'd just said. It wasn't only the tone of those words; it was what he'd said. As if Camron was talking of Lachie, but also himself. But where did Camron want to take her? Or maybe it wasn't a place, maybe it was—

Foolish! Days together and other than that moment in the cave, which she was certain was all in her imagination, there was no evidence that he wanted her. How could a mere shadow affect him? Too many thoughts this early in the morning. Maybe it was she who needed to wake up, and let this poor Highlander return to his bed.

She held out her hand to Lachie. 'Then come here, and we'll go.'

Camron took it instead.

The roughness of his palm dispelled none of his warmth or gentleness. When he gave a little tug to move her forward, she was hit with more of the Highlander. And on this quiet morning, with his easy slumberous expression and that tiny crease in his cheek, it was much too much.

She could do nothing to stop it because he clasped her hand gently, but firmly, and Lachie was avidly watching them.

'Late night?' she whispered.

Camron's eyes went to hers. She couldn't tell anything from his expression. But what was there made her feel a little warmer, a little more restless. When she tugged back, he rubbed his thumb across her knuckles and let her go.

Flushed now, Anna took her brother's hand. 'Come now, why don't we be off.'

Lachie held onto her, but he also kept Camron's hand with his other.

'He means to take both of us,' Camron explained.

Discomforted more than she could say, Anna smiled down at Lachie, who by standing between them looked up at both her and Camron.

It was almost as if…they were a family.

The sensible action would be to let go of Lachie's hand and beg off from whatever he wanted to show her, but Lachie was looking so tentative, proud and expectant, she wouldn't do that to him. But the Highlander's large hand still engulfed the young boy's, and again there was that fluttering in her chest that shouldn't be there. They weren't a family.

'Let's go quick!' Lachie did a little running jump and swung into the air.

Oh, no. He meant to—

Swing. Jump.

Anna didn't let go and neither did Camron and as they made their way to what she now knew was likely the pond, the boy's smile grew, and that odd formality he'd had disappeared.

Swing. Jump.

This was something he usually only did with Murdag and her. With family because Lachie was aware of the unevenness of his foot, and this swinging and jumping pronounced it. Yet here he was, confident that Camron would physically support him. Which he did.

This man... How was she to get over this attraction to him if he continued to be so good and kind?

When they reached the little copse of trees surrounding the pond, Lachie released their hands and ran ahead. Lachie's leaving should have immediately erased the intimate feeling that Camron was her husband, and she his wife, but it only grew.

Trying to avoid Camron some more, Anna stopped to brush her hands down her skirts to give him time to go on ahead with Lachie, but Camron kept his gait even with hers. So she could do nothing but continue towards her brother.

'I was up late last night,' he said.

His rich brown hair had been whipped around with wind, and he seemed more awake now. But that little crease was still there on his cheek, making this warrior, this Highlander, look a little vulnerable.

She wanted to press her lips to it.

Then his words sunk in. He could only be up late for one reason. Maybe his clothes weren't wrinkled from sleep, but from some woman grabbing at them.

'Oh.' She increased her steps.

A perplexed glance her way, Camron stayed in step. She didn't like it. 'You don't have to come any further; I've got it from here,' she insisted.

'He asked me to come.'

'It looks like he dragged you from bed.' She waved around him. 'I'm certain that was uncomfortable for you.'

Camron chuffed. 'I'd only got to sleep an hour or two before.'

When she'd retired for the evening, it was ages ago. She didn't want to imagine what had kept him so occupied. She didn't!

'I hope you spared him the sight of seeing your...friend lying with you.'

Camron stopped. She should have continued, but there was a tree directly in her way, and Camron blocked the other forward path.

She didn't want to go around him or even look at him to ask him to move. She truly didn't want him looking at her so closely! Just because she'd realised her attraction to him didn't make it sensible, and he'd never openly said he was attracted to her. But he wouldn't move.

Forced to look up at him, all she saw were puzzled eyes, and an upward curve to his lips. Was he pleased she'd figured out why he hadn't got enough sleep?

'I don't want him too shocked at his age,' she said, trying to soften her tone. To be *reasonable*. Because of course he could entertain other women.

People could…love someone else. She had, after all. It wasn't Camron's fault that she was a fool and had chosen a man who'd lied to her.

Perhaps Camron had feelings for this woman who made his clothes and hair dishevelled. Maybe she had lovingly traced that pillow crease on his cheek.

Maybe…

But she was too much a coward to ask, and Camron just kept looking, and looking, and looking at her.

She felt seen.

'He only has ten years; not that he doesn't know what happens between a man and a woman, but—

That curve to his mouth turned into a broad smile, that puzzlement eased into something like—satisfaction? He *was* pleased with himself. And she was a fool trying to explain something that didn't need to be spoken of.

'Oh!' Anna picked up her skirt and pivoted to move ahead of him.

But the warm hand at her elbow held her back. 'There wasn't anyone else in my bed, Anna.'

His eyes were taking in every flushed detail and imperfection of her face.

'There wasn't?' she said. Though immediately regretted it. 'Not that there is anything wrong with that. You're perfectly entitled to have… someone over.'

He rubbed his thumb along her elbow, which must be doing strange things to her balance because she placed her hand on his chest.

'There wasn't anyone.' He slowly shook his head, his eyes never leaving hers. 'I've had trouble sleeping since we've returned.'

He'd mentioned once how he and the others couldn't sleep. 'Like before? I could make you some tinctures.'

Another half-smile that threw her because she could feel her fingers on his chest curl…she could feel her *toes* curl.

'Not like before,' he said.

What then? She so wanted to ask him, but she felt…foolish. Again.

'Anna, about our journey to Colquhoun land… We need to talk.'

Did they? She was attracted to him, had feelings for him, but she shouldn't. Stepping away, to try and put some distance between them, she called, "Lachie?"

Taking a deep breath, Camron looked over his shoulder. 'He's excited to show you, and I'm up because I wanted you to see too.'

The fact he wanted her to see this didn't have to mean anything. It could be simply a nice gesture to make for an older sister. But she didn't feel like a sister when Camron still held her elbow. And his palm didn't feel warm because of any air around them.

It felt warm because he was brushing his thumb across her sleeve. When he still didn't let her go, she looked down. His large, callused palm cradled her arm, and as she watched he curled his fingertips for a moment as if to hold her that bit longer, then made it all worse when he released his hand, and brushed the backs of his fingers up her arm before his touch ended.

It wasn't a simple touch, but it was hardly intimate, and yet…it affected her. He was affecting her.

'Should we go?' he said.

Her head hoped upon hope for this man to fully

wake up soon, so that rasp of his would disappear. Her body didn't want to ignore him at all. Nor did it want to ignore anything about his easy stride, or how the morning wind tossed his bedridden hair, or how she knew if she touched him back, his skin would feel warm like she could simply snuggle up to—

Foolish again. He wasn't some quilt on a cold winter's day or a secure bed when she needed to sleep! She truly wished he'd walk ahead of her. Even when she sped up, he was right there next to her until finally they made it to the clearing.

'You took for ever!' Lachie whinged when they reached the pond's edge.

It felt like for ever. 'We're here now,' she soothed.

Faster than she could blink, Lachie ripped off his clothes and dove into the pond.

She caught her breath and couldn't release it.

'He's learnt to dive,' Camron said with pride in his voice.

It was exactly as she'd feared. So despite the pride in Camron's voice, despite the fact Lachie had approached the water like he'd seen it a thousand times before, and dived in with all the confidence he could ever display, she was still terrified.

And it all came tumbling out.

'Lachie!' she cried. 'What are you doing?'

'I'm swimming!' Lachie held up his arms. 'I'm actually swimming, Anna! Can't you see my arms? Can't you see my legs?'

'Why are we here again? I thought we'd agreed. I thought we—'

'He came to me,' Camron said.

Such simple words of…trust. So she stood there quietly. She watched Lachie splash in the water and it was nothing like before.

Lachie was swimming.

Laughing she turned to Camron. 'He's really doing it!'

'I'm doing it!' Lachie squealed. 'Now see this.'

And Lachie, paddling his arms with perfect precision, and keeping his body prone, put both his legs straight in the air. And didn't sink.

But it wasn't that which made Anna gasp. It was that he held up both feet side by side. As if one wasn't different than the other.

No, he wiggled them as if they were the same… it was as if they were each as good as the other. It was the most beautiful, glorious thing she had ever seen in all her life.

'A better showing than even yesterday, lad!' Camron said.

It was so much better than Anna could ever have expected.

'I'm getting out now!' Lachie scrambled to the

bank where he'd tossed his clothes. Without even properly drying off, he'd flung them on and scampered off. As if what he'd showed her was nothing but easy for him.

And because of Camron, it was easy for him to swim and dive. There was no foot making him different, yet he was still the same boy. She wanted to cry, to shout with joy!

Was this what Ailis talked of? Was this what trust got her? It couldn't be that simple, and yet maybe it was. She grabbed Camron's arm with both her hands, pulled herself up and kissed his sleep-creased cheek.

The man she held lightly, and so easily, stilled.

It should have been nothing. How many times had she grabbed her friends so? Or kissed Lachie or her father's cheek?

But she swore…she swore Camron stopped breathing, stopped his heart, stopped whatever strength and power coursed through every bone and tissue in his body.

Then she knew without looking up that, in that moment, all of those life-sustaining actions he did throughout the day, and everything about him that made him…him—a Highlander, a Graham, a warrior—was all directed towards her.

She wanted to let go of his arm; she also

wanted to raise her eyes. But it was like whatever had locked him into place locked her as well.

'Anna?' His low voice broke on her simple name.

She was incapable of looking up. Unfortunately, looking straight forward meant she looked at Camron's tunic hugging his broad shoulders and chest. She admired the stretch of the fine fabric and the shallow rhythm of his breathing.

What was wrong with her? But her arms felt strangely possessive of his arm, her gaze avaricious of his form.

'I'm truly happy for him, Camron,' she said. Her voice hadn't broken like his had, but it was a little frayed around the edges.

'I can see that,' he murmured.

The amusement in his voice eased something within Anna. Too entranced with the heat of his breath and body against her palms, and the minute bunching of muscles under her fingertips, she couldn't seem to release his arm, but she could lift her gaze from his masculine chest.

But for some traitorous reason, her eyes lingered as she took in the cords of his neck and the bump of his Adam's apple, the scruff of his beard that he hadn't shaved, the plump softness of his lips, his strong jaw ending with the almost tender curve of his ear.

By the time her eyes fully lifted to his, she felt as if she'd journeyed from one end of Scotland to the other. Her breaths came out just as unsteady as if she'd run that entire length too.

'You keep doing that,' he said.

His voice was definitely rough this time, and there wasn't a bit of sleep about it.

He swallowed hard. Somehow her gaze noticed that, too, though she didn't lower her eyes from his. No, not when they were this intent, and his pupils blown dark.

'Doing what?' she whispered.

'Looking at me,' he said.

She was. His hair was tangled, and so were his lashes. And everything…everything about him was fascinating.

'How can you think there was someone else in my bed last night?' he said. 'I already told Ewan there was no one else for you but me.'

So the whispers of him warning Ewan off her were true. Whatever attraction she felt, he did too. 'So it's not in my imagination.'

'What, this?' he said, sounding confused.

Had she said that out loud? Anna felt the turn of his body beneath her still gripping her hands, and in the corner of her eye she detected his hand rising slowly…to her nape? To her cheek? He was going to touch her. Where, how? To touch only, or to kiss?

She had wanted to kiss him in the cave until she didn't, but here it was again, that undeniable feeling. Even stronger than before. After everything she'd been through with Alan, did she dare? Anna looked at his lips again, and Camron let out a rough breath, a low growl that shook her. Such a plump bottom lip, such a masculine curve.

Her body didn't feel still any more. If his had turned towards hers, she knew hers had done the same. Other points of contact she could note: his chest to hers, one hip angled so that if she leaned up to kiss him back she'd feel that hip against hers.

Then...

Then what? She wasn't too old for him any more? She *completely* trusted him now?

No!

She wrenched herself from his side. Utter confusion, and loss, in those hazel eyes gone dark, his brows raised, then lowered. Camron's hand reached towards her as if to grab her again. To make her—

Shaking her head violently, she fisted her skirts. Even if she wanted this, how could she trust it? She was meant to be *past* this longing!

'Anna,' he said again, but nothing was rough or

sleepy about that voice. There wasn't any enticing seduction either. There was only loss.

As it should be and would always be for her. Pivoting as fast as she could, she ran.

Chapter Nine

Camron woke with a start, or maybe he had never truly fallen asleep. The days since they'd nearly kissed had been passing in some sort of wonder and feverish strain.

To be free to woo Anna…if she'd let him. To get so close and then miss such a kiss.

As he went about his days, he tried to both see her and then not see her, to give her whatever space she needed from him. But no matter what he did, meetings in tents or training, or seeing the blacksmith for the altering of his dagger handles, she was always there in his peripheral vision, in his thoughts, and at one bright moment, right in front of him as he rounded the cordwainers' structure.

He'd retired early to bed last night in the vain hope he'd actually fall asleep until tomorrow. Futile! He'd burned to kiss her, and from the flare in her eyes, she knew it. Yet, she'd denied him. Denied them.

Now he was fully awake, and aware of what a mistake he'd made…yet again. All his life he had given this woman space to…find some shelter within herself. Someplace where she could feel and be protected.

But he'd given her too much time and space. Anna had found that shelter within herself, and now resided behind thick stone walls with gates and a portcullis. If he waited much longer, she'd have arrow holes and ramparts with weaponry to keep everyone away.

She'd been so alive to him once, but one Maclean, one cursed man, had come, and she'd allowed him to take all her joy away. Did she think she had nothing left to give another man?

Oh, he could still see remnants of it when she played with Lachie and talked to her friends. He'd see it in the softness of her eyes when she shared words with her father.

And it had been there in the cave in the fire's flames, and again by the pond. No walls, no barriers, and so bright he wanted to capture it.

But she'd pulled away again. He'd seen hesitancy in her eyes, a certain anguish, and he'd let her step even further back. But what he couldn't deny was that despite those other emotions he'd seen, there was also desire.

Desire for *him*. Knowing that, he shouldn't have let her go.

With a curse, Camron yanked off his quilt, got out of bed and dressed.

His home was quiet, and not many sounds came from outside. Was his clan asleep? Was Anna? Somehow, instinctually, he knew she wasn't.

He stepped out the door. The moon was full, bright. The spring weather a little warmer now, with no mist and clear skies.

He knew where she was.

Keeping to the shadows so he wouldn't be seen, so that when he found her they would be left alone, Camron strode to the edge of the thick copse of trees by the river's side, near the tiny inlet where the women often bathed.

Steadily he walked under the dark canopy, until moonlight emerged again up ahead, and almost touched the tips of his boots, and there she was. And it was like seeing her that very first time all over again.

No, it was different…better. Infinitely more.

She wasn't sitting or combing her hair. Instead, she was bent half over, her chemise damp, and the abundance of her hair was wrapped tightly in her fists.

There was no mere hint of curves, or anything left to his imagination. No, the damp fabric and her bent posture highlighted every shadowed hollow and perfect line of her.

He wasn't a child this time, but a man fully comprehending the absolute thrilling beauty of this woman bathed in moonlight, and knowing what it meant when her eyes widened with the awareness of her own desire.

For she had wanted his kiss earlier.

And he wanted her…

Another step, and a branch cracked. She stopped wringing out her long hair and spun around.

'It's me,' he said, fully emerging into the light.

She froze as if he hadn't announced himself. Her hands still gripping her hair, her eyes wide with surprise. Her bare toes digging into the earth at her feet, as if at any moment she'd run.

Releasing her hair, which fell over her shoulder, and curled around one breast, she said, 'What are you doing here, Camron?'

Wasn't it obvious? 'Finding you.'

Another step, and her eyes darted behind him. 'Are you alone?'

Did she believe this was the daytime, and he

wanted to bring her brother to swim? Or worse, his brother and friends to drink mead? This spot, at night, this very bit of crushed grass and mud, was theirs. Always theirs. 'Do you believe I'd share you?'

She fully straightened. 'I'm bathing.'

'You were. I missed it again?'

She got a delightful crease between her brows. 'Again?'

'I've seen you here before.'

'You've been watching me?'

'You know I have,' he said. 'Despite you not wanting to talk of it in the cave.'

She opened her mouth, closed it. Shook her head as if answering her own question. 'Recently?'

Even at this distance, he could see the questions in her eyes. In the past, certainly in his youth, he would have answered all her questions, appeased her in some way, allowed her that bit of comfort and familiarity.

There was a part of him that certainly wanted to. Perhaps if they had met somewhere else tonight. Maybe outside of her own home or his, or in the chapel gardens. But they'd met here, a place in his mind that was almost sacred. Blasphemous, he knew, but it was a feeling he couldn't shake.

So he behaved like any man would at a reverent

moment in front of a woman; knowing that everything was at stake, he whispered. He enticed. He would not completely appease her curiosity because he did not want her to feel comfortable.

When Anna was comfortable, she hid behind her walls. That was what had happened ever since they'd returned from Colquhoun land. Anna thought she was safe there. Oh, he may have overstepped in the cave, but they were alone again, and now wasn't the time for retreat. However, unlike the cave, he would not force her walls down; he had to coax her out of them.

So he would.

Here, under the moonlight, next to lapping water, he would have his Anna.

Another step, the smallest curve to his lips he could not contain, he answered her. 'Not here, which is why I told you I'd missed you.'

'You told me you'd missed seeing me bathe *again*,' she said, with a bite to her voice. 'Which means you've seen me here before.'

'I saw you the first time here, and I've not seen you since. But between those times and now I have watched you in all the thousands of ways you've shown me.'

'Am I supposed to understand you?'

'Do you want to?' He took another step. 'Because I'm here now if you want to understand me.'

Her hair was sopping wet. Water ran down the black curl of it, further dampening her spring chemise. Damp, wet, the linen clung to reveal the warm hue of her skin across her plump breast, just the fairest hint of the pebbled tip he would give his right arm to taste.

She straightened a bit more, her lower lip clenched beneath her upper one. She said no words to dispute him. None. Whilst Anna was thinking about understanding him, he wouldn't dare move.

'Why do you watch me?' she asked.

Camron closed his eyes to savour this one moment. The one question he'd wanted her to ask since his return. And as his heart soared, his blood ran thick and pulled low.

Opening his eyes, he replied, 'Why does the moonlight cast its rays on your curled tresses, and the reflecting light of the river shine in your eyes? If you can answer these questions, you would know.'

Her hands went to her hips, then slid off. 'I don't even know who you are right now.'

'Who am I?' He was the man who loved her, who wished time had worked out better for them. That he hadn't been too young when Maclean had taken her heart. Or that she'd looked his way even once since.

He'd never regret giving her time to recover after that, but it was too much. His brother was right, he'd waited too long. And now some drunken bet he didn't even remember had forced his decision.

But he didn't really need the bet. He just needed her here in the moonlight.

'Camron doesn't say teasing sentences and give me riddles; that's more your brother's way. Why come out and bother a woman who is having a bath and then ask her such questions?'

Because he had questions of his own. 'How do you always know it's me? I have a brother who is identical. Yet still you know.'

She huffed. 'These questions will get us nowhere. I'm to bed.'

'You'll never have the answer to your question if you go now.'

She lifted her chin. 'Maybe I don't want to know any more.'

'But that means you did.'

She gaped. 'This isn't…suitable at all.'

There, he'd made another mistake. All his life, he'd held back, but in all that time, he'd done nothing to dissuade her that he wasn't still a child.

No more mistakes. A bet, and the drumbeat of more war, was letting him know he could waste no more time.

He took another step forward. 'You don't want suitable.'

'How do you know what I want?'

'Because I want you.'

She pressed her lips and looked over his shoulder. There were a few paths she could take to get back to her home. But all of them meant that she had to step through the surrounding trees. All of it meant that she had to step towards him to do so. She was essentially trapped.

But her eyes never showed any wariness, nor fear. Instead, there was fire, and a bit of annoyance. There was also an aching awareness that she displayed with her restlessness: the fluttering of her eyelids, the almost infinitesimal tremor in her voice.

Just a few weeks he had been home again. And in those weeks he was not the Camron that she thought she knew. She had seen him naked, and she had willingly touched him.

'What are you saying?'

'Do I need to say any of it? I've returned, and you came upon me bathing. I was naked. You never turned away.'

'I was… I was stunned,' she stammered.

'Because it was me you were seeing.'

Her eyes told him the answer. Only a few more words, a few more points to make. The portcullis and gate were open, and his lass was standing right in the threshold. A few more steps and she'd be out of the fortress she'd built around herself.

'That's what I thought,' he said with satisfaction. 'This isn't just in my imagination or yours, Anna. It simply is. Why else would you have shown me your form in the shadows of the cave?'

'I didn't do that for you—'

'And when you clung to me and kissed me when pride swelled your heart because Lachie could swim?'

'I was grateful.'

She was more than that, and she knew it, because if he lied she'd be gone. But she stood here, argued, and more than that. She didn't attempt to cover herself, though she had to feel the way the chemise clung to her curves.

'You held onto my arm as if I belonged to you, leaned into my frame so sweetly, and you didn't let me go.'

She shook her head once, twice, as if disagreeing with him and with whatever internally she was protesting.

'Tell me why you didn't let go,' he demanded.

She made some sound. 'I did! I left.'

But she'd clung to him first. 'What made you turn away?'

Such a pointed question and she knew it by her

suddenly lowering her eyes, that darting tongue telling of his forwardness. But she was brave, his Anna, and she lifted her chin when she said, 'You were going to kiss me.'

Briefly, he closed his eyes at finally hearing the truth between them. 'And you were scared.'

'No, because I didn't, *don't*, want it,' she said defiantly. 'I'm to bed.'

Did she think to flee? Fair enough. 'If you go to bed, Anna dear lass, it'll be with me.'

That hitch to her breath went straight to the root of his every desire.

'It's where you belong. It's where you've always belonged.'

She blinked a few times, and Camron knew he'd do anything to provoke that astonished look on her face again.

'In case you missed the point, I want you,' he said bluntly. 'Now tell me you don't want me.'

'Want me?' Brows draw in, lips tight, she retorted, 'You can't possibly know what you want.'

Not want her? Camron almost growled. If that Maclean wasn't married now and living a league away from here, Camron would happily break the man's nose for him.

For now he cursed his former reserved self for ever letting this woman doubt he wanted her. He'd thought if he showed maturity and patience, she would finally see him as a grown man. Instead, he should have been impulsive and taken what he wanted.

Which was her. Always her.

'I know I want lamb pie, and good ale. I know I want that bite of frost across my face to tell me of the change of the seasons. And I know I want you.'

'You compare me to food?' she scoffed. 'I'm not something you eat.'

Her words held some of the derision he was used to hearing in her voice, but it was not enough of a deterrent. Not when her eyes darted around them looking for distractions, but not finding any.

He wouldn't let her find a distraction. Not when she was right in front of him, the night was cool and the moonlight on the water illuminated everything.

Not when she was right in front of him and he had her all to himself.

She may be fighting it, but she still felt it. Felt that she was his. Not food? She was his every sustenance and he wanted to devour her.

'I wouldn't be so sure of that.'

She gasped, and he didn't hold back his knowing smirk. Oh, he liked how her mind worked so quickly. So easy to get right there where his thoughts were.

She took a step back. 'I'm older than you!'

As if that was ever an obstacle. 'It only allowed me to notice you all the sooner.'

'With wrinkles around my eyes.' She held up a strand of loose hair. 'And grey beginning.'

The hot, heavy bolt of pure lust shuddered through him. He'd have to woo his woman and fast or else he'd be upon her before she was prepared for a proper Highlander man.

'I know of those appealing strands streaking the black. I dream of your hair, my fair Anna. I long to feel it, to see it tumbled against that grass behind you and spilling against my bared chest.'

Another hitch to her breath as she registered his words. If there was light enough he knew there'd be a blush. If he could place his lips against the column of her fine neck, he'd feel the heat there.

He licked his lower lip as he tracked her hard swallow.

She took a few steps to get around him. But there was nowhere to go. There was him, the river or that knoll he'd described, and he'd have her in any direction she went.

'What is wrong with you! My nose is crooked.'

He barked out a laugh. 'Aren't you full of surprises showing me things about you after all this time.'

'Showing you things! You have seen my nose for years.'

'But I didn't know how you felt about such a fair thing.'

Her frown would be fierce, if the blue of her eyes wasn't glowing with wonder. Maybe he was getting the hang of wooing her. He'd swear those gates of her fortress were open now, and the portcullis was safely chained up.

But she hadn't stepped out from the safety of the threshold yet. A few wrong moves on his part and he knew she'd retreat once more.

So close she was, he could just take—kiss her until she was well seduced. But he wanted all of her, every bit. And she still needed to be coaxed.

'You don't know anything about me,' she objected.

Or maybe he needed to say a few more words because his lass was wilful. 'I know you prefer parsley to all other herbs. I know you play with the tips by running them through your fingers before you nibble it.'

She put her hands on her hips, which slid off, and she put them back on again. 'It's parsley, everyone likes parsley!'

'None of them flutter the leaves against their lips first.'

'They're—' she blurted.

'They're what?' Camron asked, and held his breath. 'Tell me, Anna. You accuse me of not knowing you, and yet you hold back? Tell me because you want me to know.'

'They're soft; they…smell like spring,' she huffed. 'This is ridiculous.'

'Not ridiculous, not foolish, not a waste of time or any other untruthful description you'll be giving to it because I know you like this conversation.'

She opened her mouth, then closed it.

He leaned in. 'Not willing to ask how I know you like talking to me?'

She shook her head.

'That's too bad,' he said, slowly, easily, as if he hadn't a care in the world when in fact this conversation was everything. 'I was looking forward to telling you how I know you. How with that tilt to your head, your fingers clenching into your skirts, you're trying to hold your chemise away from you so I don't see how my words are affecting you.'

That pause she gave was delicious, and he thought…he hoped she'd take that final step away from the keep, until she squared her shoulders and said, 'What words? You talk of moonlight and water as if they make any sense.'

'If not my words to woo you, what of my actions?'

Her hands fluttered at her sides before she clasped them, then shook them free.

'I don't know what you're talking about.'

Oh, she did.

'I'm fond of your brother. Care for him deeply, and if his life was at stake, I'd save him at the risk of my own. But all those occasions when I taught him to swim, I wasn't coming to your hut to find your brother. I was coming to get you. And you know this because I've watched you watching me.'

She sucked her bottom lip.

He saw the flash of her teeth, her tongue. Knew she nibbled on that plump dip that he wanted to trace with this finger, with his tongue.

Moonlight. His Anna alone, and he wanted that lip between his own. To taste her finally... She didn't know it, but she was fast running out of time.

'So you took care of my brother; how am I to equate that with your...with your wanting me?'

Stubborn lass. 'And all the years I've watched you?'

He said it, though it didn't need saying. She

knew he'd done it, as did the entire clan. He'd caught enough jests over it when he was young, but after a while, everyone had let him be with his obsession.

Because it was true. Right.

Because everyone in this clan knew Anna was his, and now it was past time to claim her.

'I've always watched you,' he repeated.

'Then you'll have seen my hips are wider.'

The sudden laugh was unexpected, as was her remark.

'What?' she said, her chin going up.

'Got a bit of vanity about you, do you, Anna? Nose crooked, grey hair and a curve to your hips,' he chuckled. 'Trying to be humble, are you? Let that go for it's a lost cause. You *should* be vain. You are a very desirable woman.'

Too desirable. The last time he'd caught her alone at night at the water's edge was all those years ago when he'd first fallen in love with her.

Then, like now, her hair beckoned him. But it was worse now. Then he'd thought her untouchable, otherworldly. Now she was a woman, whose height he knew would align them perfectly together. A woman whose curved breasts he craved to cup in his palms, and his mouth watered to pull taut her nipples between his teeth and tongue.

He rubbed his hand over his mouth when he

looked back up. She was eyeing him in horror, and not a bit of intrigue.

That was heartening. Very.

'What are you about?' She waved a trembling hand in front of her. 'I don't know you. Or this… whatever this is.'

Now those were fighting words. That little tremor in her voice showed she may be pretending not to be affected, but she was…and so was he. 'Don't know me? Look closer and you'll discover all you need to know.'

She looked to argue; instead, she kept obstinately quiet. But her eyes…they spoke clearly to him when they went from being frustrated at his challenge to accepting it.

He almost groaned when she capitulated. Almost, as her assessing gaze stayed frustratingly on his face, then flickered to the width of his shoulders.

'Eyes lower than that.' He stayed still.

He liked her eyes on him, very much, liked the way that moon's light reflected in the glorious blue of them. She could deny it all she wanted, but she was more beautiful to him now than ever.

'Lower still…' he cajoled, because her eyes were almost there to discovering the irrefutable truth that he desired her. There. *Now.*

'Who. Are. You,' she whispered again.

It was the fixation of her eyes on his breeches and the startled awe in her voice that was her undoing.

'I'm the man about to kiss you.'

Chapter Ten

But still he didn't kiss her. He held back, restrained, as if some invisible hand pressed against him. Anna felt as if a fist was squeezing her own heart at his obvious...*wanting* of her.

Desperate to look anywhere else, she took in his hands seemingly resting calmly at his sides, but one was fisted, the other tapped against his thigh.

What did he want?

What was this...this force between them? She'd come here for calm, for answers, and he'd wrecked it all like spring foliage in a gale.

On a cry, Anna wrenched away, and when he reached for her, she held up her hand. She wasn't running; she just needed a moment.

'What are you doing here?' she repeated. Why wasn't he kissing her?

She didn't understand this conversation, his

presence or what was happening with her. Oh, she wasn't naive. She'd shared a few kisses with one or two men, even before Alan came. She knew desire and want and need.

Thought she knew. But whatever crackled between her and Camron wasn't anything close to what she'd felt for any man before.

It was part of the reason she didn't run this time. She wouldn't. She'd already done that before at the pond when Camron of Clan Graham had looked at her like he wanted to kiss her.

She knew why too.

Because a large part of her had wanted that kiss. Could almost feel it when he'd looked at her the way he did. Now that she'd got as close to him as she had, she knew that intriguing scent of his, the unique salty taste of his skin and the scratch of his hastily shaved cheek against her lips.

She wanted more than that kiss, but that wasn't all that was compelling her to stay.

The other part of her, the most astounding part, was…she wanted to believe him.

She knew he helped Lachie because he was a good man. But she also suspected, as did her sister, that he did it to court her.

And maybe her sister, Beileag and her brother were all right. Perhaps it was time to let what Alan did stop ruining their lives. She knew those who loved her took the brunt of most of her grievances.

She hadn't been kind to anyone for months, and then she was rabid about seeing betrayal around every corner.

There was a wound, a splinter or fracture inside her still, and maybe it would always be there. But she wasn't that same girl Alan had betrayed, and she'd done much good for her family, for her clan, since then, and when she knew her over-protectiveness became too much, she'd tried to let go…at least a little.

Except for the last few weeks since Camron had returned, she'd fallen back into old habits again. A little more bitterness to her voice with her sister, those accusations towards Lachie's friends.

She was ashamed of how she'd been acting. Shaken up, because it shocked her. She couldn't settle all day today, and had come here to ask herself questions, to find answers. Because even if there was no one, if Camron hadn't returned, she couldn't go on like this. Maybe she needed to let it all go.

It wasn't the first time she'd thought of changing; she wouldn't have come so far already without trying to make her life different and succeeding to some degree.

But she'd thought the rest of her life would be as a good friend, daughter and sister. After all, why would any man look at her as anything else after Alan?

But with Camron's gaze, the way he'd felt against her at the pond, maybe she *was* desirable. At least to this man. Maybe he didn't see her as old or rounded or greying.

Just a few steps separated them. He wasn't saying anything, wasn't moving an inch, and yet, there was something dangerous about him. Something that was affecting her.

He was handsome, and if she was held at sword point she'd admit out loud he was far better looking than his twin. Hamilton's easy smiles weren't appealing to her. Camron's brooding patience was.

As was his hand tapping against his thigh. Why was she so intrigued when he did that?

She wanted to feel that hand, place her own against his thigh.

She wanted to believe Camron.

The belief went beyond her family's prodding, or time passing. The difference, the wanting to take a leap of faith, was because of this man.

Because he was different. Because he was constant. Yet the truth was several years did separate them, and her nose was crooked, and her hair had grey.

And despite catching glimmers of belief, she still had doubts.

'Why did you watch me as a child?'

His contemplative gaze turned pleased, and that curve to his lips flipped something in her heart. 'Only then?'

When was it she was last flirted with? When did she last enjoy it? 'Let's start then.'

'There's another question I didn't think you'd ask me...or at least not as if you truly wanted to know the answer. The cave would have been one moment, but why here?'

'Why? Because I asked.'

'But what use is a child's desire between us now?'

Oh, that crackle, that tension, was far worse with that statement. She felt it, but so did he, and let her know.

But he didn't kiss her, and she didn't kiss him, and right now, she wanted to know the answer. She'd always wanted to know.

She didn't ask when he truly was a child. Back then, she could have just teased him like the rest. At the time, she'd argued with herself that she'd give the boy some dignity.

If it was a childish attachment, it'd go away.

But he'd never stopped. It wasn't only her who had noticed. She'd witnessed his friends giving him a difficult time over it, but he still did it from time to time.

She wasn't worthy of such devotion. No more than anyone else.

She was just…her. Older sister, daughter, friend. She looked like her mother, but her sister and Beileag were comely, and yet they were not watched by anyone.

'I never asked you then.'

Another swift grin. 'I may have wished you'd asked earlier, but I'm glad you didn't. Whatever odd spouted words I would have given you then wouldn't have been eloquent or accurate. I didn't properly understand it myself.'

There. He was admitting she wasn't any more or less than anyone else; that was fair, and true. And for some reason it made her want him more. Because he wasn't mad or obsessed. What he was saying was simply the truth. At least for him.

And that might be even more heady than Seoc's mead.

'You know what I like about this conversation?' he asked in that low rumbling voice.

Everything. She liked…everything. She hadn't felt like this before, didn't know she could feel like this. There was something between them.

She was fighting it because she couldn't trust it, but then…it was Camron, wasn't it?

'The play of moonlight and shadows on your face doesn't hide your thoughts,' he said in that low voice. 'And what I see in your expression is heartening.'

She wasn't trying to hide her thoughts. She was…a little undecided on this newness she was exploring, but her heart liked it.

And Camron stood still, his brown eyes roving over every bit of her like he couldn't get enough. As though he liked everything too.

She wanted his touch.

'I thought you wanted to kiss me, not talk,' she said.

A long pause before he slowly exhaled, and his swift grin faded.

'Shouldn't tease a man when he's this earnest, lass,' he said. 'Do you believe because we're talking I'm not seeing you nibbling that bottom lip and wanting to do the same?'

Oh.

If anything, his dark eyes darkened again. The look became more intense. If anything, she wanted more of everything.

'Best get on with this talking, then,' he said, his voice that bit rougher. 'You decide when it's enough and you want me to kiss you.'

'But you already decided to kiss me,' she pointed out.

'How long ago did you think that was?' he said. 'This morning at the pond? At the cave? Just now? Years, Anna. But you decided you needed more words, and so I'm giving them to you.'

That simply, all the doubts in her head quieted, and her heart didn't question further. 'I don't need them any more.'

Camron became utterly still. 'What are you saying?'

'I've had enough words.'

There was a shift to him as if she felt him everywhere at once, but he didn't move.

'Not good enough,' he said.

Not. Good enough. He'd said he'd kiss her once she decided.

'I've decided,' she said. 'I've decided those were enough words.'

A long breathtaking pause, before he answered, 'But your words aren't specific.'

Not specific? She was having trouble catching her breath. If he wanted a longer conversation now she'd decided she wanted that kiss, she might faint. 'But you said once I was done with words, you'd kiss me.'

His eyes dropped to her lips. 'And have you

used the actual words telling me you want my kiss?'

No. But then he hadn't said she needed to. Wasn't her standing here before him enough?

The cool night breeze off the water made it known that her damp chemise was hardly any barrier. But with Camron before her, even that flimsy bit of linen she wanted gone. She hadn't done this since Alan had gone. Hadn't wanted to, and even then...this wasn't the same. She quaked with her decision, and he said it wasn't enough?

'You can't change the terms on me.'

'I'm not changing the terms on you, lass,' he said. 'Because after the cave, after you ran away from me at the pond, you need to let me know exactly what you want.'

'You keep mentioning the cave, but nothing happened at the cave!'

He raised a brow. 'Didn't it when I watched your shadows? When you gave me more of them? And are you implying you felt something at the pond this morning?'

He'd said he would kiss her. Why wasn't he kissing her? And she knew full well what she wanted from him.

But he was asking something of her. He had stated his intentions, and she'd agreed to them.

But she'd never stated *her* intentions, her wants.

And now, he wanted them very badly. His fingers were no longer tapping either, but with his palm resting on his leg, he splayed his fingers once, twice, again. Trying to release a tension that truly only had one outlet.

He wanted her words, her actions. *Her.*

'Why do you want to know?' she said. She needed to know the reason.

His eyes warmed as if pleased she'd asked. 'Because it's been too long, and there's so much… Because I like to see you flustered. That rose to your cheeks, that fluttering feeling inside of you…it's just the beginning of what is between us. And I like that I'm doing it with only my words.'

'What you're doing is frustrating me,' she said crossly.

'I know.' He moistened his lips. 'Use your words, Anna, and put us both out of our misery.'

He was holding her gaze long enough to make her heart skip.

'I don't know if I'm miserable.' She attempted to make her words light, piqued, but knew she'd failed.

There was a dangerous glint in Camron's eye, and everything else about him seemed to grow, expand. If she was forced to, she didn't know if she could fully describe him. Gone was the un-

derstanding patient man. In his place was a feral
predator heavily laden with pure hunger.

Though her thoughts cautioned her, everything
in her thrilled at that look. She needed to trust
this man. Trust him not to break her heart. Because he wasn't just asking for a kiss, was he?
He wanted it all.

And that look in his eyes…it was absolute. But
she couldn't do that in return. She wasn't whole.
There was an ache inside her heart that wouldn't
allow it. That fluttering inside her wasn't anticipation. She wasn't ready.

'Where'd you go?' Camron said gently.

'I can't do this,' she said. 'I'm not running.
We're…past that. I want to be past that. But I'm
not ready for everything. I might never be. But
I'm here, if that's what you want.'

Pressed lips, nostrils flaring, Camron looked
over her shoulder at the water still lapping under
the moonlight until his gaze snapped back to hers.

He'd said the shadows didn't hide her expression, but the moonlight wasn't so kind to her. She
saw the lower part of him, but his torso, his expression, was hidden in the tree canopy's shade.

At first she'd thought that would make it easier,
but she was wrong.

'Then come to me, Anna, one step at a time,'
he growled. 'And I'll go the rest of the way.'

She took a step towards him.

'Words too,' he commanded.

Some words were simple, weren't they? 'Thank you for helping with Lachie, thank you for being fierce in not overprotecting him and letting him grow with confidence.'

His hands relaxed at his sides.

Thank you for that wrathful demeanour when Alan wrecked my heart. You and my father were the only ones. No pity, no comforting hugs, just vengeance in your eyes. I took strength from those eyes.

Words. Ones she wasn't prepared to say. Words that took her by surprise because she hadn't fully realised they were there, in her head.

But now, it hitched her heart to know she hadn't been alone then. She wasn't alone now.

Everything about this was easy, and yet not. He was asking for so much. Couldn't she just get a kiss and be done?

But then with him, she'd always known it was never going to be just a kiss. Was that why it was almost easy to be with him like this? Because in one important way, she knew him?

Releasing a breath, taking another step forward… 'Thank you for your friendship—'

'I want more than your friendship.'

'I know,' she whispered. 'But you've got at least that. Some people don't.'

He rocked on and off his heels, releasing the mud around his boots.

'I want to touch you.' She took and held another breath. 'I don't understand why.'

Some sound of amusement from him.

She huffed. 'I understand why I'm attracted to *you*.'

'Tell me.'

That eager demand sent a thrumming pleasure through her heart, but also a skittering vulnerability. He wanted so much, and he was standing there waiting for her…to give herself to him.

Alan had simply taken. Just taken, and because she didn't know better she gave everything away.

His betrayal had left a fracture in her heart and now Camron wanted her to expose all her weaknesses.

If it was any other man, she'd be gone. But he was a constant in her life. She knew him. Had watched him as he watched her.

Maybe this was too fast by any other measurement, but for them it had been years. Or maybe all of this had truly happened in the last few weeks. She didn't know.

She *had* been different since he'd returned,

but then so had he. Familiar and yet…that day at the pond when she'd come upon him naked had changed everything. Now, he'd caught her here at this place, and they could share a kiss, couldn't they? But he wanted her to take those steps.

'I like the way your hair waves and curls at the back of your neck,' she murmured.

A shuddering breath from him.

'And when you crouch in front of the little ones to become their height when they are nervous to talk to you,' she said. 'I feel like you're doing that with me now by just standing still. I like that you're standing still—'

'You like that I'm *standing* here?' One brow rose, and the corner of his lips curved. 'I believe you just like *me*.'

She did. Was this something she'd always felt, or something new? She looked around her. 'I still don't understand why you're attracted to me. I'm older than you. I'm certain to get fatter before you. I'm—'

'Anna,' he growled.

He was right, it would be easier if he met her halfway. But he wasn't moving. When did he get so stubborn?

She took the last step and placed her hand over his, which rested on his thigh, and said the words he'd truly been asking for. Maybe for years.

Maybe for things she didn't fully understand, but she could make these little steps. They'd be enough.

'Kiss me.'

enough ...
Kissing.

Chapter Eleven

Camron had dreamt of a thousand ways of kissing Anna, and a thousand more of how she'd respond.

But he couldn't comprehend what it would feel like watching her bravery, nor her vulnerability, as she took those few steps towards him.

Some primitive part of him revelled in her showing him this…vulnerability. Another part was possessively proud in her certainty. Could any woman be more beautiful?

'Enough?' she whispered.

For now.

He was caught between two demands, to both give and not give Anna any more time. He was done waiting, done watching her run. But she gave words to her desire and her hesitancy.

One kiss, one touch, wouldn't erase what that bastard did to her in front of the entire clan or

mend her heart. Which he knew was still frag-
ile. He knew he'd take the best care of it, but she
didn't know that yet. She didn't.

The true issue, however, was that once he held
her in his arms, there was no way he'd be able to
hold back. He'd wanted her for so many years…

'It's been too long,' he said. The words easy,
but he almost couldn't get them past his clenched
jaw. He was a man possessed, obsessed with this
woman, and her fingers were caressing against
his, whilst his heart thumped hard against her
other palm.

And he wanted to go to his knees because of
that small frown between her brows.

'You don't understand,' he tried again.

She shook her head.

But her hair was still wet and he felt the drips
against their entwined hands. Felt the brush of
her thumb against his inner wrist, the tiniest tap
of her little finger against his thigh. All the while
her hand at his heart fluttered, but held steady.

And he was lost.

'I can't give you any more time,' he said
hoarsely.

So many years lost. But his dreams weren't
close to the reality of threading his fingers through
Anna's thick black hair, of tilting her head to align
her lips to his.

Of feeling her notch her chin and press close enough to meet him halfway. Of sharing breaths and the barest hint of a true kiss trembling between them.

'Kiss me,' she whispered again.

Crushing his lips against hers, Camron drank deep that little cry of surprise when he could no longer hold out. The joy of her not pulling back.

Of her accepting his kiss.

If his fingers dug that bit more into the lushness of her wet locks, she matched him with the threading of her own at the back of his neck.

Her hands finding the unguarded tender place right above his tunic sent shivers down his spine and heat all the way back up.

If his palms pressing against her cheeks were similar to the grasp of a drowning man at the banks of a raging river, her arms arced up his chest and around his shoulders were just as desperate, just as tight. And so sweet. Like her breath, her mouth.

He took her upper lip between his own and pulled, nibbled on the plumpness of her bottom one. Kissed and flicked his tongue on each corner. Everything about her a delicacy to be savoured.

Especially her whimper as he pressed his lips that much more heatedly against hers.

His body wanted to fold itself against her. He

ached to be closer, whilst his head told him to go slow.

She'd said she wanted answers. Asked him a specific question he would have answered. Then she'd tossed it all away.

His body didn't give a damn about words or questions or answers. His heart didn't either. Any reasonable man would have taken her at her word. But half of him had been driven mad.

She'd offered him what she could; he could have simply taken it.

But he'd tortured them both by demanding she meet him halfway. The man in him wanted her to walk towards him. So he'd stood still, whilst he silently begged her to leave that fortress she'd built, and walk across her threshold. He thought he'd come out of his skin when she took those final steps. When she'd answered him a thousandfold.

He was coming out of his skin now, on her throaty moan as he slid his tongue against the seam of her lips. His tongue sweeping in. Sweet. So sweet. That hint of bright parsley, the taste of pure Anna, heady. Addictive. That tremor running through her begging him to deepen the kiss. Her melting into his frame. Giving him her softness.

Not yet.

At the end of this kiss, and everything else she

was willing to give them, she couldn't have any more questions. There were so many more words to share, but when it came to him, to them, he wanted there to be no doubts.

Pulling away, he breathed hard, and was rewarded when her breaths came as fast. Something feral within him sprung up, wanted to yank her back to him. To guide her down onto the wet ground and cover her lithe frame with his.

Against her lips, he answered her question she'd thrown away about why he'd watched her years ago. 'When I was a child, I couldn't sleep one night. I came here, and you were bathing in the moonlight. It was nothing untoward, but you placed an enchantment on me. I kept watching you, believing at any moment you'd release me from your spell, but you never did.'

'What?'

Gentle kisses, light flicks of his tongue along her jawline up to her ear. 'I'm telling you of the time you bewitched a boy.'

She pulled away, opened slumberous eyes that, if possible, readied him even more for her.

She ran her hand along his jaw, looking at his face as if trying to see him as that boy. 'What was I doing?'

'Combing this hair.' He cradled her head and massaged his fingers through the thick volume.

She leaned her head back, parted her lips on a hard pant.

He almost lost every bit of his control. My God, if she was like this now from one shared kiss, what would she be like when he could truly touch, truly taste…

Careful, he warned himself. *Slow*, he told his body. He could have a lifetime with her if he didn't lose her now.

She'd walked out of her fortress for him, but the door behind her was still open for her to run back to. He could practically see it, feel it, the way she trembled, the way her eyes searched his. She'd said she wasn't ready for everything yet. He knew what she meant. He was true to her, but she didn't trust them fully. Not yet. So he'd talk of her combing her hair.

'You clutched a section and ran a comb through it. One, two, three times before you released it to gather another.'

Her eyes opened and stared at him. He let her. He'd let her do anything.

'You watched that closely?' she said curiously.

'When I think back on that memory, I know you did it with such efficiency. But there are times, I swear, I felt the release of each individual strand.'

Her eyes widened.

Had he said too much? He had no barriers or games to play with this woman. Was he supposed to use them?

'I didn't sense you there at all,' she said, looking far away as if trying to remember him being there. She wouldn't, he had hidden in the shadows.

'I stayed until you were done with that brush. When I thought you'd catch me, I escaped.'

A curve to those red lips. 'Escaped?'

'I was under a spell, remember?' he said. 'Escaping was all I could do. Until later that afternoon and I saw you folding laundry in the sunlight and it was just as bewitching. I was so angry at you after that because you clearly refused to release me from your enchantment.'

'Whilst folding laundry?' At his nod, she added, 'You are a strange man, Camron.'

'Oh, but I only told you the story about a little boy.'

Humour in her blue eyes, bemusement wrinkling her brow. When she chuckled, a hard throb pulsed in her neck, and he ducked his head, ran his nose up that delicate column. The softness and scent of her skin drove him mad.

More, his body demanded.

When she gasped as he licked and kissed the shell of her ear, he complied with another kiss.

This one certain of its destination. No more almost or hesitancy. Not tasting, but devouring.

She was delicious, and everything feminine. Soft where he was hard. One palm still at her nape, the other snaked around her waist, and gripped her hip. Spanned his fingers to feel the swell of her bottom.

This time he aligned their bodies until she gave him her weight and she slipped her arms around his back.

He slanted his mouth and she matched him. Nibbled on his lips, pulled on his tongue. Rock hard, he groaned. When he pulled away, she protested. That was heartening.

Her eyes as dark as the night narrowed on his lips. 'Why are you smirking?'

He tucked a tendril behind her ear. 'Because this is fun.'

'Fun? I thought you wanted to kiss me.' She licked her lips, and he almost dipped his mouth there again.

'I do, but…' What was he doing? She only wore a chemise. He felt the hard tips of her breasts pressed against his torso, the slight movement of her hips as she sought him through his breeches.

Years of agony, and he waited? No…he was savouring. Another brush of his calloused hand against her soft cheek, another brush against her ear until she shivered.

'When I became a man, I was resigned to your spell.'

It was her turn to smirk. 'Oh, you were, were you?'

He liked this flicker of fire in Anna. Knew it was there, hidden for so long, and loved that she shared it with him.

'Because beside this glorious hair, there were other…bits I noticed.'

'Bits?' she said. 'You *are* smirking.'

'Can't help it, you should see your expression.'

Rubbing his hands up her sides to her elbows at his shoulders and back down. Then again.

'You never truly showed me anything as you were always clothed.'

'Unlike you,' she said pertly.

'And now you're gloating.' He grinned. 'Keep in mind your chemise was wet that night and as the years went on it became more sheer, and then you added to my torment all the other times I saw you whenever you bent over or nibbled on parsley.'

'What am I supposed to keep in mind?' she asked.

'What my imagination did with those images of you…and my hand.'

On a shocked cry, she slapped a hand on his mouth.

This was so good, so right. She was at ease with him. Part of this was because they were familiar to one another, part was because she was believing him, beginning to trust him.

'I'm only saying words, Anna,' he mumbled against her palm before she huffed and dropped her hands to his chest again.

'I don't need those any more.' She plucked at the hem of his tunic. 'Especially those words.'

All right, they could do both. He reached behind him and yanked it off.

Wide eyes on him, she held herself away from him. No touching at all, but she looked. And looked again.

It was more, much more, than she had done at the pond either time. Because they were alone, there was no one awake to interrupt them. Because he'd stated his intent, and she hers.

Now there was only anticipation.

'Should I tell you how those dreams became more detailed?'

She shook her head resolutely, but her eyes didn't stop their exploring. He wanted her hands on him. He took her palm, placed it in the middle of his chest and warmed it when she didn't immediately remove it.

'Do you doubt it?'

She shook her head. 'How can I when you stand like that in front of me? Why have I never seen you here before?'

He didn't know. 'I came here at night many times.'

'I was here,' she said stubbornly. 'I came here too.'

And she wanted him to know that because she'd imagined them like this? He closed his eyes at that truth, and felt the keen loss of years. Held her closer, as if she'd run away, or disappear, or go back to where they were before.

'Tell me how this could be any better, Anna.' He almost couldn't stand all he felt. Her damp chemise, the press of her hand against his heart. The warmth of her body. 'It is impossible to improve on your crooked nose, and too big feet.'

A rough chuckle. 'I never said anything about my feet.'

'We'll discuss those some other time.'

She sighed half pleased, half wary still, and he felt that too. He knew it was right to keep this slow. It may kill him, but it would be worth it in the end.

'There are still the years between us.'

'I told you, the fact you're older than me only made me notice those curves earlier. You're a boy's dream, Anna my dear. A man's every desire.'

Through the chemise, he slid his fingers along the bottom curves of her breast. 'The plumpness of this breast.' Ran his thumb over the tip. 'The bead of this nipple. You were my first dream of a woman, and I haven't stopped dreaming of you since.'

'Oh,' she panted.

She *was* his dream now. Her cheeks flushed with colour, and he wanted to nibble down the delicate curve of her neck and chase how far it went. So he did, and every slight nick of his teeth and soothing glide of his tongue echoed in her eyelids fluttering shut, and her lips parting on small gasps.

Harder than he'd ever been in his life, caught between clothing and too much distance. Everything in him strained to touch her.

If this was a bet or wager, she made a pretty prize. But this wasn't a game when her hands explored up to his shoulders caressing down his arms, then up again to begin at the top of his chest and over…and then down to the very core of him.

Resting her head against his heart, Anna's gaze stayed on her hands as she drew circles against his stomach's corded muscles. He shuddered hard.

'I want to kiss you, Anna, touch you, lie with

you, but you need to trust me for any of that. I'm willing to be patient.'

'How patient?' she murmured.

He didn't know. Exhaling roughly, he looked over her head to the moon. Everything in him was strung tight like snapping linen in a gale.

'Because I've been patient enough.' Her fingers went to the waist of his breeches. 'I don't want more stories, Camron, I want you.'

Chapter Twelve

Camron entwined his fingers with hers and stopped her from pulling more on his laces. Raising her head, Anna searched his eyes.

'One more question for you, then,' he said.

He cradled her body against his from head to toe, trapping their hands between them. She didn't know why he kissed her the way he did, told her of his want and need and then talked so much. How long could they talk?

She felt like she was at some breaking point. Wait too long and she couldn't do this. Instead, the longer they stood in the night whilst animals scurried in the brush, toads splashed in the water and the mist rose…the more she felt the rightness of it.

The more her wariness left.

She knew she could take all the time she needed here alone to sort her feelings, but still it would always come to this. To the desire to test herself. Is this what Ailis had meant when she talked of trust? That she would trust when she'd learned to trust?

'What?' she dared to ask him.

He brushed his thumb over her knuckles. 'How do you always know it's me?'

With her thoughts fixed on the expanse of his chest, his uneven breath, the rumble of his voice, his question made no sense. 'What are you talking of?'

He gave a quick grin. 'Who is standing before you?'

'You are.' She tried to release her fingers from his, tried to get to his laces, but he held firm.

'Yes, but how do you know it's *me*,' he repeated.

'You answer to your name?'

Their fingers danced, and with every brush of a palm or a calloused tip, she felt the slight movement of his hardness against her stomach and that sent an aching heat everywhere their hands were not.

It made her palms damp and sweat prickle in the small of her spine. Her breath which he took with each kiss now became nigh impossible and he wasn't doing anything except running one finger up to the tip of hers, then down the vee between fingers and pressing there. It felt indecent, and heady.

Now she knew what he meant by waiting too long. She felt if he kissed her again, any other touching wouldn't matter.

His lips curved. 'I like that bit of fire in you, lass. But I need the truth more. We play with time between us. You told me you don't want to wait, I don't either.'

This was a test. Again she was reminded that if he was any other man, she'd have run away. Was she brave enough for this?

'We've lived in the same clan all our lives, so of course, I've seen you plenty of times before.'

There came an edge to the corner of his eyes, as one brow raised. Whether he meant to or not, he pressed harder into the vee between her fingers.

'How do you always know it's me, though?' he pressed. 'I'm an identical twin. Same height, same hair, same colour eyes, same voice. How do you know I'm not Hamilton?'

When he kept rubbing one calloused finger across her inner wrists back and forth, back and forth, she snapped.

'You tap,' she said. 'On your right leg you rest the heel of your palm and you tap your fingers.'

His eyes narrowed. 'I don't do that all the time.'

'You do whenever you watch me.'

'Such a small detail. So…miniscule.' His brow eased and a dancing light entered his dark eyes. 'And so all becomes clear.'

At her flummoxed expression, he added, 'You watch me as I watch you.'

Nothing was clear to her. She didn't know why he did such a thing. And he was so smug she wasn't about to tell him of all the other ways she knew it was him. Even when he stood out in the far fields next to his brother, she could always tell them apart.

Everything about him was different. From the way he rolled his shoulders or held his head. From the way he spoke, or smiled, or…breathed. She always knew it was him.

But he was right, that wasn't…typical. Her sister didn't even know the twins like she did. Camron was right. She did watch him as he had her. Even despite their age difference, despite falling in love with the Maclean, she knew this man before her to his bones.

Maybe that was why when his eyes darkened more, when he told her to hold still, she did. He disentangled their fingers to hold the chemise at her hips. She knew what he wanted, and she wanted it too. At her nod, he yanked the garment up and over her head until she stood naked before him. On a rough exhale he threw the chemise down to where he had discarded his tunic on the grassy soft knoll sans any mud.

Sneaky Highlander, he'd made a bed for them.

The cool air and his intent stare raced goose pimples from the heels of her feet up the backs of her legs and over her body. Traces of the cool night wind brushed across her bared nipples, more heat from his gaze racing across that. Until she shook and trembled before him.

'Camron,' she pleaded.

With a groan he lifted her, and laid her down on their clothing on the soft bank. There was no cold now, as he took her lips, as he parted her thighs with one of his own. No more did she feel that wariness. He was right, she had watched him. He was different from any other man.

He was Camron and she wanted him.

A soft breath against her cheek, more kisses along her jawline and lower. She stretched her neck to give him access. Arched her back to give herself as he held himself aloft. Not much, just enough to drive her mad.

Hands and lips going lower yet, her sinking her fingers into his thick hair. His rumble of approval at her demand to move his kisses from one breast tip to the other. And on each tip his tongue fluttering…no, tapping.

She stilled her hips, and realised his hands at her hips, his roughened palms, his hard fingers, were doing the same thing.

'What are you doing?'

He lifted his head, and smirked. 'If you have to ask there will be words involved. Do you want words now?'

'I thought you were the quieter one,' she said wryly.

'Don't know everything about me, then, do you?'

She couldn't believe she got to touch this man, brush his hair away from his cheek, trail her fingers down his jawline to his neck. Feel the roughness of his stubble end in soft warm skin, down to his big thick shoulders peppered with freckles that she knew were there, but it was too dark to see.

'What are you doing?' he rumbled. His voice partly a rasp, partly a moan, and everything she ached to hear from him.

Whilst he stayed mostly dressed, she was completely bare to another man. Camron had asked her permission, and she'd given it. That was telling.

Maybe she could do this, maybe that fractured splinter that was left in her heart a year ago would simply get smaller and fade away. She could believe that with the warmth of his body against hers. He felt good, right.

'I miss seeing your freckles,' she admitted.

'My freckles?' he said.

'On your shoulders,' she added.

He made some pleased sound. 'How long have you been looking at me?'

For ever.

'Since you were naked,' she said.

He chuckled. 'We'll remedy that next time, yes?'

More of this? She nodded, and he smiled. One that reached his eyes, warm, soft. Good. Until he lowered his head, and began those intent kisses, those searching hands all over again.

She clung to those curls at the back of his neck, and when that wasn't enough, she anchored her nails on the tops of his shoulders.

His breath harsh now, whilst hers became a mere pant. A lick along the underside of one breast, a hand sliding down one thigh, opening her wider for him.

But always, always, that rhythm of his driving her part mad, part craven.

'You're tapping,' she said. That's what he'd been doing this whole time. That crazy fluttering heavy feel of his fingers, of his mouth, his kisses. Tapping. Everywhere.

He huffed against her belly, circled his tongue until it dipped, clutched her hips which she couldn't still.

'Just letting you know it's me.'

Oh.

Around he went again, with ardent thrusts of his tongue, until she felt that pleasure deeper inside, more piercing. His grip tightening as her hips rose to meet him. But his hands, his mouth, his tongue, weren't yet where she needed them.

'Camron.' She licked her lips, trying to draw moisture there to make any words. 'Are you...? Are you being patient again?'

'Savouring,' he groaned.

She opened her eyes: his head bowed, his hair brushing against her belly, his hands, so big, so good, gripping her waist.

His shoulders spanning wide... She desperately wanted the daylight on them so she could see. Wanted—

Another fluttering of his tongue, a tapping of his fingers. The heat searing fast and strong. Enough of the savouring.

'Camron!' she demanded.

He laughed this time. 'Don't want me tapping here, or...here?'

Yes, but more! 'No,' she said.

'Can't tell it's me yet?' He huffed. 'What about here?'

Sliding his hands down her thighs, he tapped against one, then the other. Which should have felt foolish or light, or anything else, but what it actually was, was a drumbeat of her pulse, a rhythm of her desire.

'Not there,' she moaned.

Another hum, another slide of his hands to her inner thighs. Opening her more, until she felt the cool of the night, the heat of his breath against her dampness.

Camron paused.

She couldn't have it. Fingers raking through his hair, hands pressing hard on his shoulders. Hips rising towards him.

'Still,' he commanded.

But she couldn't.

He pressed his own fingers into her tender flesh until she lay quiescent, and finally heard him speaking.

Resting his head on her belly, his eyes feasting on all that he'd revealed, Camron rasped, 'Years I've watched, waited. I wanted, dreamed, and all that time you held these secrets, these treasures, from me.'

Did he expect words from her; she barely knew how to open her eyes!

'I want your kisses,' she said desperately. 'I want you.'

He raised his head then, his eyes burning. 'I wanted to take this slowly. We shared our first kiss just moments ago.'

They had, but this wasn't like anything she'd experienced before, and he… Everything told her this wasn't the same for Camron either.

They were different together.

'Maybe slow isn't for us, maybe we've done slow already.'

'Anna.' He tenderly kissed heated flesh. Everything about his touch and kisses was different now. There was still that drumbeat, those heartbeats, but they were hurried, needful.

Hands now sliding up her sides as his mouth went lower. Her hips still as she braced her feet flat giving access to any and all of her.

And Camron took. No, he *gave* all to give her pleasure. Every kiss along the crease between her leg and mound, every breath against her damp folds.

He flicked and slid his tongue, separating her delicately, revealing even more. A finger notched low, a curved tongue tapping at her entrance. A gasp from her, a low chuckle from him.

'It's you,' she gasped. 'I know it's you!'

'Now you make me want to do it more.'

And he did. Until she was clenching the sides of his body with her legs and clutching the top of his head. Until she broke on a keening moan. It didn't end.

Still pulsing with pleasure, Camron wrenched from her grasp.

'About to spend!' Kneeling, he shoved at his breeches, his braies. Kicked them down until they snagged on his knees around his boots.

But she didn't, couldn't, pay attention to the rest, until with a groan he clasped his length hard at the base, and threw back his head at the thwarted pleasure.

She'd never seen anything so magnificent in her life. Never wanted anything more.

'No more going slow,' she said.

Maybe they didn't know everything about one another, maybe there were still secrets. She didn't care. When the head of him beaded, and he ran his palm over it only to stroke back down again…

She didn't. Care. Jerking up, grabbing anything of him she could reach, she tugged him down on top of her.

He complied.

One hand braced by her head, the other stroking the back of his finger up her thigh, he said, 'I don't believe you want me tapping here, Anna.'

No, she didn't. She wanted him higher. *There* all over again.

He seemed to know it, too, when he lowered his hips, bowed his head and kissed her. Pressed that hand on her thigh, and then his length along her folds.

'How about here,' he whispered as he nipped and licked her jaw, her chin. Sucked in her lower lip until she arched her back.

And he sank his body lower yet, his arm giving out until he was on his elbow with his extended fingers gripping her dark strands spilling out over their clothes underneath them.

He hadn't notched his shaft, didn't sink into her as she thought he would, but the heavy base of him was there at her centre, and she felt the weight of him right at the tip of her folds. Right where she needed him.

'There,' she breathed out.

A hitch to his breath as if she'd surprised him, so he rocked his hips, and dragged his length through her.

'Again,' she demanded.

Camron held still. 'Tell me why?'

She didn't want to say. What they did made no sense except to the two of them. But aloud? It still made no sense. She shook her head, felt the wet grass through the discarded clothing beneath them.

Felt the hard press of a man everywhere else.

He snapped his hips. Dragged the base of his length up to the tip and down hard through her soaked folds.

'Why?' he demanded.

'Camron,' she warned. She was going to break again. The moonlight barely reaching them both, she couldn't see him as she wanted to, but felt him. But she needed more. Why wasn't he giving her more?

'I'm right there, too, Anna,' he rasped low in her ear, the words piercing through her as surely as his touch. 'I'm right there, say the words. Why the tapping?'

Words. Deeds. He wanted her to meet him halfway again.

'So I always know it's you,' she panted.

He raised his head; his gaze held hers. She wouldn't let it go. His breath nothing but ragged gasps as he held his control, whilst she was losing hers.

Coils, spiralling outward, feeling him swell against her outer lips, his hips rocking and snapping more tightly against her, driving her upward, ever tighter. She couldn't stop the pleasure cresting.

'Camron,' she cried out.

'Now, Anna,' he groaned as he spilled. They shuddered and breathed out together. 'Now it's enough.'

Chapter Thirteen

'Why are you here again?' Murdag said. 'You never come here.'

'*You* never come here,' Anna argued, though she'd promised herself she would make an effort to stop arguing with her sister. This didn't count, did it?

'I do when I want fresh bread,' Murdag retorted.

But her sister wasn't simply grabbing a loaf and dashing off, she was helping in the ovens. That bore some discussion, but not now.

'I'm here to apologise,' Anna said, taking the bread peel from Murdag and walking the few steps to the table to shake out the loaves before putting on two risen loaves and handing it back to her sister. The movement was completely unnecessary since her sister could easily carry the peel and take the two steps to the tabletops herself, but it allowed Anna to be close enough to say the words that needed to be said.

'I've heard your apologies before.'

'I'm doing mine here in the kitchens where anyone can hear.' Anna handed her the peel.

Her sister hesitated for a moment before taking it from her. 'What's changed?'

So much.

As much as they argued, they *were* sisters, and Anna wasn't surprised Murdag knew she was risking her pride by being overheard.

Was Camron good for her?

If she went with everything she knew of his past, or his reputation, she'd recommend him as a good husband to any of her acquaintances. He'd always been kind to Lachie, never once treating him different than any other boy.

On Colquhoun land, he was well received, and Ailis teased her about his protectiveness of her and how handsome he was. But…was he *good* for her?

Ailis had said she had to learn to trust in order to trust, which had made no sense to her at all until last night. But she did trust Camron. She must, or else she couldn't have shared what she did with him.

Except… She was still scared, and he'd taken

all her reasonable excuses to stay away from him and touched and kissed them away.

He wasn't a child; she wasn't too old. He'd burned away all those insecurities until she was nothing but simply her. She hadn't been that way since she'd first met Alan.

No, she was different. There was still the hurt Alan had caused, and she could never be that free with herself again.

When Alan came to Graham land, he became the very air she breathed, his smiles the sun. She hadn't been the only one to welcome him with open arms. And when Alan chose her out of all the available maidens, she had heedlessly thrown herself at his every smile and touch.

Was Camron similar to Alan? Until this spring, she wouldn't have even compared them. She only did so because…she had feelings for him.

'I talked to Ailis.'

'That was two weeks ago,' Murdag said. 'You've already told Father and me how she was doing.'

'I didn't tell you of the bits of wisdom she gave me.'

Murdag stopped. 'Gave or pummelled into you? Because I'm going for pummelling.'

'She's pregnant, and I couldn't exactly run

away. So I had to stand and take it. Does that count?'

'Good.' Murdag gave a small smile. 'What did she tell you?'

'She told me to learn to trust…and then I'd trust again.'

Murdag shoved a few loaves on the peel, then slowly turned. 'What does that even mean?'

'I had trouble with understanding that too.' Pushing the hair strands that stuck wetly to her cheek, Anna stared at her sister.

Because that's what scared her too. She'd kissed and touched Camron. He'd waited and been patient. It was her who'd begged him. Wanted him. And she felt…right about doing everything they'd done. They'd felt right together.

She wanted more of last night, and that was something she never could admit. She was no virgin. Alan's false promises and her own recklessness had ensured that, but Camron's touches were nothing like Alan's.

They way he'd looked at her, his brown eyes burning with truth in the moon's light. He'd followed her to that bliss, that joy…that connection. And when it was over he'd given her such tender care. And an even gentler kiss to her temple.

Even when they stood, he'd cradled her in his arms for the longest of moments before he bundled her up and made sure she took the path first and alone to return to her home.

What did he mean that it was enough?

He hadn't been pleased with her telling him she couldn't give him everything. She'd felt his disappointment, but he'd still kissed her, held her.

Was it enough for now? She hoped so. Maybe with time, maybe that pain in her heart at the memory of Alan would eventually fade. Maybe she could trust Camron. Fully trust him.

She wanted to.

But she knew she had to come here first. Had to face her sister and apologise. Truly say she was sorry and mean it.

'So what is it?' Murdag put the peel back in Anna's hands.

'It's something I realised last night.' Turning her back on her sister, Anna released the baked loaves on their table and shoved the new ones on.

'What about last night?'

How much to tell? Her knuckles white around the handle, Anna tried to loosen her fingers. Her sister was looking at her strangely.

'Will you be forgiving me?' she said instead. 'I know I haven't been easy to get along with. I know that I will probably struggle again, but I think I can try.'

'Because of last night?' Murdag pressed.

'Can you not say it so loudly? Or maybe we can go somewhere else?' She was fine apologising to her sister—she wasn't fine telling the whole clan of her and Camron. At least not yet.

Murdag's eyes darted to the open doors of the baking ovens back to her. 'Can we stay here a bit longer?'

So her sister was here for more than fresh bread. 'What are you not telling me?'

'It's Hamilton,' Murdag blurted.

Anna blinked.

Pressing her lips closed, Murdag turned to release the next loaves in the oven and then turned back. Recognising that closed-off expression, Anna sighed and took the peel from her, loaded fresh loaves again, then handed it back to her sister so she could place them in the oven.

More voices surrounded them as they continued working with the fresh and baked dough. They'd arrived in the kitchens early when there were only a few people about; now it was getting on in the morning, and it was filling up.

Murdag sighed. 'It might be all in my head.'

Anna felt that way about what had happened between her and Camron. For how could someone youthful and vibrant like Camron really want an older woman? Yet what they'd shared couldn't be denied. She had trusted him, and she had his touches and stories to back that up. This morning, she couldn't help feeling differently.

'What's in your head?' she asked.

'Since his return Hamilton's been everywhere I am,' Murdag whispered heatedly. 'As I'm cleaning out the stables or grooming the horses. If I'm at the blacksmith's, he keeps trying to talk to me, instead of letting me get on with my day.'

It wasn't like their homes were far apart, and they'd been friends for all their lives, so him conversing with her sister wasn't anything new. But her sister being concerned about it was.

Maybe…was it possible Hamilton liked her sister?

Murdag stopped, looked over Anna's shoulder before she leaned in and whispered. 'But then all of a sudden, he's not anywhere. But it doesn't matter because I keep looking over my shoulders like I'm being followed. You know I hate being followed, and watched, and…supervised.'

Did she ever. 'I always thought you actively went to places you weren't supposed to, so as not to be watched. Ravines, into wolves' dens—'

'I never went into a wolves' den,' Murdag denied.

'You were walking that way.'

Murdag blew a raspberry. 'I was a child.'

'Imagine what you would have done if you were older and had longer legs!'

'What about you?' Murdag said. 'What's with you being here, and last night…and you *look* different.'

'Not here.' Anna grabbed her hand. 'I have to talk to you outside.'

Murdag grabbed a warm loaf and followed her out. Feeling an ease in her heart, Anna grinned back at her sister.

Out of the kitchens, she felt a sharp bite of pain in her stomach, feet stepping on hers as Anna ran right into one of the growing children.

'Ach! Raibert, what are you doing right here?' Anna let go of Murdag's hand and held the boy's shoulders. 'Did I hurt you?'

Raibert, a boy of about twelve, straightened himself out, as did she.

'Anna! Anna!' Lachie ran up to them with Roddy, Raibert's brother, fast on his heels.

Anna held still.

'What is it?' Murdag tore off a piece of bread and handed it to their brother.

Murdag didn't seem to be stunned, but Anna was. Here was Lachie, running with Beileag's siblings, Raibert and Roddy. Her brother, who'd never quite fit in because of his foot, was…joyous.

The sun was bright, and she couldn't control

her emotions, but this wasn't because of her…it was him, because her brother was so happy.

Anna brushed his dry hair with her fingers, which was already getting crumbs in it. 'What else do you have to show me today?'

Roddy made a funny sound. Raibert, who the eldest of this bunch, turned red. Lachie was simply pure sunshine with rays of mischief. 'Oh, it's going to be good,' Lachie said around a mouthful of bread.

Anna looked to her sister, who shrugged.

But Raibert looked like he was about to be sick, and Roddy looked down at the ground and kicked dirt.

'Maybe we should stay quiet about the whole thing, huh, Lachie?' Raibert said.

Roddy tried to grab Lachie's tunic. 'Yeah, Lachie, let's go.'

But Lachie for once was too quick as he skipped around her. Normally he walked as steadily as he could to cover up his foot that wouldn't cooperate, but this time he displayed the little limp in front of these two boys, in front of anyone who could see.

Except the two boys looked suddenly uncomfortable. They were acting like whatever Lachie was about to report wasn't good at all. Something inside her flared hot and curled black like a dying ember.

Hands on her hips, Anna said, 'What are you two up to today?'

She swore…she swore if they didn't tell her they intended to harm her brother she didn't know what she would do. Roddy was the same age as Lachie, but Raibert was older, so surely he could see it wasn't right? They couldn't play some cruel prank on him…

Trust.

Lachie stopped skipping. Stopped skipping so suddenly he had to hold onto her skirts to keep from falling over, and her heart just tore out of her chest seeing his stalwartness and fragility. And these boys, these *boys*—

Raibert glowered, his arms going about his waist.

'I wanted to tell you…' Lachie said, his expression a mix of his former happiness and confusion. 'I only wanted to tell you we're to play this greatest game.'

'Leave it, Lachie,' Roddy said gruffly. 'We'll go and see you later.'

'Oh, I know what this is about…' Murdag said.

She did? Because to her it looked like the boys were about to set up Lachie to take the blame for some jest they were about to play.

But her sister was still chewing on bread, and there was a mischievous light in her eyes.

Murdag pointed to Beileag's brothers. 'Guilty expressions.'

Anna looked closely. They did look sheepish, a little red around the ears too. But they held still for inspection. If they were going to be cruel, wouldn't they have just taken off?

Trust, she repeated to herself.

Anna looked at her brother, who had lost some of his enthusiasm, but he, too, was standing there as if he couldn't wait to tell her.

Anna smiled at Murdag and pointed to Lachie. 'Too excited?'

Murdag nodded slowly. 'What were you boys going to do to Oigrhirg?'

Oigrhirg was Beileag's younger sister, but older than the boys. Oigrhirg wasn't quiet or shy like Beileag. In fact, she was quite the force.

'We're putting beetles in her bed!' Lachie exclaimed.

Raibert's arms went out. 'Lachie!'

The boy shoved bread in his mouth. 'Murdag asked me.'

Anna, so relieved, but a little horrified, asked, 'Why?'

Roddy mumbled, but Anna couldn't catch one word.

'Say that again,' Murdag laughed.

'We were getting her back for pouring water in my bed,' Roddy said.

'And pretending he peed on it,' Lachie said conspiratorially.

Murdag choked on the next laugh.

Raibert growled. 'It's ruined now.'

Hands on her hips, Anna shook her head. 'No, it's not. Go get her.'

'Anna!' Murdag exclaimed, as the boys ran off before she could change her mind.

Trust. Little by little she could feel herself come back. Could remember what she was like before Alan. She wasn't quite there yet, but she could almost see it. Almost feel it.

'What happened to you?' Murdag said, not without a little awe.

Winking, Anna turned. And there was Camron, with his half-smile, and tousled brown hair. Always handsome, this morning he took her breath away.

'Do you want to go for a swim?' he said.

Mouth gaping open, loaf half up to her mouth, Murdag gasped. 'Last night, huh?'

Of course her sister understood, of course she forgave her for the past year. If possible, Anna's smile grew wider yet, as she grabbed Camron's hand, startling them both. Oh, she may not ever be as free as she once was, but did she ever want to be that naive, that trusting, again?

This was enough.

'All day?' she asked.

His hand tightened around hers, and his half-smile grew. 'All day.'

Chapter Fourteen

'If you smile any wider people are going to think you're me.' Hamilton spit blood off to the side.

'Impossible.' Camron kept his stance wide, and his arms out. His brother often attempted to distract him and show off with chatter when they sparred.

Now, however, it was late, and many people were preparing for dark. But Camron had spent the day with Anna, swimming, talking, walking. The entire clan had seen them and although there had been times of hesitation, and an almost shy wariness about her, she didn't leave his side.

Needless to say, even when the sun was beginning to set, and though he'd barely slept the night before, and had stayed occupied all day, he couldn't contain himself.

The only person mad enough to take him up on the offer to train was his brother. They'd had an audience at first, but now it was just them out in the fields, near the forest and the orchards. Nowhere near children or mothers tsking because of their enthusiasm.

Since they were so equally matched, and had trained together all their lives, the grappling and dodging quickly took care of the excess strength he had. But before he could call it off, his brother had struck a solid blow, and now they faced off in a true stance.

He was only waiting for Hamilton to— There! Camron leapt and struck. Unbalanced, or surprised, Hamilton staggered back. When he registered the strike, or perhaps the pain, Hamilton came after him with fists raised.

Camron ducked the first one, but Hamilton's other fist was a solid blow across his jaw. Camron saw black. This time he stumbled into his brother, and they both hit out again and again. A couple more strikes and they agreed to call it quits.

Bellowing breaths as they sat, Camron and his brother looked out on the damp field and leaned their backs against two of the bordering orchard trees.

'What was that all about?' Camron asked curiously.

'You said you wanted to train.'

Camron had just wanted to have fun with his brother. 'You hit me and it hurt.'

'You should have ducked,' Hamilton said. 'And you hit me next.'

He had…mostly out of surprise and then they just hadn't stopped. Camron was thoroughly exhausted, yet his brother looked knotted up with his thoughts.

'Want to do it again?' he offered.

'If I thought it would do me any good, I would. But I can't feel my arms now.' Hamilton patted his arms on one side, then the other.

That brought up memories. 'Isn't that how we got here the night we arrived?'

'That was our legs not moving because of the mead, remember.'

When Hamilton went quiet, Camron said, 'You want to talk?'

'You wanted to train, and I agreed.' Hamilton tossed a pebble out towards the sodden field.

'That wasn't training. What's bothering you?' Camron picked up his own pebble and threw it towards his brother's rock. It was too small to tell if it went further.

Hamilton chuckled low and tossed another. 'Sometimes I hate it that we're twins.'

'I forget that we're twins,' Camron said.

'Madness!' Hamilton stretched out his legs and

crossed his ankles. 'Not only are you fortunate to look like me, but imagine all the jests we would have lost over the years.'

'Unless I'm staring at my reflection in the water all day like you, I forget you look like me.'

Hamilton picked up another pebble, but didn't throw it. His face had grown pensive again.

Bending his knees and resting his forearms on each one, Camron said, 'It's because of Anna. She always knows it's me and not you.'

'And because you love her, it's important she can tell the difference.'

Camron nodded. He hadn't meant to hurt his brother about being a twin, though.

Hamilton opened and closed his hands around the pebble. 'You do know it's because of that tapping thing you do against your leg.'

He felt it went further than that, but until Anna had said it, he never even knew he had a tell. 'Why didn't you ever say anything?'

'What's the point, you only ever do it when you look at her,' Hamilton said. 'And we all know you wouldn't stop watching her.'

'I could truly murder you right now.'

'Well, get in line. You aren't the only one,' Hamilton said morosely.

His brother was always getting into trouble, but this seemed different. 'Whatever it is, just say it.'

'I wish this tree we leaned upon had ripe pears.'

The trees they leaned upon, all the trees in the orchard, were in leaf and still blossoming but were far from bearing fruit. 'I'm not intending to sit here until autumn waiting for my answer.'

Hamilton clenched the pebble in his fist. 'I saw you with Anna today. That looks like it's going well. Any hope for me may be lost.'

Camron turned his head, winced at the bite of pain in his jaw. His brother had swung hard.

'Wooing Murdag not going so well?'

'Murdag? No, that's fine,' he said.

Fine, when courting anyone, was never good. 'Shouldn't there be passion? A kiss? Holding hands. Held eyes?'

Hamilton bowed his head. 'There's that. And that's the problem.'

That didn't make any sense, and Camron was feeling too sore to force his brother, who didn't want to tell him. The fact Hamilton was so secretive about it was concerning. His brother usually liked to talk out his problems, whereas he told no one about his.

Even his feelings for Anna would have been a secret if he hadn't been a child who couldn't stop staring at her. Instead, his brother was staring pensively at the open field not looking for answers…simply looking lost.

Whereas he'd spent the day with Anna and felt found.

'So it's good, then.' Hamilton turned his head. 'You and Anna? You were gone all last night.'

Attempting to contain the flare of heat at just the memory of last night, he answered, 'I was with her all today too.'

'But I'm your brother, so I want details on last night,' Hamilton said.

His brother's words were teasing, but there was no matching light in his eyes. He knew he'd been distracted with Lachie and Anna since he'd returned from Colquhoun land, but what had happened to Hamilton in that time? Though his brother was less boastful than usual, he wasn't usually this subdued. When he could barely contain his joy, it unsettled him to see his brother so.

'You will tell me what's wrong,' he asked again.

Hamilton exhaled roughly. 'We made a bet, and it's all turned out well for you. How could it be wrong when you finally have Anna?'

Again, his brother denied him a straight answer. 'I told you, I don't remember making that bet.'

Hamilton's eyes grew intense. 'Does it matter if it turned out so well?'

Well was hardly a description of all he'd shared

with Anna. They still had much to discuss and a long way to go before that wariness of hers fully left. But they'd shared their lives through stories, their bodies by the river and an entire day of simple, small enjoyments.

Anna was a terrible swimmer, but knew it, and splashed as much as Lachie had when he had begun to learn. Her laughter and exuberance...the sheer abundance of her company after years of being denied, it was overwhelming. 'It is good.'

Hamilton threw the pebble. 'Then all is well, especially if she doesn't find out about the bet.'

Camron's stomach sank. He'd forgotten about that. 'How would she find out? We only told Seoc.'

Hamilton quickly looked away.

Camron groaned suddenly. 'I forgot. You told Beileag, didn't you?'

Hamilton stood. 'She won't tell Anna. She promised. But I needed—'

'To gain her help to woo Murdag? To win a meaningless bet!' Everything was becoming clear to him now. Hamilton's troubled mien... Seoc's telling them of how much time his brother had spent with Beileag versus Murdag.

'Please don't say that. It's not like that!'

'You think I went after Anna because I made

a bet?' Camron said. 'Then I'll make it easy for you. You win. The bet's over.'

Hamilton's eyes skidded to the side. 'But you haven't asked her to marry you yet. The game hasn't even been properly played until you ask and she agrees.'

Hamilton still wanted to play the game when there was so much at stake for him and Anna? 'You're spending more time with Beileag than Murdag. Admit it. You only want to keep the bet going because if it's not, there's no excuse to go after what, or who, you truly want.'

Hamilton opened his mouth, closed it.

Shoving his brother in the chest. 'Seoc was right, we are fools, and you most of all. Do you think you need a bet to tell Beileag how you feel?'

'If we end it…what reason do I have to talk to her? You know how quiet she is. Trying to win the bet gives us a purpose to speak.'

'That is the reason you use? You truly don't deserve her,' Camron said, disappointed. 'And after all these years, I don't need a bet between us to win Anna. I've had her in my arms. The bet has already been won by me.'

Filled with disgust, Camron strode out towards the field. He wouldn't return to his bed this night either. But instead of the elation of last night, he was only filled with dread that Anna would hear about that foolish bet before he could confess to her himself.

He had to remedy this, but how to even tell her when she was still so mistrustful and wary?

'Say that again,' Murdag said.

Anna didn't want to say it again. It was difficult enough the first time. When Camron had held her by the river two nights ago, when they'd kissed and touched, she'd given him so much, but still held something back. When he'd asked her to swim yesterday morning…she'd given a little more of herself. She'd thought it a perfect day.

A day of sunshine, of more stories, of finding out how far he'd travelled, the prepared food he didn't like. No subject was serious as they swam and walked. It seemed he'd sensed her reservations and kept matters light. She was so very grateful because she hadn't freely walked with any man for over a year. Ever since her clan had witnessed her total humiliation with Alan.

When the day had ended, it had been difficult parting from him.

Too full of happiness, she hadn't wanted to sleep. So she'd wandered off to think. Since returning to the river wasn't going to help her gain perspective any more, she'd walked amongst the flowering pear trees, but it was soothing to weave in and out of them.

Then she'd heard two voices on the other side of the pear, pine and birch trees. Two voices she'd recognised as Hamilton and Camron.

After all the words they shared, she'd know Camron's voice anywhere. She'd walked closer to them to reveal herself, but then Hamilton said her name and she stopped.

She'd thought, foolishly now she realised, but she'd thought if she overheard what they said, her final doubts regarding Camron would finally ease.

Though she'd heard only smatterings of words, they were enough to find no comfort in anything at all, for they'd talked of bets and marriage. Her time with Camron had been false, the result of a bet between the brothers. Her emotions since then had been a cross between despair and rage, and she could find no in between. Unable to be kind to Lachie or anyone else this morning, she'd begged her sister and Beileag to a council here in her bedroom.

She didn't know what to expect from either of them, but Murdag's request for her to tell the tale again, and Beileag's obvious discomfiture, made her doubt they could help her. Still, she'd try.

'Last night,' she began…then had to clear her throat of the large lump in it.

'Why make her repeat it?' Beileag said gruffly.

'Why make her repeat it!' Murdag echoed. 'Because I can't wrap my head around it. There's no reason for it… And why have you suddenly gone all pale?'

Beileag put her hands to her cheeks. 'I'm not pale. And even if I was, maybe I'm just…troubled?'

Murdag was right, Beileag was paler than usual, but more than that her eyes kept looking at everything in the room except for her. Something was different about her too.

She didn't have the strength for any more secrets! Stumbling back until her legs hit the bed, Anna fell backwards, grabbed the extra linen and pulled it onto her lap.

Exhaling roughly, Murdag slumped against the opposite wall, and Beileag delicately took the only chair.

She stared at her sister and their friend. 'There's no other way to interpret their conversation. Hamilton and Camron made a bet to marry, and whoever got married first won.'

'What would they win?' Murdag asked.

What would they win? 'What does it matter!'

Anna cried out. 'This isn't a game! They bet on our lives and I…'

Murdag looked at her closely. 'You what?'

Beileag gasped, her hand back to her mouth. 'Oh, Anna…'

'We did more than spend the day together yesterday. The night before, we might have…kissed.'

'You kissed him?' Murdag's eyes locked with hers. She could never hide anything from her sister. 'What else?'

'Does there need to be anything else?' she said. She was loath to tell them she did a lot more than that with Camron. *Wanted* a lot more with the Highlander. All those words and gentle kisses were dead to her now.

She feared if she did tell them, her sister and friend would believe more of her feelings were involved. And though Beileag would be shocked, Murdag might force her to marry the Highlander. Either that or shoot an arrow through him.

'You'd tell us if there was, wouldn't you?' Murdag warned.

'There's nothing to tell. We're not married! He didn't ask the question, and if he asks me today, he'd better like black eyes and a broken nose for an answer.'

'He kissed you, you spent the day together and

then he left you with no words?' Murdag said evenly. Too evenly.

Trembling with something she couldn't contain, all of Camron's gentle caresses and murmured words of comfort had been everything to her. The way he was so careful today. There'd been that moment her father had looked too closely at them, and Camron had been at ease with it all.

No boasting, or hand-holding. Shaken to her core with what they'd shared, she'd been grateful he hadn't pushed for more.

She felt like he knew it too. Maybe he did. Maybe he'd watched her for so long he knew exactly how to play on her feelings.

She'd thought what she had started to feel was trust, hope. Hope there could be love for her. Children. Trust that not every man was Alan.

'I returned to my room alone last night,' she whispered. 'And today, you all saw how we were.'

Murdag crossed her arms. 'Why am I feeling like you're still not sharing everything?'

'Murdag!' Beileag said.

Her sister was watching her too closely. She didn't like it. In fact, she may not like being watched ever again.

'Am I supposed to share everything with you

now?' Anna wanted to cry. 'How much shame do you want me to feel?'

'How are we supposed to protect you from betraying males if you don't let us in on the truth!'

Crying out, Beileag slapped her face in her hands to hide.

Her sister hissing out the same words that Anna had repeated to Murdag several times over the last year felt like a slap. 'I thought we were done with arguing,' she said numbly. 'Aren't you cross at all? The bet included you.'

Murdag closed her eyes briefly and sighed. 'I don't want to argue with you either. I don't know why I even—'

'Because I've been saying it myself?' Anna said to meet her sister at least part way in this. They'd fought enough.

Murdag gave a tentative smile. 'Those twins are always making senseless bets. I'm certain if you talked to Camron, it would turn out to be merely a game, or something for fun. At least it explains why Hamilton was always trying to gain my attention.'

'Still?' Beileag's eyes narrowed. 'Is he still doing that.'

Murdag shrugged one shoulder. 'Not truly, but it was humorous at least.'

'Humorous? This isn't a game!' Slamming her

hands in her lap, Beileag pulled herself in. 'Or it's not a game to Anna at least.'

She was more than upset now. When had she ever seen Beileag so distraught? Never. But then Anna had never talked to them about anything like this before.

When Alan broke her heart, she'd refused to talk of it again. Of course, everybody knew what had happened with him so she didn't have to. At least Alan was gone for good, and at least Alan wasn't someone everyone respected. She was nothing more than a bet made by brothers, and twice a fool!

Alan had practically destroyed her, and she'd stayed away from everyone ever since. But once, only once more, she'd taken a chance on someone, and see where it had got her.

She'd spent the last year warning everyone about men and betrayal, and then softened her own stance. She'd risked it all and tried to learn how to trust again. That fracture in her heart from Alan was nothing compared to the canyon that Camron's bet had created.

'You didn't hear everything they said, so maybe we have it wrong,' Beileag added.

Anna could imagine no other interpretation.

'I would have gone closer,' Murdag said. 'I

would have got right in his face, slapped it and then had a good laugh about it as they grovelled.'

Laughing wasn't possible, especially now that anger was taking hold again. 'I could still harm him.'

She wasn't that woman she'd been with Alan. Perhaps she should have demanded something of Camron. But what? His head? Because even if she pleaded with him not to humiliate her…he'd already made the bet. She was already shamed even if no one else found out about it and he never asked her to marry him.

Still…

'Something needs to be done,' she said firmly.

'Why? Can't it just be left alone?' Beileag pleaded. 'Maybe you just don't have to see him again.'

There truly was something bothering her. Beileag was a gentle woman, but when it came down to protecting a friend, she was fierce. Yet her suggestion was to leave him alone?

'Why aren't you giving me any other suggestions?' Anna said suspiciously. 'You don't believe those two deserve at least some retaliation? Do you also think it's just a game?'

Beileag opened her mouth, closed it. 'What if this is all a misunderstanding?'

There was no misunderstanding. Alan had

played a cruel game with her, and with other women in other clans. Now Camron was doing the same. Even if he did it in jest, that only made her an object of entertainment. She was tired of being lied to and tossed around like some sheep knuckle in a game of chance.

'Why don't we turn the tables on them?' Anna suggested.

Murdag pushed off the wall. 'Oh… I like this idea.'

'You do?' Anna said. Heart hurting, shame at being duped again. Throw in every emotion she'd ever felt in one chaotic mix, but that vindictive thrill of giving back as good as she got sliced through them all, and she held on to it.

She wasn't the same girl Alan threw away. She was stronger now, and no men and their petty games were going to get between her and her sister any more.

'What idea is this?' Beileag said.

'We'll switch the game back on them,' she said. 'I'll go after Hamilton whilst Murdag goes after Camron. It'll be sister betting against brother. We'll make our own bet.'

'Oh, I… I don't believe…' Beileag stammered. 'What if Hamilton—?'

'We already know Hamilton doesn't want

Anna or me,' Murdag said. 'He's not even surprising me with that ruse any more.'

'He's not?' Beileag's hands fluttered in front of her, her brows were raised in shock, and Anna swore she had sweat on her upper lip. 'But how will this work? What if Anna proposes to…to *Hamilton*…and he says yes so that he wins his bet?'

'I'm not going to propose to him!' Anna said scornfully.

'Oh,' Beileag answered with far too much relief. 'Good. You'll just forgive them, then?'

'No!' Murdag said.

Why was Beileag struggling with this conversation? Murdag had played loads of jests in her youth, and Beileag was usually by her side. 'We'll just make Hamilton believe I prefer him with words and deeds. They don't have to like it or react. Just know how it feels to be made a fool of.'

Beileag went even paler. Was her friend about to faint?

'What is it?' Anna asked, alarmed.

'Camron hurt you.' Beileag looked from Murdag back to her. 'So you'll hurt him in return? When has that ever been you, Anna?'

Murdag huffed. 'Maybe that's been her issue. Maybe the men of this place believe they can walk all over her.'

Anna slid Murdag a grateful look. This was the sister she wished she'd had when Alan left. Someone who was on her side.

'You don't even know if that's what they intended to do,' Beileag said. 'You haven't talked to Camron or Hamilton yet!'

'Don't you believe I'd prefer a different interpretation?' Anna said. 'All night I've thought about this. When I could think of nothing else, I had to come to you two for help. But you're not making suggestions to make this better either, and I'm tired of being thought of as being someone without any feelings to hurt!'

Beileag strangled her hands. 'What if they did make the bet, but there was an honest reason why?'

Why was her friend defending them? 'I. Am. No. Game! Maybe before the… Maclean that might have seemed acceptable, but how could anyone make such a bet knowing what happened to me? Only a heartless person would do such a thing.'

'Or one who was a fool,' Murdag added.

'Are you defending them?' Anna said.

Murdag put her hands out as if holding her away. 'No, I'm all for retaliating.'

'And you want to do this because of honest reasons. Because they hurt your sister?' Beileag said. 'Or because Hamilton bothered you?'

Murdag shrugged. 'Maybe both? My loyalties lie with my sister either way.'

'Beileag, if they want to have fun at our expense, why can't we do the same?'

Beileag shook her head as if she was trying to come up with different answers but couldn't.

Anna couldn't think of any reasons not to do this. They'd made a bet to make her and Murdag look like fools. Or maybe it was an honest kind of bet, although she couldn't think why. She didn't need the reason. It wasn't fun for her after how badly Alan had hurt her.

Maybe the brother who'd suggested it was an idiot for making the bet, but the other twin could have held him back.

She could see it all now. Hamilton making the bet, Camron agreeing.

Reasonable, kind, gentle Camron agreeing. Not telling Hamilton he was a fool, or pointing out that maybe they shouldn't play around with Anna and her fractured heart.

That maybe this one person who had only recently let up on her lectures, and her overprotectiveness, and was finally joining in on what used to be painful conversations, should be left alone.

Poor Anna, who'd begun to feel desire again… and renewed hope.

At least she was stronger now. She was. And maybe that's why her heart hurt worse than last time.

A foolish bet. Well, she hoped it was worth it and it had given them some laughs, because it was time for her to have some too. She didn't intend to take any of her flirtations or taunting far. She wanted nothing to do with either twin.

But maybe it would show them it wasn't nice to play with people.

Chapter Fifteen

'Now this is the last place I'd thought you'd be this late in the afternoon,' Camron said.

Anna only came to the chapel gardens when she wanted to be left alone. In truth, he'd expected her to be with her family on this day or off to bed catching up on sleep like he wanted to. But he hadn't seen her all day, and before he retired to bed, he wanted to catch one more sight of her.

Even better, she was here, alone, with a basket at her feet. It was an almost perfect opportunity for them to share words. All day he'd needed to tell her of the bet. He feared he was too tired now to tell it properly, but he couldn't have her knowing about it before he told her. How would she trust him again?

She spun at his voice and stood rigid as he approached. When he got closer, she widened her stance as if prepared for a fight.

'Deep in thoughts?' He gave her a smile and slowed his gait. 'I didn't mean to scare you.'

There was a tenseness in her shoulders, and an edge to the corners of her eyes. 'You didn't. I'm busy with Beltane coming and have much to think about.'

So were they all busy. Tomorrow, they'd celebrate the beginning of summer. It was a day and night of much merriment and promise, both for the future of the clan, and in many cases between two people. Many became pledged to each other on that night.

Though he hadn't thought of it as such, what would he now give to drive the cattle between fire, and then claim this woman before his clan on Beltane? That would be a subject he'd rather talk of than the bet.

But given Anna's closed expression, even addressing the bet seemed challenging. Dark circles under her eyes, and terse words from her lips. Ah. Here was another secret he didn't know of his Anna. She liked her sleep, and maybe like him, she hadn't been getting enough.

He took the remaining steps to her, lowered his voice, but increased his smile. He could think of several places and ways they could find rest together.

'Any of those thoughts about me?'

'Yes,' she said curtly.

He waited for the rest, or some acknowledgement of what they'd shared, but she went back to attacking the rosemary bed with her trowel.

She…ignored him. Her behaviour gave him pause. This wasn't wariness or some sort of caution after the day they'd had yesterday, and the night before that. There was no one else in the gardens, no one to overhear their conversation, and only a few who glanced their way over the hedge. Maybe she needed him to acknowledge their recent time together and what it meant.

'I couldn't sleep at all last night,' he said. 'Didn't want to sleep because then I wouldn't be thinking of the way your breath hitched when I—'

'Can you not talk of that.' Eyes narrowed, she looked over her shoulder at him.

She wasn't pleased with his topic, and her movements were jerky, her hand trembling. Maybe she was hungry.

'Did you miss last meal? The bread was still good. It'll beat the charred bits they'll put up on Beltane—'

'Don't talk to me of bread.'

No blush to her cheeks, no desire in her eyes. Her voice was firm. Definite.

'No bread, then, but the stew.'

'I'm not hungry, only…' She trailed off.

He wanted the end of that sentence. 'Is there a reason you're not hungry?

'My stomach is fine if that is what you're asking.'

She stared at him so coldly. So different than when she'd gently entwined their hands together after their swim yesterday. Too different. She wasn't tired, or sleep deprived or hungry.

No, she was turning back to her tasks, tossing her trowel only to pick up her shears, snipping herbs as if she was trying to kill each and every plant.

Frowning at them as if they gave her grave insult.

This wasn't the look he'd shared with her two nights ago, that moment right before her pleasure broke. That pliant softness of her limbs as she'd curled up in his arms straight afterwards. Or the following day, when they'd splashed water at each other before swimming away with laughter. She was angry.

Patience. It had brought him this far. He'd waited until their age difference didn't matter, he'd observed her with Alan, and then counted the months afterwards for her heart to want to mend. Oh, it was past time for them both, and he wouldn't retreat any more.

But it was hard to be resilient after he'd tasted

her passion, impossible to hold on to the strength to step back when his body reminded him repeatedly how she'd unravelled underneath him… against him.

'What is this?' he asked.

Not looking over her shoulder she snipped another branch. 'What is what?'

One day until Beltane, and he knew any chances of claiming her then were too soon. He'd waited a long time for her; would his patience run out?

Maybe we weren't meant to go slow.

She had said that to him. Step by step, every moment they spent together as they walked side by side with the backs of their hands touching, it had seemed like she meant it.

'What is the matter, Anna?'

'What do you care?'

For one full perfect day, he'd had everything he'd ever dreamt of. Anna by the river at night and a day spent like their whole lives could be. And for once the restlessness that had plagued him since Dunbar had eased. Now, it seemed he had nothing.

'Anna, please turn around so we can talk.'

The only sound was the snip of her shears. Cursing silently, Camron exhaled slowly. He was tired, and it further frayed the last remaining bits of reason he had.

'You can turn around now, or later, but I'm not walking away.'

'Are you ordering me?'

After what he knew Alan was like, he'd lose her if he dared to try. 'We need to talk.'

'We spent the day together yesterday—it was enough.'

It was never enough. 'Anna—'

'Hey, brother!'

Camron released his breath and turned to Hamilton, who was loping over.

'Are you going out to the field tonight? Seoc—' Hamilton peered over the hedge and saw where Anna was crouched.

'Oh, Anna!' Hamilton licked his lips, and paused.

'Hello, Hamilton.' She slowly stood. Her expression almost thunderous before it turned sweet. Too sweet, and none of it reached those beautiful blue eyes of hers. Then she rounded the hedge and walked towards his brother like she never had before. Suddenly, Anna became all swaying hips and huge eyes. His brother, who was looking at her full basket and the shears beside it, didn't notice, but Camron did, and he didn't like it at all.

'You and your sister seem to be doing similar tasks today,' Hamilton said.

Tapping slowly on her lip, bringing every man's attention there, she asked, 'Similar tasks?'

Hamilton changed his stance, and glanced Camron's way as he answered her. 'She was at the blacksmith's helping to sharpen shears.'

Anna dragged her finger down her bottom lip, to between her ample breasts and around one hip before resting it there. 'Maybe we're alike because we talked this morning.'

Hamilton cleared his throat. 'That's. Good.'

By the time she was done with her slow caress, Camron was hard and furious. And wanting to grab those feminine hips accentuated by her pose until they were right back where they were at the river.

Hamilton was another colour. Pale. Which was good, because he was seeing red.

What game was she playing with him today? Avoiding him, then ignoring him, now flirting with his brother.

Slowly shaking her head, her gaze solely through her lush lashes, she said throatily, 'It is good, isn't it?'

Hamilton looked panicked. 'And Beileag, how has she been occupied today?'

Her gaze grew sharp, but his brother didn't see

the fire there. So Anna was back to being cross again. About what? His brother came to the gardens because he was here, then he saw Anna and commented on Murdag's whereabouts. All while Anna had flirted with him…until he'd mentioned Beileag.

What was his brother up to? What was Anna doing?

'I'm not making it to the field tonight,' Camron said curtly.

'Probably best,' Hamilton said. 'Seoc may have been meddling with the ale again.'

'If you came to take your brother to the fields, Highlander, why talk of Murdag and Beileag?' Anna asked sweetly.

If anything, Hamilton grew more wary. He should be. If Anna knew he was only toying with her sister, and now wanted her friend, it wouldn't bode well for him. Was that why she was cross with them both?

Then why flirt with Hamilton herself?

'What is it, Hamilton?' Anna said. 'My sister not good enough for you? You need Beileag as well?'

Anna sauntered up to Hamilton, until she was within touching distance, but when she placed her hand in the middle of his brother's chest, Camron was done.

Slapping his palm on his brother's shoulder, Camron sunk in his fingertips until Hamilton winced. 'Come, brother, it's late, the sun is almost set.' Anna's scathing blue eyes and pursed lips were all he needed to know she didn't like him taking his brother away.

And then, right then, he dreaded the reason why. But his brother was here, and he was too damn tired to fight with her tonight. But he vowed he would soon.

Chapter Sixteen

Camron waited until the light broke the horizon to wake his brother. One swift shake of his shoulder, and roughly growled words, were all he needed to rouse his sleeping brother. 'She knows of the bet. They all do.'

Groaning, Hamilton flopped on his back, and threw his arm over his eyes. 'I only went to bed an hour ago.'

'That's on you, not me.'

'I hate it when you're awake,' Hamilton grumbled.

'I'm always awake before you.' Camron yanked off the bedding. 'Get up. They've agreed to stop yelling and actually talk to me, but I want you there too.'

Hamilton stood and stretched. 'Why do I need to be there when you talk to Anna?'

'Not her,' Camron said. 'I already woke Beileag,

who actually cursed at me, if you can believe it, but she agreed to wake Murdag and meet us in the woods. And can you hurry up? Any more time wasted won't be in my favour.'

'You want to talk to Beileag and Murdag about Anna to get some advice?' Hamilton cringed.

Camron felt like growling, but since Hamilton was getting dressed, and rather quickly, he was almost generous in his patience which was past frayed.

Hamilton secured his breeches, threw on his tunic and sat on the bed. 'Is this about last night at the gardens? She was rather...beautiful, wasn't she?'

'That act she put on wasn't about *you*.' Camron did growl then. 'It was to hurt me. Anna was angry even before you arrived. But you mentioning her sister, and her closest friend, didn't make it any better.'

Hamilton stopped securing his boots. 'You think she knows about the bet?'

Camron gave a slow nod. So close to earning her trust, and then this had happened.

'Beileag wouldn't have told her,' Hamilton said with certainty.

He hadn't even asked Beileag if she'd told her. 'Doesn't matter how she found out; I was a fool to make it in the first place.'

Hamilton winced. 'You would have pursued her anyway.'

That was what he'd been telling himself this whole time. But he'd wanted to wait...to tell her about the bet once he had gained more of her trust. Coaxed her out of her fortress a bit further, for longer.

They could have argued about it, but the deed would have been done, and she'd have had to tell him what was wrong so they could solve it. Instead, she'd run away from him again, and he'd let her.

He cursed, and when that wasn't enough, he kept doing it all while they wound around the homes trying to see as few people as possible. As fast as they were, it still took too long, and his biggest fear was that Beileag and Murdag wouldn't be there to yell at him some more, despite Beileag's promise not to, and then help him.

'Took you long enough,' Murdag said when they finally came through the forest and into the small clearing.

Camron was so relieved they were here he didn't point out the fault of his brother.

'Why does he have to be here?' Beileag's eyes narrowed on Hamilton, who was looking anywhere but at her.

'He's my brother,' Camron said. He hadn't even

questioned why he needed to be here. Maybe this was more of a twin aspect than simply a brotherly one. That bore some thought.

'You think it's going to stop Hamilton from making any of his own mistakes?' Murdag laughed.

A crashing of some branches had them all turning.

'What?' Ducking his head from a low hanging branch, Seoc entered the small clearing. 'You thought you all were being subtle? I could see you from the field.'

They were all here. He didn't care about that, he only cared if Anna was there. He turned to Beileag.

'As I told you, she went to bed late,' Beileag said. 'She won't be up for a while.'

Camron's obsession with her had ensured his courtship of her had never been quiet within the clan, but this needed no audience other than who was here.

Murdag, who paced, and Seoc, who leaned against a tree, didn't know what to do either. Though Beileag and Hamilton kept looking to this little clearing off the side as if there were answers there.

When Hamilton caught him looking as well, he could swear his brother flushed.

'How does she know of the bet?' Hamilton asked accusingly, frowning at Beileag.

Beileag fisted her hands at her sides. 'I didn't tell her!'

Murdag rolled her eyes and looked to Seoc. 'Am I the only one who didn't know of this marriage bet before my sister overheard it?'

Seoc shrugged.

'Overheard who?'

Turning back to Camron, Murdag looked half murderous. 'Apparently, while you were nattering away with your brother in the pear orchards, you didn't look behind you.'

He and Hamilton had leant against the pear trees and looked out towards the fields. Anyone could have been behind them. They hadn't looked because there usually wasn't anyone there at that time.

'What was she doing in the orchards at that time of day?' Hamilton said.

'You're a fool.' Murdag glanced at Hamilton, then back to him. 'And so are you.'

'As am I,' Beileag said with a sigh. 'I already knew of the bet when we talked in the bedroom.'

Murdag glared at Hamilton, then at each of them. 'Am I the only one who hasn't betrayed her? Did none of you think to mention it to her so she'd have some defence against it!'

'Murdag…' Beileag said placatingly.

'Don't!' Murdag bit out through her teeth. 'At least now I know why you were trying to reason with her that it was all simply a miscommunication.'

'*I* asked her not to tell,' Hamilton muttered. 'There's only one evil person here, and that's me.'

Camron stared at his brother. It wasn't so much the words he said, it was the tone of anguish and uncertainty.

Murdag seemed to hear it too, for the venomous light in her eyes eased, but she kept her eyes on Beileag when she added, 'At least we know where your loyalties lie.'

'I'll tell her I knew.' Beileag stared directly at Murdag as if one flicker of her eye would tell another story.

He may already have lost Anna over this stupid bet; was he to lose all his friends as well?

'Maybe we can repair it now,' Camron said. 'It's why I wanted you all here. Please don't leave.'

'Oh, I'm not leaving,' Murdag scoffed.

'I thought I was doing something right.' Beileag pointed to Camron. 'It's *him*, Murdag. You know if there's any chance for her, it's him.'

Camron was lost completely, and Hamilton and Seoc looked equally flummoxed. Yet the women weren't leaving. There was still a chance to repair this mess, but they were running out of time. The sun was already higher in the sky, and more of the sounds of people had infiltrated the little copse of woods. Anna may be rising, and no doubt she'd look for at least her friend or sister.

'Whose idea was it for Anna to flirt with my brother,' he said through clenched teeth.

Murdag smirked. 'Hers, and I was to taunt you. Although I think you're tortured enough, and I couldn't bring myself to even think of trying.'

Camron rubbed his forehead. This wasn't on them; he was the one responsible for this disaster. For not being more forthright with her, and yet…it was all over a drunken bet he didn't even remember making. It held no consequence because he'd been pursuing her since he was a child. Surely she'd see that?

Beileag looked at Hamilton, then back to him. 'Foolish idea or not, she's very upset.'

Anna had every right to be upset, but to retaliate like she hated him didn't seem true to her nature. But then, he'd been gone, hadn't he; maybe she'd changed more than he thought? 'Has she done this before?'

'Been betrayed by a man?' Murdag said.

'Murdag!' Beileag gasped. 'You know what he means. The twins may not be the men we hoped they'd be, but that doesn't mean she had to retaliate the way she did. I told you it wasn't a good idea.'

Seoc laughed, Hamilton looked strangled and Camron cursed.

Useless! Something else had upset her. 'How has she been since we returned from Colquhoun?' Camron pressed on. They were here, they could talk. He might not have this opportunity again.

'My loyalty lies with my sister as you well know,' Murdag said.

'She didn't overhear everything we said, did she?' Hamilton pointed out. 'Maybe with a good conversation this can all be resolved.'

'Anna is past a good conversation,' Murdag said. 'In truth, I don't think she should give you any moments. Because even if you talked, what does it matter? The bet was made.'

'But she clearly didn't hear that Camron was against it all along,' Hamilton said.

'How against it could he be when he made it?' Beileag said, but again she didn't look at Hamilton.

Camron didn't know fully what was occurring between his brother and Beileag, and had no time to worry about it.

He had always been truthful to Anna, and she knew what he wanted from her. Perhaps a conversation would help, but she insisted on avoiding him. And hadn't they already shared words and stories? Shouldn't she know where his heart lay, despite the bet?

He only needed one more moment with her again, but feared she'd refuse.

Patience? He barely had any left, and what was there was severely weakened. He needed to get her to talk to him, and to stop hiding behind her walls, but how?

'Are you going to stay quiet on this?' Camron turned to Seoc, who was leaning against a tree, and looking far too amused.

At Murdag's one raised brow, Seoc huffed. 'I'm with Murdag on this; you're all fools. Bet shouldn't have been made, and, Hamilton, you shouldn't have agreed to it. I told you all that before.'

Hamilton made some face that raised the hairs on the back of Camron's neck. Was it guilt? Shame?

He was plagued with those emotions himself, so maybe it wasn't odd his brother felt the same.

'Does it matter if I don't remember making the bet?' he said wearily.

Seoc slapped his chest. 'You're blaming my mead?'

He was blaming himself. He'd thought he had loved Anna before, but it was nothing to how he felt for her now he'd spent time alone with her. How could she…how could *they* possibly be any less than everything together?

How could one kiss turn into touches, then turn into her responding to him as she had? He'd always thought her beauty unsurpassed, but there were no words for what she looked like when she came undone in his arms. Now she was in pain because of words he had carelessly spoken.

They would talk when he saw her, but the way he felt now…he didn't know if he'd fling her over his shoulder before his apologies poured out.

'It's Beltane today,' he announced.

'She won't want to go,' Beileag said.

Because of Alan's lies or his own deception? He'd find out. Beltane was about renewal and love. So many people pledged themselves to each other. And it was public, so she couldn't simply avoid him with people surrounding her, could she?

She could humiliate him, but then he'd already done that to himself when he was a child gawking at her.

'You'll get her there,' Camron said. 'Near the fires and the biggest crowds. We'll surround her, and I'll…talk.'

Seoc snorted. Camron didn't blame him; it

sounded like a weak idea to him, but he'd figure it out as he went.

Beileag looked to Murdag, who eventually and very slowly nodded. 'I wouldn't want to miss your humiliation in front of the whole clan.'

Seoc did laugh then, and with a nod to Murdag, they walked away.

'Beileag?' Hamilton glanced at him. 'Can I talk to you first? Alone?'

Beileag clasped her hands, released them, only to clasp them behind her before she shrugged. 'Later; I have preparations to make.'

Camron watched a thousand emotions cross his brother's eyes. What secrets was he keeping now? Yet for once, because he had a thousand emotions of his own roiling in his gut, Camron felt, at least right now, he could actually be a twin to his brother.

'I'm talking to her father,' Camron said to his brother when they were alone again. 'I'll need to get his understanding first before I approach her.'

'Don't envy you that,' Hamilton said.

'I may have to talk to Padrig, but if you pursue Beileag, you have her family to persuade.'

'So you've guessed.' Hamilton huffed. 'They'll never approve.'

Camron stayed quiet on that. It was possible Beileag's mother would never forgive Hamilton for the jests he played as a child. 'Between Seoc's words and your own forlorn expression, and what we discussed at the orchards, it wasn't difficult to surmise where your heart is leaning. You hold off on your troubles, until I get my own repaired.'

'Scared to lose the bet to me?' Hamilton smirked, but it didn't reach his eyes.

'No more bets.'

Tonight had to work. If she was surrounded by her family and friends, if he could announce what a fool he was and get on bended knee in front of everyone, maybe she'd free some of that pride and forgive him.

All he needed to do was stay calm and apply some reason. All the traits that got him here, to this point, but that he'd feared were gone.

If she didn't give him an answer, he could… force her hand in front of the clan. He was mad to even consider it. Out of any other ideas, he might be desperate enough to do it. Of course she'd hate him for the rest of his life if he did.

Even so, he'd have an answer and it would end whatever purgatory she'd put him in since he was ten years old.

Chapter Seventeen

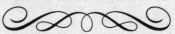

'You thinking of joining the rest of us for Beltane?' Padrig stomped into the house, tapped his shoes on the outside and again on the straw inside. It was enough noise to make Anna jump, and she was glad she was in her bedroom so he couldn't see it. It was bad enough her father was checking on her without adding how jumpy she was to the mix.

'I'm tired.' She walked into the main room even though she honestly didn't want to be anywhere near here. If it was possible to leave for Colquhoun land again, she'd do it. She knew Ailis would welcome her when no one else would. Especially if she promised no mint or parsley tinctures.

'Those dark circles under your eyes could be from lack of sleep or worry,' he pondered.

'Dark circles? Is this your form of flattery?' she said.

He took in the rest of her rumpled form. 'I'm thinking worry.'

It wasn't worry, it was disappointment, and she didn't know if it was more with Camron or herself. 'And are you going to close that door?'

Huffing, Padrig closed it. 'Dark in here. How can you see anything?'

'I wasn't intending to.' The dark room suited her empty mood. She was, however, a husk of who she wanted to be, and felt like all she did was go around and around with her thoughts.

Padrig pointed behind him. 'How are you going to sleep with that noise outside? You should go and join in.'

She wasn't going to sleep or join in with the festivities. 'I didn't attend Beltane last year either.'

'You did,' her father said. 'Because I came in here then too.'

Anna rubbed her forehead and sat down. The noise from outside was barely muffled, but her head was aching from pent-up tears and anger and lost hope. 'So then I can skip it now.'

Her father yanked out a chair and sat down at the table with her. For the longest time he didn't say anything, just watched her breathe and blink.

When he crossed his arms in front of him and leaned back, she knew she was in trouble.

'What makes this year different than last? Should have been worse last year, huh? We'd discovered that Alan fellow promising a betrothal to several women as well as you. I could see how you'd want to miss it then. But though you protested, you still showed up. You didn't hide then.'

'I'm not hiding now,' she said. 'Maybe I don't want to see the pitying looks again, or worse, maybe I don't want to—'

'See anyone else being happy?' Padrig said. 'I can see how that would upset you last year, but not now. So what aren't you telling me?

She couldn't say.

Padrig stretched out his arms and tapped his fingers against the table. The movement reminded her so much of Camron her chest ached. 'I don't think I've apologised for not helping you enough.'

She raised her gaze. 'What?'

'I wish I'd helped you with that man. Made some enquiries about him, talked with him of his family. Could have spared you some pain, perhaps?'

Her father regretted stepping away when she was with Alan?

She laid her hand on top of his. 'Wasn't your fault.'

'And it's yours?' Her father squeezed her hand. 'Maybe there's a time for these things, huh? I saw you and Camron walking about side by side the other day.'

She didn't want to talk about fault or Camron. 'There's no time for that.'

'It's not what he told me,' he said.

Anna pulled her hand away. 'He what?'

Her father shrugged one shoulder. 'Came to me telling me of his intentions.'

'And what were those?'

'To marry you. Not to worry, I told him I expected it.'

'I don't want to marry him,' she said, appalled.

'You want me to get a haircut first?' he teased.

She wanted to smile, for them to be able to slip into their usual word games and challenges. She couldn't when her emotions were impossible to contain and just the low embers from the fireplaces and the occasional popping of logs were an irritant. 'He's not the man for me, Father. I admit I thought he was, but he's not.'

'Because of Alan?' he said. 'It's been some time since we ran him off. He was decent looking and a good talker, but was he really worth these long thoughts?'

She shook her head. 'Maybe at one point I would have thought that, but him making promises to women in several clans dissuaded me of even wanting to say his name.'

'Yet, you've pushed away everyone, even your family, ever since.'

She'd purposefully avoided everyone by hiding in here so she didn't have to voice these thoughts. But if Camron had come to see her father...

'Did he tell you of the bet he made with Hamilton to marry me?'

Her father flashed a grin. 'And a fine bet it was too. He's won.'

Everyone was impossible! 'You think I appreciate a game being made with me again?'

Her father lost his smile. 'You think that pushing away others is going to help you learn to trust again? Or will you just keep spinning your own thoughts?'

Why did her father know her so well? 'Ailis gave me the same opinion, Father, and it didn't work either. She told me to learn to trust and then I'd trust. I know I haven't been easy over the last year or so.'

She looked back up. Her father kept his gaze on hers. 'You've never been easy, Anna. But you're loyal and a fine sister, daughter and friend. You've only been a bit more of all of those things this year.'

Had she? Was that all it was?

'You'll be happy to know I softened my opinions with Murdag and Lachie…and then Camron. But when I discovered the bet, it was as if Alan was happening all over again. It *is* happening all over again! I'm not a game to be played.'

Her father drummed his fingers one more time and pushed away from the table. 'Tonight's Beltane, isn't it? New promises and all that. Maybe you'll simply try that trust again.'

She couldn't imagine anything worse. 'I'm still too cross with him, Father.'

Padrig swung open the door and stepped out. 'Then you'd better get out here so you can let him know that.'

Anna watched her father walk away. He'd left the door open again. She could see people talking and laughing, a few slowed down by her door and waved at her. It would be impossible to stay inside now they'd seen her.

Frustrated at herself and her father, Anna stepped out and closed the door behind her. Seeing the revellers, she sighed. Already the large fires were lit and men and boys held the cattle, preparing to herd them between them for the saining.

She could take a few blessings herself right now. Perhaps if she drank a couple of cups, she could do this. Could walk through her clan, though everyone knew she'd missed most of last year's festivities.

After another hour, she knew she couldn't. Trying to breathe through the constriction in her chest, she weaved around people, and nodded to those she knew, but everything was so awkward and forced.

Maybe perhaps because she still hadn't found Murdag or Beileag, so she didn't have their comfort. Perhaps because everyone was so…happy.

She'd been betrayed yet again. Even if it was a jest that meant nothing at all, it had still been played on her. And Alan had already done that. Done more than that for two years. She'd been played so perfectly she'd had no indication until it was too late.

She'd believed she was safe with Camron. He was from the clan, knew of her, her family and they of him. He knew when Alan became false. They'd all known.

He was supposed to be better than that.

Years of Camron watching her from a distance, and him spending time with her family and friends. Years of him being nearby until Alan. Then Camron left for scouting and missions and training. Each time he'd come back a little different. A little *more*. She'd thought she could trust those years, and his steady brown eyes.

Blinking hard against the sudden tears, she set her cup on some nearby log.

Worse, maybe it was the ale or the raucous dancing and the fire's flickering light, but she swore every once in a while that she spotted her sister or Beileag. But whenever she drew near they disappeared.

A roar in the crowd had her turning. Ah. Men with large sacks high over their heads came out.

Some of her anxiousness eased. In those many sacks would be broken pieces of bannock, one piece of which would be charred. The person who chose that piece would get the honour of jumping across the embers from the dying fires. They'd have their own special blessing and good luck.

Oddly, the sacks were deeper than usual. Was that a tradition started last year? She couldn't remember. But entire bodies could be held inside them. Which meant everyone would be reaching deep and sticking their torsos in to get to the bread at the bottom.

At least everyone would be occupied with the new game, and maybe she could sneak off. No more forced smiles or pleasantries for the rest of the night. Maybe tomorrow she'd— There. That was certainly Murdag; it couldn't be anyone else standing on a boulder by one of the large fires.

Was she brandishing a goblet? Anna shook her

head and rubbed her eyes. Couldn't be her, but it was. Hadn't she learnt to not stand on boulders? And there was Beileag by her side!

Should she go over to them, or return to her home? Had she been out here long enough to satisfy her father? But was her dark silent bed going to give her any relief from these thoughts?

Curling her hands into fists, she tried to release the sudden wave of powerlessness and anger. Of helplessness. Before she knew it, she was winding her way across the large field. Weaving around people who kept thrusting sacks in front of her as if she wanted to play a game. As if she deserved good fortune or protection.

Didn't they know good fortune fled when she was near? She could reach in every sack and never come up with a charred bit. She wouldn't put it past Fate that she could grab every single broken bit only to discover there were no charred ends in her sack.

Maybe Murdag sensed her approaching because her gaze snapped up and she hopped off the boulder. Anna walked faster. Another sack was shoved in front of her, but at this one she didn't even bother to stop and smile and say no to the carrier, as she barrelled by. Ill-mannered she knew, but maybe they wouldn't notice.

At least this was providing enough distraction

from her thoughts, and as she went through, she still couldn't see the twins, or Seoc. Maybe they were all avoiding her like she was avoiding them.

She'd been so angry when she'd taunted Hamilton in the garden. Could feel Camron's gaze turn from confusion and surprise to displeasure and then anger. While she hated approaching Hamilton in any bold way, she'd taken great pleasure in Camron's discontent.

But that glee had only lasted an hour or two. She'd talked briefly with Murdag before bed to see if she had approached Camron in front of Hamilton, but her sister hadn't. The relief that had flooded her because her sister hadn't flirted with Camron had only made her cross again. And that had lasted longer, so she couldn't sleep through the night.

Who was she any more? Despair or Anger? She'd always been the calm one in her family, but now she couldn't contain her emotions.

And now she was wondering if maybe her sister had flirted with Camron today. She could imagine it and the weight in her heart was crushing her.

Another sack on her right. Without taking her eyes away from her sister, she gave a tight smile and a dismissive nod. But when she stepped around it, it was shoved at her again.

She tried to sidestep it, but this time she looked up at the insistent person and would have fallen, if not for the large and very capable hand wrapping around her wrist to prevent just that.

'You!'

Chapter Eighteen

'Me.' Camron released her wrist slowly, partly because he didn't know if she'd run, partly because even in this small way he was touching her again.

Mostly because when she recognised him fully, he wasn't certain what she would do with that hand. Possibly throw the sack at him or punch him.

He'd welcome both.

He'd hurt her, or what she'd overheard had hurt her, and she'd jumped to her own conclusions on everything else. But when Alan had been revealed to be a liar, Anna hadn't fought back. Instead, all the joy had simply vanished.

But his Anna, the one standing before him, wasn't a shell of her former self; she was angry, shocked, and…magnificent. He couldn't help it. He grinned.

Letting out some choked frustration, she tried to go around him again. He wasn't having any of that.

'Your fingers are green, lass,' he said.

That drew her up. 'What are you going on about now?'

'Why are your fingertips green? Had a bit of parsley, did you?'

'I made some mint broth for everyone for later,' she huffed. 'Get out of my way.'

Oh, he liked it when she played with her herbs. 'Maybe you should clean them on this sack.'

She eyed the sack he held, which looked like the same sack as everyone else, though his was different. Something she'd discover if his plan worked to his, *their*, benefit.

'I'll clean them in my own time; now leave me be, Camron. I don't want to talk to you. I would like to talk to your brother, however.'

Camron knew why she pushed back, but still he didn't like it. Stepping in her path, he dangled the sack again. 'Put your hand in the sack, Anna.'

'I don't know why you're here,' she muttered low, so only he could hear, 'and I don't care. I do care that my sister is—'

'Right here,' Murdag said from behind her.

Anna gave a forced smile. 'All is well, then; you can stick *your* hand in the sack. Wasn't there something you wanted to talk to Camron about? Now let me—'

'What about me?' Beileag added.

Just as they'd discussed before these festivities started, Murdag and Beileag came up on Anna's sides. Essentially, they blocked her in, but they were far enough away that she hadn't realised it yet.

Of course, she could pivot right now, but then Hamilton would reveal himself.

'What is all this?'

'This is the sack you're to reach into to see if we're to jump over the fire.'

She batted at the sack. 'I'm not reaching into this sack and I'm not jumping over any fires.'

It was well into the night, and everyone was into the revelry, their cups and each other. The cows had gone through, and now it was simply people and fires, and far too much ale. He thought she'd come out of her house earlier than this.

The day had been busy with preparations, and he'd seen Anna carry more than her weight in food. So when she didn't immediately come out to enjoy the feast he'd thought her resting.

But then the day had turned dark, and far too many people were now well into their cups. Which may go to his advantage while Anna yelled at him.

He deserved it, but she looked ready to do more than that, and he didn't know how his body would react if she punched him. He'd probably kiss her, or simply throw her over his shoulder and walk off with her. He felt unchecked heat flood through his veins, burning away the little remaining reason he had left, and all she was doing was standing in front of him!

'I told you we'd talk. So here I am.'

Straightening herself up. 'There is no discussion; I didn't want a discussion, and that's something you should have known since I've ignored you.'

'You've avoided me.' He leaned forward. 'Because you're afraid.'

She pulled back. 'Afraid?'

'You are,' Murdag said.

Anna rounded on her. 'Since when?'

'Since the Maclean,' Beileag said.

'Camron lied to me!' Anna exclaimed.

'He didn't; he just didn't tell you something, something that didn't really matter anyway, but you'd know that if you talked to him,' Murdag said.

Camron stood holding the sack, watching the play of emotions cross Anna's face. He'd caused this, but…they were right. And he was humbled and grateful they stood by his side as he tried to earn this woman's trust and love all over again.

'You didn't avoid all of us after Alan,' Murdag pointed out. 'Something's different this time.'

Anna stood staring at one friend and one sister. Staring at him. Frustration, anger and hurt were fleeting across those blue eyes, but she held firm; she didn't pivot and storm off.

She argued.

He'd hoped that's what would happen, that she'd stand her ground against them and fight, and that soon…soon the poison that the Maclean had poured into her that had never been lanced would bubble to the surface.

That soon—oh, so soon—that fortress she'd built would be thrown away stone by stone.

'I'm not avoiding you all,' she said.

Eyeing Murdag, then Beileag, he turned to Anna. 'Prove it,' he said.

He wanted conversation, not arguments that went in spirals and never ended. His Anna was hurt, angry, her breaths coming in mere puffs as if she couldn't draw it in fast enough.

Oh, this battle was between them now, and he barely held in his restraint, but when they truly talked later on, after he'd managed to persuade her away from here, he didn't want her throwing up excuses like her family not understanding what had happened. And though it wasn't necessary to declaring them married, he wanted witnesses.

If not for the battle needing to be won, he didn't want any distractions or words from anyone else. He only wanted this woman.

'We're here, together. So speak, Anna. Tell us all your thoughts.'

'You bet Hamilton you'd marry me,' she said. 'Why?'

He could only give her honesty. 'I made the bet when I was drunk; I don't remember making it, nor do I know why I did so. There was no point.'

Jaw clenched, she batted at the sack he held. 'So you suggested the bet, and everything we've done since you've returned was following a bet you can't remember making, and yet that doesn't matter? What is wrong with you?'

Nothing. He was simply following his heart, but he wouldn't confess that in front of witnesses…even though they already knew.

'It doesn't matter even when I knew of the bet,' Beileag interjected.

'What?' Anna shook her head. 'I told you of it.'

'No, I knew before you did.'

Anna took a step back, and another. She was wary now. Looking from one to the other of them, realising she was circled.

'You already knew of the bet? You lied to me

too?' Anna said, her voice strong, but at the end there was a tone to it he'd do anything to never hear again.

'I didn't lie.' Beileag clenched her hands in front of her. Three of her fingers were wrapped up, and as she pressed them together, some blood seeped out. 'I didn't say anything because I hoped it would be resolved. I hoped... Can't you see it wasn't that terrible? That it's—'

'It is! Because that jest was at your *friend's* expense,' Anna bit out.

'Anna,' Murdag started to say.

'No!' Fists clenched, she barrelled forward. 'No more.'

'Stay,' Camron said. 'Don't avoid us again.'

'I'm not your dog. Get out of my way now, Camron.'

'The bet doesn't matter, and you know it,' he said. 'It's an excuse for what truly ails you, lass.'

'You?' she retorted.

Stubborn. Magnificent. Hurting. If he could, if she'd allow him to hold her, he would. He wanted her to give herself time to heal, for her to trust again. Not just him, but herself too.

She always ran; she wasn't going to give them that time. So he was taking it now, but his plan to simply get her to talk wasn't working. She'd break through the little circle they made, and then what was he to do…chase after her?

'It was an excuse to pursue you, but not the reason I did. You're the reason.' Her expression wasn't full of hurt or anger, only confusion. 'Did that Maclean's lies—'

'*Your* lies,' she said low, but they hit him in the gut.

'I didn't tell you of the bet, but I didn't lie to you either,' he answered. 'You are the reason I pursued you. You, nothing else, no bet or wager or sword tip to my neck. You. It was a foolish drunken bet that meant nothing because it wasn't the *reason*. Believe, Anna, in what I'm saying, because it's…me saying it.'

If he could get her to trust him, then maybe next she would trust herself. If he could…

She opened her mouth, closed it. Looked to the sack, to him. To more of the crowd gathering around their declarations to each other.

And they were declarations…just not ones filled with the usual joyous laughter and passionate embraces of Beltane. What they said to each other was true, raw and necessary. No matter if he had to surround her here all night, so they could say all that they needed to.

It would be said. If she still rejected him afterwards, if she still insisted on being stubborn, then he could at least say he'd tried everything. He would do everything he could while there was a chance she was listening to his words and realising them to be truth.

But that stubborn fire within Anna, the one he wanted for her, was a strength that would work against him.

Thus he wasn't above the Grahams surrounding her and using the distraction of a sack.

'You know what I *believe*?' she said. 'I believe the Grahams should celebrate Beltane with sacrifices again, not with these bits of—' She reached into his sack and pulled out a handful of flowers.

Her thunderous expression turning to perplexity was one he'd remember for the rest of his life.

'They're flowers,' he offered helpfully.

'I can see they are flowers,' she said slowly. 'Why are they not pieces of bread?'

'Because flowers are for wooing you.'

She dropped the crushed petals from her palm. 'There is no wooing.'

'Then why did you pick out the flowers?'

With one contained screech, she reached into the bag again and threw a handful at him. 'I'm not picking them. I'm throwing them at you!'

Oh, she was mad, and letting all the clan know. Soon, he'd take her away from here where they could talk about what was truly between them.

Not the bet, which was foolish, but easily forgivable. No, she fought him for another reason. A deeper one.

One that he regretted because he'd had a part to play in that too, when he'd stepped back and let Alan take her from him. Young or not, there was still that moment when he should have punched Alan and declared himself to her.

That was what needed to be rectified. She likely would have still chosen Alan, and he'd resigned himself to accepting that. She had been happy with Alan, and Camron hadn't yet proved himself.

But if he had declared himself to her back then, at least she'd believe him now instead of doubting his loyalty and love and doubting herself. And he couldn't have that.

'You may be throwing them at me, but I'm feeling every soft petal, lass, of their fertility rite,' he goaded. Prodded. He'd do all he could to provoke the one outcome they needed. 'Throw some more petals at me, love, let's see if they're right.'

'Love!' she cried.

'Love.' He declared to her, to their family and friends, to his clan, to all the Grahams who surrounded them. This wasn't exactly how he'd envisioned saying the words. Oh, he didn't protest letting the world know; he just protested that he had to say it without her in his arms. Without soft gentle caresses and even more intimate words.

No, he had to say it like it was a cold truth, and one with a bite. Because Anna was angry, but he needed her truly spitting in order for this to work.

'You know it's love.' He smirked and cringed a little inside whilst he did it. 'It's always been love.'

Eyes like daggers, and face turning red, Anna yanked at the sack they both clutched. Kept yanking until she completely forgot their audience. When he raised one taunting brow at her, she growled.

Something primal inside him answered her frustration. The need for her, the desire to get away from others, the delay in having her. He wanted to… He wanted to suddenly throw her over his shoulder and—

'Oh! You!' She reached in, got more handfuls of petals and chucked them at him.

Most didn't touch him, but the few that did, he felt. Felt her pain, her anguish, her doubts, felt her want. As if each soft touch was a calling to him to answer her. To answer her finally and truthfully with everything in him.

Feeling the eyes of their families and clan on them, he ordered himself to calm. To have patience just a bit longer, but he could no longer feel it there. It was gone. He was simply a man full of longing and desire. And the more she reached into the bag, the more flowers she threw his way, a terrible thought entered. He was supposed to use the bag as a distraction. But what if he used it as a true trap? She may hate him, but he was done. He had nothing left. She hadn't listened.

Another handful, then another as she finally bent inside to reach the bottom of the bag. As her rump was displayed and her torso disappeared, and she growled and hissed…

He answered her and his impatience. With a quick movement, he grabbed the sack's excess and wrapped it around her body.

'What!' She pushed and shoved to get out of the sack. 'Let me out!'

Elbows going, her feet attempting to walk or run from him, but all in vain, for he had the sack and his arms securely around her. She wasn't going anywhere.

Leaning close to her ear, he said, 'Say please, Anna, and I'll let you out. All you have to do it say please, and I vow you'll never see me or hear from me again.'

She utterly stilled, her chest heaving. He wasn't worried for her breathing. Wasn't concerned about how her pride or his was being pummelled as surely as her fists and elbows had tried to get at him.

Because as surely as she held her breath now, he held his. Oh, he was done waiting. She was his, but she had to agree to it. She had to agree to it all or everything was lost. He wanted her heart, thoughts, soul. He wanted her everything, but that meant she had to meet him halfway.

Because she may be trapped inside the sack, but he was still coaxing her out of that fortress to give him hope for *them*.

'Let. Me. Go. Camron. Or I swear you'll regret it,' she spit out between clenched teeth.

Not one word of please which was more than good enough for him. When he tightened the closing string, she lashed out again with her arms, but he barely felt them. Barely registered anything but Anna's lush rump up in the air, and her angry thrashing rubbing all over him.

He needed to get her out of here before he proved the flowers' fertility potency in front of an audience. Hoisting her over his shoulder, Anna shrieked. But by then there wasn't a Graham who would come to her aid. This whole clan knew their story, and he was done waiting any longer to claim her.

More than done, his arm across her thighs pinning her to him, every curve pressed against him. It didn't matter that her legs were dangerously close to emasculating him, or that she was cursing him from now until well past the grave.

He'd have her now. Here at Beltane, if he took her away during Beltane night, many would believe them wed.

She knew it, too, but she wasn't saying the right word. She'd stilled and had taken in his meaning as he'd repeated it. One simple please from her, and he'd let her go for ever. She was angry, she was hurt, but she didn't truly want to end what was between them.

That was heartening.

Hard thumps against his back he ignored, as Camron said to Hamilton, 'Where's the horse?'

'Behind me.' Hamilton pointed to Anna. 'I'll help you up with her.'

'You're all right on your own?' He pointedly looked at Beileag. He didn't know fully what was happening between them, but he knew his brother was losing.

'Murdag will protect me,' Hamilton said with a wink.

'I won't,' Murdag quipped. 'We were supposed to stand here and talk, not trap her like…like a chicken. And I won't protect you either, Camron, when you finally get that sack off my sister!'

He laughed. 'You're still in agreement with

me, though, since none of you are helping her to get out.'

An elbow to the small of his back had him bracing and slapping his other arm across her curves, which stilled Anna immediately. She knew where his hand was as surely as he did. He'd known some altercation would occur between them, and had Hamilton ready a horse. Passing her off to his brother, then back to him, wasn't exactly how he'd envisioned them mounting it, but it'd do.

Hamilton grinned. 'Go well, brother. It's safe to say you won this bet.'

Anna's cursing began again, this time aimed at them both. But she still didn't say the word that would truly end this for her, or him.

Or for them.

And Camron, who finally had the woman he'd craved for more than ten years pinned solidly to his shoulder, couldn't contain his enormous satisfaction.

Chapter Nineteen

Anna gave up any verbal fight as her stomach pounded against Camron's stubborn shoulder.

Only once she was deposited in another's arms, Hamilton's no doubt, and then transferred up on a horse and between Camron's legs, did she stop with the elbows. But that was only for her own safety, not his. She refused to talk whilst he secured her in the ridiculous sack. Blushed whenever she thought about everyone seeing this.

But she knew the moment it was off her, she'd bolt, and he must have sensed it, too, because he kept it on as they travelled. Wherever he took her wasn't far for he soon slowed to a stop. She could hear the babbling of water, feel the deep breath Camron took.

'When I take off the sack, what are your intentions, lass?' he said.

To elbow him a few times in the stomach, vault

over the horse and then curse him so long and loud that even his ancestors knew of it. But she said nothing. Refused, in fact.

Another breath, more waiting, whilst she felt the heat of him against her back and his unique scent of wool and leather and *him* permeated through the heavy linen. Whilst she became aware of how his arms wrapped gently around her, his hands, holding the reins, rested in her lap. The weight of them, the warmth.

The very way his heart beat against her, the minute movement as he swallowed, the tilting of his jaw briefly resting against the top of her head. Camron held her, surrounded her, and her body…sung for him.

She hated the sack. Hated it. And yet, she hated this awareness more. But she wouldn't talk. What little pride she had, that tiny voice inside her, drew the line there. She'd been penned, herded like the cattle between the fires and her family tonight. They'd blocked her in. She realised that now.

She was meant to see Murdag on top of the boulder, meant to go to her directly and for Camron to intercept and surround her, for him to dump her in a sack!

The sack which she should be fighting with all her being, and yet she docilely sat on a horse trying to contain her body's reaction to this man who put her there. But her heart didn't seem to care if she'd been caught and trussed up like a chicken. Her heart, loving the warmth of him, the steady way he breathed, wanted him to hold her that bit tighter, to press that bit firmer.

She feared if she spoke it wouldn't be words of hate or anger or betrayal. They'd be ones of want. Desire. Longing. This was how he'd break her.

So she waited…she waited until her breaths weren't steady, and her heart not calm at all. She waited, biting her tongue and clenching her teeth…and trembling.

Trembling which he must have felt for he released the reins, his hands caressing up her arms and back down, which should have only aggravated the fact she was trapped in heavy linen.

But it was sweet, and comforting, and it spread whatever unwanted desire she was feeling even further throughout her.

She wouldn't beg, she wouldn't! Tears built in her eyes. She didn't want any to fall for this man; she merely wanted out of this suffocating linen. She wanted to be away from him. She needed—

Firmly holding her waist, Camron dismounted.

'Jump, Anna,' he ordered gently.

Her pride screeching at her now, Anna tilted towards him, until he caught her, and let her go.

She was free to release herself, but she waited

again. Because though she stood there looking like a fool, wiggling and struggling whilst her arms were trapped at her sides would be worse. She stood still whilst Camron loosened the cord around her thighs and yanked the entire thing off.

It was night, the moon wasn't full and, though they were near water, they weren't near her bathing area, the clan or the fires. It was dark, and her eyes strained simply to see Camron's raised brow and his own gaze fixed on her hands at her sides.

All of those dramatics for this quietness? To be somewhere far from people? She knew the Beltane celebrations invoked many to partake of too much ale, mead and intimate relations.

Some became marriages, most did not. But always it was with flowers and words and skipping off behind some shrubbery or inside the closest shelter. You couldn't live in a clan and not accidentally see many things occur between adults on Beltane. But here was somewhere else altogether. No people except for them, and only muted music and loud chatter that floated across the misted air.

Here was only a gentle little meadow with a stream flowing nearby enough to be able to hear the uneven rhythm of it. The grass underneath them was dry.

There wasn't anything here except the thundering of her heart, and Camron, who still kept his eyes on her hands. She couldn't stand the quiet of it.

'What?' she demanded.

'Frankly, I'm waiting for you to punch me,' he said. 'Or curse me and all my descendants with some vile pestilence.'

That was what she'd intended too. That's what she was doing when he'd first trapped her in a bag like root vegetables. But he'd changed that uncontrolled anger by keeping the bag over her, taking her away from the revelry and holding her the way he had.

He'd regret that. She wasn't angry like a raging fire; she was angry like the blade being held to that flame.

'How dare you!' She spun away from him. 'In front of friends, in front of family.'

'I dared, and your friends and family thought it a wise idea, too, or they would have stopped me,' he said calmly. 'As for what I did, what do you think that is?'

'You think they approve of you putting a sack over my head?'

'They approve of my loving you,' he said.

Steady brown eyes on her, Camron didn't flinch or avoid her anger. He acted like he wasn't in the wrong, that he spoke the truth, and it did odd things inside her.

Like making her want to believe him, and the same time her heart was screaming what an accomplished liar he was. What was she to believe when she doubted herself?

'That's your declaration of love?' she spluttered. 'And you believe I'll accept it, or worse, return it?'

'You already do.'

He held up his hand as if to stop her so he could make his *point*. Too bad. She utterly rejected his meaning.

'Like hell I do,' she said.

She expected him to wince at her retort. To step back to become gentle, patient. To soften his tone, but he did none of those things.

There was a sliver of moonlight; they could barely see each other even though they stood in a meadow under no tree canopy. But something of Camron's presence grew. Maybe it was the change of his stance, the lowering of his chin and the tightening of his jaw. Not threatening, never that, simply...formidable.

He wasn't here to negotiate, nor would he change his stance. He *meant* this.

Something like heavy dread, like cornered fear, grew. Suddenly the babbling brook, the light breeze in the trees and this quiet, secluded meadow took on a new meaning.

Love? He told her of love? He'd declared more than that when he took her away from everyone on Beltane.

'Take me back.'

'Not yet.'

Then she'd take herself. Anna stepped away from Camron and his demands, his assumptions.

'It's done. Even if you ride back at this very moment, we're already married. I took you away in front of witnesses.'

Pivoting around. 'I refuse!'

He took a step towards her and she held her ground. If he wanted an argument, she'd argue until he regretted his wanting and needing and *watching*. Regret whatever madness he'd insisted on with trapping her this way.

'You already accepted our bond when you lay with me by the river, when you let me kiss you and touch you and hold you. When you spent the following day with me in front of the clan. And even before that, when we travelled alone together to Colquhoun land.'

All those times, she'd trusted him, but he'd held a terrible secret.

'What I accepted was not real; it was a bet for you and a lie for me.'

'You hold on to that bet as if it means something, when you know it doesn't,' Camron's low voice growled. 'You argue that one drunken moment makes everything that's happened false between us? You lie.'

'Never!'

He darkly chuckled. 'You're lying so hard that you even believe it yourself. What of the stories we told each other that night by the river?'

He thought a few shared tales made whatever they had true? 'How many stories did Alan tell me?' She spun her hand in the air, and sank as much disdain in her words as possible. 'All those tales of dangerous escapes and narrow misses. Oh, but the best ones were his feats of valour and the challenges he overcame.'

'You compare our truths to that man's bragging? You compare any of that night to what you had with him?'

Camron was utterly still; his words, however, were dark, potent, and hit her in the heart. Her heart shouldn't be touched by any of this. He couldn't possibly be speaking any truths...and then she knew why.

'You keep saying the bet meant nothing, and should mean nothing because of all our shared moments, but there are arguments against that.' She held up her thumb. 'One, you still made the bet.'

'My brother said I did, yes.'

Everything inside Anna pressed against her. Embarrassed by how she'd reacted to him in front of the Grahams, how he'd so easily carted her off.

She stood before this man in this gentle meadow in the pitch dark of night, but she felt as if nothing in her could be contained. She was both here, and in the past, and in the future, and so full of emotions she couldn't possibly undo them enough to understand. But she'd try, if only to get her fervent wish, that he, and every other man, would leave her alone.

'Whether or not you did, you still held to it.'

'I held to none of it, other than a mention. You overheard some, but not all, of that private conversation in the woods between Hamilton and me.'

She hadn't, that was true. 'But you don't deny the bet was made.'

'Why should I doubt my brother's words? Would it make you feel more secure about my true intent if he lied? Why are you making us repeat this again when you already know that, underneath it all, there's something else we should be talking about? I put a sack over you, Anna, and rode with you here, and you keep acting like I have any patience left. I don't.'

That spoke true. Who was this man? One moment he acted like he could wait for her for ever, and then the next…a sack went over her head, or he was naked by the pond!

Why did Camron, whom she'd known since he was born, keep surprising her? Was it another form of lying? Everything in her protested at that. Despite telling him otherwise, she kept believing him. Like now.

'Hamilton has no place here,' she said finally. 'But since he was a participant in that foolish bet, you won't stop me from having a little conversation with him when I return. After all, that bet was for him to marry my sister, wasn't it, while you were to marry me. Except…'

'Except what?' he said.

'Why is Beileag upset? And why did Hamilton tell her of the bet?'

Camron looked over his shoulder and exhaled roughly. 'Anna, can we for once have this be about us? I feel like I've been fighting others as well as time when it comes to you.'

If she hadn't had Alan's betrayal, or if Camron hadn't made that bet, his words would have floored her. As it was, she kept her defences against him. Maybe she could make this about just them so she could leave this time behind them. It was one she didn't want to go through again. As for Hamilton, her sister and the rest, she'd talk to them at a later time.

She nodded.

His expression almost eased. Had she surprised him? She wasn't unreasonable, she also wasn't some…pawn in his game of needing a bride.

'So now can we talk of our words?' he said. 'For everything we've said to each other has been true.'

Hers were; she doubted his were. She'd been trying to trust him. How could she try again? 'Fancy words to gain kisses.'

Camron made a sound of dismissal. 'Then forget the words, what of the deeds?'

The deeds… Travelling to Colquhoun land and their time in the cave. That growing awareness between them that had kept her warmer than the fire they'd built. And knowing he'd watched her moving her hands above her head. Why did she do that? For her…or for him?

He'd described the feeling, when he was a child, of coming across her at the river like she was some fae in the moonlight. Did that make him a fae prince?

The fact the twins had fine looks was obvious from the women who always giggled as they strode by. But Camron was altogether different for her. He was different for her now.

His features shadowed by night, she could only gaze at his form which looked like he was both part of the rough-hewn nature around him, but also apart from it, like some predatory creature.

So much of their time together repeated in her mind. Things that she wondered now if they were true. Had his voice stirred through her that night at the river, had she arched for more caresses from his calloused palms?

She couldn't grasp all that had happened, and couldn't forget it either. How could she, when he stood there in the moonlight, and she was still so intrigued by him? She hated it and wanted to dismiss him all the more for that.

'Deeds? Is that what you call basic bodily functions?' she jeered. 'As if any of that meant anything more than… More than…than just a release.'

She couldn't believe she'd said it; neither could Camron, for a taut silence dropped over him. So long did he stare, unblinking, all she could do with the time was remember the moment of their last mutual pleasure and blush.

Then blushed some more.

'I meant how you trusted me by walking towards me that night, Anna,' he said, his voice no more than a gravelly rasp. 'But I more than appreciate the direction of your thoughts.'

That seductive low timbre of his voice had no place here in this meadow. *She* had no place here.

Pacing away from him, taking in the trees, the sound of the stream, the stillness of the sky. Was it even night any more, or was day soon to be here?

'Where are your thoughts now?' he asked.

Something fluttered in her chest. She'd been here too long already. His intent around the fires had been all too clear, and she had reached in his sack over and over, chucking flowers at him as if she….as if she was declaring her love for him over and over.

Was it, as he told her, too late for her to announce to her family or clan there was nothing between them? That splinter, that fracture Alan had made, was still buried in her chest, and Camron had made the poor organ all that weaker. Was she stuck with a man her heart doubted?

'You've played with my life like I'm a pawn in some game.'

'You are not a pawn. You're my wife. We are married. You just haven't said the words. But every witness on Beltane's Night knows it when we left to seek privacy together.

'We didn't *leave* together.' She would never walk on quiet moonlit nights again! 'First the bet, then this capturing me when you knew what people would think. And you say you're playing no game.'

He didn't even flinch. 'I regret you believe that,

but my bringing you here is as much on your shoulders as mine. We exchanged words that night by the river, many words, all to make certain of your wishes.'

Over and over again he had done that, but it wasn't enough. She waved around at the soft meadow. 'What of this? There were no words exchanged to make certain I wanted this. How could you force this on me?'

'Force? Oh, no, you don't get to claim that when you came so sweetly into my arms. And I say it freely because I am not ashamed, nor will I ever be. I claim that night and you freely. As you did me too. This—' he pointed between them '—is merely a continuation of that night.'

'False claim!'

'You knew what I wanted, what we both wanted, and took the steps towards me of your own accord. You said the words! One step. Wanting to kiss me. Another step. We touched.' He looked away, down to his feet, then his eyes locked with hers again. 'You may say there were no words exchanged. You also may say you don't want this, but tonight in front of everyone you could have walked away, but you chose not to.'

'I argued with you to leave me alone.'

His smile was one she could see in the dark. 'You didn't say please.'

She froze. That moment when he'd put the sack over her, when he'd muffled all other sights. When it suddenly became his dark voice that was the only sound she could hear.

She'd been livid and embarrassed, but he'd repeated the word twice. Had he truly meant it as a way out? If so, then her treacherous heart had ignored it.

Her heart couldn't have wanted him; it was her body, her desire. Hadn't it already betrayed her in the cave and by the river? That had been merely lust, wasn't it?

Yet even now she gazed at the breadth of his shoulders, down to his hands, to his fingers tapping on his thigh as he watched her. As she watched him. Did he know what that did to her? Of course he did!

'You tricked me!'

'Tricked? When I've been patiently waiting for you to come to the only conclusion there could be between us?' He ran a hand through his hair. 'On my oath, you are so stubborn.'

His words. His demand that she say please to be released. Was it true? Could it be she wanted him? If so…did she doubt him…or herself?

No, she was right. She had to be. Otherwise, she'd learnt nothing from Alan's betrayal.

'And you're not just as stubborn as I? What

other man would pursue one woman his entire life? How much rejection do you want heaped on you? Never did I look at you. Not when you became a man, not when Alan claimed me. Now you'll be humiliated when I return to my family, unclaimed by you again even though you stole me in front of everyone.'

If a man could become a sword and a predator, a storm that ravaged the earth and the mountain defying it, Camron did it all in that moment.

She'd gone too far. She knew when her words had sunk into him as certainly as any sword in his gut. She felt the give of his emotions like flesh, the tip hitting his impenetrable pride like solid bone.

One moment, two. A pause that waited. Too dark to determine his emotions, too deathly still to gauge his reaction.

Camron lunged.

Chapter Twenty

Camron wanted to laugh when Anna fled, but the meadow was small and she was stuck between trees and water. She was trapped here with him.

One, two steps, and he had her back in his arms. Her eyes narrowed, her lips pressed together, but she didn't fight him, didn't struggle, though something close to battle blood coursed in his veins.

Unclaimed by him?

They were as good as married. Neither her father nor their laird would allow him to truss her up in front of witnesses and take her somewhere private, on Beltane moreover, and not make it official afterwards. But he wanted more than formalities and clan certainties. He wanted everything.

Thus, his position was to persuade her to want this marriage. The only issue was his stubborn lass was back inside her fortress on the ramparts she'd built and was busy lobbing flaming stones at him.

This was no longer a siege or negotiation. Once entrenched, the enemy had no path to manoeuvre, so she was attempting to fell him where he stood, with whatever was left in her arsenal.

She'd meant to hurt him with that jibe. Perhaps his younger self would have felt it, but he knew what a weak parry it was.

She'd started to listen to his words. To believe that he genuinely didn't remember the bet for a bride. To believe the years of him wanting her meant more than a drunken moment of weakness.

This was his Anna listening to him, and beginning to doubt herself. Her walls were crumbling.

He hated that more words needed to be said for he knew they'd hurt, but he wouldn't give up. He'd hold true for them. To ease the upcoming pain he'd inflict, he kissed her.

Cold tight lips, stiff frame fighting the press against him. As he intended, this kiss wasn't a crushing of lips, a melding of their breaths. This kiss was a brief tap. A butterfly would have felt more substantial.

Then he pulled his kiss away.

She blinked, a bemused fire in her eyes. 'Release me.'

'No.' He wasn't holding her tightly. She could break free, but she stood. Staring at him with eyes that were too dark to be blue, with a face he'd memorised a thousand times and yet he still stared because he always discovered something new.

Because he didn't want to look anywhere else.

Another press of lips, no more than the last, a different angle, a different intent. His arms holding her firmly, but she could still break away, his every silent thought towards her telling her she could say *please* but wasn't doing so. All she had to do was say it, and he'd step away.

Not for ever. No, he'd given her that chance only once. He wouldn't give it again now when they were alone in the meadow, and he could feel the stone in her fortress begin to crack.

Her body more pliant, her eyes wide, but her brow still furrowed in confusion. She gripped his arms, pushing away a little more this time. So he gave her that space, only to take one of her hands. Rub his fingers against the tips of hers.

She yanked that hand back, so he clasped the other and brought that one to his lips, for his kiss, for a taste. Welcomed her shocked gasp.

'Parsley,' he said.

'Give me my hand,' she said unevenly.

He licked around the tip, tasted the bright green on another. 'I've missed your green fingers.'

Her hand trembled, fluttered, but was held so softly in his a sigh could break their hold.

'What are you on about?' she said. Her words, her voice, that bit different. 'You're mad.'

'You like parsley, and so do I. The garden's run rampant, and I love that you're doing everything you can to pluck it.'

'Let go of me,' she said weakly.

Never.

Her eyes narrowed on him. 'Please.'

He released her immediately and stepped back. Cold night air, wet now with mist. There would be much dew on that May morning. But there was no light, only darkness which he felt to his bones.

He'd thought himself in control, his touch gentle when it came to her. Yet, his breath came fast and ragged through his lungs; his stance was widened to brace himself against the desire raging through him.

Her eyes darted from his brow to his toes, then back up again. He wished he was bare to her, but in this dim light did it matter?

He *was* bare, vulnerable to her despite the clothing he wore. She could leave now. Take the horse, and ride away. He'd follow her and have this argument another day. Anna didn't move.

'I said words to you,' she said.

All true. Only a little of the biting frustration

and anger was still in her words, in her stance. But he knew it wasn't his kisses or his touch that had softened her; it was her own words, her own fears. They still had far to go.

'Hurtful words, angry words, so your response is to kiss me?' she continued.

Oh, she was behind that fortress, but she didn't realise it was nothing but stones at her feet. Still she stood tall to face him. Brave, proud woman that she was.

'You said those words to me, and yet you stand before me?' he said.

'I don't understand you.'

'Yes, you do. I'm waiting for your apology.'

Brows had gone up, her mouth agape.

'I've been patient, and I've waited. But not one moment more. I'm done. I let you have your freedom. Let you have Alan to find your happiness.'

A quick breath, her expression flashing with pain. It would hurt to mention that bastard now when she had no stones to hide behind.

'Let me?' Brows drawn together, her chin raised.

'But you never found your for ever happiness with him, did you?' he said. 'No, you wouldn't because it wasn't with me.'

She looked to argue, but as stubborn as she

was, so was he. 'You are mine. You have always been mine. Now say it.'

Hands on her hips, then off, then back again. Her agitation at his words was enjoyable as was her stabbing her finger towards him. 'You *let me*…and I'm *yours*? I am not some possession that needs to ask anyone for permission. And you want me to say I'm yours?'

'No, I want you to say you apologise because you didn't intend to say those words to me.'

'For—' She stumbled over her words as she realised what he wanted the apology for. A softening of her expression before another flash of anger, of hurt, and she turned to get on the horse.

'I'll never apologise!'

Words could wait. He scooped her up, her momentary shock stilling her, so he kissed her cheek, her forehead. The tip of her nose. He continued even when her fists pummelled his shoulders, his arms. Even when she kicked him, he kissed the top of her head, her ear.

'Please!' she spit out.

This time he almost dropped her until she found her footing.

Pulling on her skirts to straighten them, she sneered, 'You should have never given me that word.'

'It was a gift I could take back,' he said, expecting the umbrage to stiffen her shoulders. When it came, he continued. 'But I won't, and you know why. Because I'm not him. I mean and do what I say. Because you care for me as much as I do you, you won't say it again.'

Victorious expression, she pursed her lips to announce the first consonant—

He kissed her again.

But this time it was different. He made it different. His hands cradling her face, holding her still for the slanting of his mouth, the parting of his lips. He pressed, her lips no longer cold, but soft as he licked the seam. She let out a whimper, and her hands clasped his arms. Her fingertips dug in; would she pull his touch away?

He groaned as she slid her hands upwards. He shivered when he realised they were chilled. Shuddered as she threaded trembling fingers through his hair at the nape. She tasted just like he remembered, like his every wish and want. Unsaid words between them still, more to be resolved.

But this…this she allowed and, after their time apart, they needed it. He needed it after he'd stopped her storming to her sister. A pull that became insistent when he'd mounted his horse and held her as they rode here.

He hated the Beltane sack as much as he knew

she would. He'd used it merely as a distraction, as a prop to block her.

Why had he done that, why had he put any more layers between them? He'd always meant to carry her off, and had imagined a thousand times her swung over his shoulder with her curves in the air.

He'd imagined his hand caressing her bottom. Like he did now, trailing his hands down her back, to the perfect plump swell of it, pressing in with his fingers.

His blood thundered through him. It became a chant, an exulting reminder this was Anna, his Anna, who stood on her toes and aligned their bodies together.

No terrible sack separating them, only thin clothing that his body begged to rend, to get to the woman he kissed as if she was his very air, his life.

She kissed him back just as passionately. The little sounds she made, her hips shifted enticingly, shot lust from every point they touched, to every part that was waiting for her.

On a groan he broke the kiss, and eased his hold.

He gave a deep sigh, then rested his forehead on hers. 'Can you at least trust in this?'

'What *is* this?'

'It isn't just a *release*,' he teased.

Resting her head on his chest, she groaned. 'Who are you? I thought you were the reasonable twin, not the unpredictable twin.'

'Both,' he said. 'I'm both…because of you. To woo you isn't easy. I had to strategise, to plan with your family and trap you.'

'I noticed that,' she said dryly.

'Would you believe me if I said your stubbornness inspired the sack?' he said. 'And when I surprise you, you have this startled yet pleased expression I'd do anything for.'

Her brows drew down, but a challenging gleam lit her eye. 'When you released me from the sack…was my expression pleased then?'

It was full of fire, he was pleased to see. 'How could I fault my plan when it brought you here.'

She frowned. Fiercely. 'Don't you dare do it again.'

He laughed. To bring just that determined expression back to her face, he would certainly think of another way to do it again. Reasonable, sensible Anna, it seemed, could be encouraged to be more free, and he along with her. It was a revelation.

Just when he thought he could not want her in his life any more than he already did, she proved to him that he could.

'Why me?' she asked, the fierceness in her gaze and voice dimmed.

'It was more than how I saw you as a child,' he said. 'It's how you are so dedicated to those you love. Fierce even in the face of adversity and pain. It's in a thousand ways that matter and don't because it truly all comes down to how we feel when we are together.'

Such simple words to say, and yet so profound the easing in her blue eyes was as she gazed up at him. How could she not know her worth when he'd hurdled himself over every obstacle she could have thrown at him?

'But, Anna, the true question you should ask yourself is why me?' he said. 'It can be as simple as that. You keep throwing obstacles in front of us, making it all about why I might want you, but is there actually a reason you want me?'

A strange hiccup of sound quickly doused by her broken laugh. 'I'm afraid to answer that.'

'Is it more than my watching you?'

He felt her head nod against his heart. 'Why did you fight me so hard, then?'

'The bet—' She pushed at his chest. When he stepped back, she walked to the edge of the trees circling the meadow. It became harder to see her, to hear her breath and steps. In rushed the sound of the water tumbling over rocks and the muted cheers of celebrations.

When she still didn't talk and he couldn't stand the distance any longer, he walked to her again, wrapped his arms around her and pressed his front to her back. When he nipped the back of her neck, her breath hitched.

'This can't be true,' she whispered.

'It's true. This is all true. How you feel when we're like this is right. You in my arms is exactly where you are meant to be.'

Awash with the scent of her, her curves pressed into the cradle of his hips, the desire simmering between them flared again. He'd had no thought of how difficult this would be when he'd brought her here. He thought they'd talk, argue, then the kisses would occur, but he should have known better.

Anna was stubborn, and she had been hurt. Her pride was at stake, but so was her heart. She wouldn't give anything away so easily.

'I trusted you that night at the river, and when we swam together the next day.'

'And you were right to.' He curled his fingers into the giving flesh around her hips, notched her more firmly against him. Felt himself pulse, and knew she felt it, too, when she stilled.

Coaxing his Anna from her fortress, from her

doubts, would likely send him to an early grave. Pushing her hair over her shoulder, he pressed lingering kisses down the lines of her neck. Wanting so much more than this small expanse of skin available to him but revering the sensitivity he'd discovered there all the same.

Heart pounding in his chest, lust pumping hard in his blood, he slid his hands from her hips across her thighs and back up to her belly.

Anna dropped her head to her chest, so he repeated the circling movement with everything in him craving to wrench up her skirts and dip his hands between her thighs.

Not yet. Stilling his hands again at her waist, he stepped back. 'I know you're still a little cross with me about the bet.'

A lowering of brows. 'Don't tell me what I'm feeling.'

'I'll tell you what I'm feeling.' He bent his head and nipped her neck. Her body shuddered, and he smiled against her goose pimples.

Another held moment, on a soft pant. She'd yet to say the word for him to release her, and his blood ran thicker.

'Tell me you know the bet isn't the reason I'm here with you now,' he rasped. 'That it was nothing but a game between brothers.'

A hitch to her breath. 'Didn't feel like nothing to me.'

He lifted his head. 'Nothing is a game when it comes to you because what we have is true. The bet wasn't anything other than an excuse to finally be with you.'

Still nothing whilst the wind played with her black tresses, and her blue eyes showed nothing but darkness. Just the faintest outline of her as she looked at him, and he her.

Until again this woman brought him to the brink of who he was, and he demanded impatiently:

'Tell me, Anna.'

Chapter Twenty-One

Tell him what?

Anna stared at the man she could barely see. She'd walked to the edge of the trees and they doused out any of the moon's light. This time of night had clouds and mist and there were no stars. Other than them being outside again, it wasn't anything like the last time they were together at night. She knew that now.

There was an anticipation already between them.

And as cross as she was with him for getting her here all trussed up in a sack, and all that she distrusted between them still, some of her earlier fears just weren't realised. There wasn't any doubt now about what he felt for her, or about him wanting her. And despite everything, she wanted him still. Barely a touch, a kiss, from him and everything in her became right.

How did she feel about him? Had one bet truly made the difference between him being a good man and not? No. She didn't like it, but if she hadn't been… If it wasn't for Alan, the silly bet wouldn't have mattered. Should he have known better not to make it?

Yes, but then, she wasn't ever supposed to have known. She'd overheard it. But there lay another issue… Would he have ever told her himself?

There was only one answer for that…yes, Camron was not a liar. If it came up later, they may have even laughed about it. The reasons here were complex, but if she untangled them all it actually became quite simple.

Did she want Camron despite all the past anguish with Alan? Could she see him as her husband? Because despite the years separating them, besides her constantly telling him she was too old for him, she did not doubt him being attracted to her. It went far beyond the years leading to this moment. It was in the way he held her right now.

She laid her hand on his cheek, felt the rough stubble there, his warm skin, his heated breath. Rubbing her thumb along the line of his jaw, she felt his hard swallow, his skipping pulse.

What did she believe?

That she'd need to talk in depth to Beileag and Murdag about keeping secrets and her lack of trust. Certainly, she'd need to apologise to Hamilton, who had gracefully eschewed any of her advances. Possibly Seoc, too, for reasons she couldn't recall here, but no doubt existed. After all, she'd changed over this last year and not necessarily for the benefit of her friendships or her own soul.

She'd thought of all these matters before, but if she dwelled on them too long she became more emotions than words. When the pain became too much, she'd avoid trying to make sense of her feelings. Now this man, all he wanted to do was talk. Yet this…

How could his skin feel so soft on her fingertips, but also prickle her palms? How could his eyes, already dark in colour, further obscured because of the night, seem darker the longer they looked at her? Why did she feel that gaze physically, as it roved from her dishevelled hair, over the curve of her ear and down her pointed jaw to her lips that were too large for her face?

Why was it when he was watching her, there were times when it felt he could see right through to her soul?

It wasn't fair Camron knew how sensitive her skin was on her neck, that he kept touching and kissing, and nipping it like she was some treat. It wasn't sensible that she liked it.

She was intrigued and curious of him, and it wasn't simply because he tapped those capable fingers against one imposing thigh, the same rhythm, the same pace, and she still didn't know why.

It was also because he'd demanded she answer his question, and he still waited. How could one man be part patient…part not? Who rushed toward battle, and then held out for a siege? She felt like she was held prisoner, with nothing but his arms and that gaze. If she was surrounded by her friends and family, she could distract herself.

Yet in this solitary meadow, they were suspended in a time apart from everyone; is that why he'd borne her here to be by this lapping water?

That he wanted her for himself wasn't a surprise, even though he was full of those. She knew this man, and yet didn't. He confused her, though she should know everything about him.

'Anna…' he rasped when she trailed her fingertip to the shell of his ear. An innocent touch, but maybe not with her on her toes and pressed against him to reach such a vulnerable spot.

'Simply seeing if you have any weak spots,' she said. If this was a siege, shouldn't she test the enemy's strengths?

He leaned into her touch, at the same time he took his arms and hands away as if it was suddenly too much to return her touch. 'All of me is weak when it comes to you.'

Oh, he had her then, completely, her heart, her body. One honest revealing of vulnerability and she was defenceless against him. And it was true, everything in her knew it as he held still for her touch, and for her eyes to see everything he showed her.

It took much to stay true to her course. 'Not when you place bets on wedding me.'

'Won't happen again,' he rumbled.

So quick with his answers, his neck was warm, inviting. Was he sensitive there too? Palm against soft skin, she tugged on his nape. Obliging her, he bent his head.

She kissed him there, tasted the salt, tasted him as his skin prickled and she laughed, causing the hairs to raise more.

'Anna,' he groaned.

'I didn't like the bet, Camron,' she said against his ear.

'Won't happen again.' His repeated words and breath rushed out.

There was a trap with those words. He wouldn't bet on her again because he already considered them married, not that it was wrong. He exhaled roughly as she licked his lobe and asked again. 'Camron?'

'Won't happen when it comes to you,' he replied with a raspy voice. 'Can't say a bet won't happen otherwise.'

It was good enough because the more she kissed and touched him, the less important words seemed to be.

'All these touches, all these demands.' He turned his head, whispered against her neck. 'What of my demands of you?'

The harsh rasp of his stubble, the heat of his breath and the fact he still did not touch her, that it was she who was angling towards him as if seeking him out, wasn't fair, just or sensible, and yet she didn't want to stop.

'What about me?' she said, her voice gone soft. 'You think I'll apologise?'

'I do,' he said.

His expression and words were certain; he expected her to believe him. When his lips met hers, and his arms wrapped around her middle, lifting her up to meet him, she almost believed him.

But it wasn't until her own arms went around his neck, and Camron bent his head to somehow deepen the kiss to something insistent and unrelenting, that she knew she was in real trouble.

Especially when he made some low rumbling in his chest she felt against her very core. She suspected only some of that was caused by her legs being wrapped around his waist, but mostly she knew it was him.

'Anna, we have more to say,' he said again. Was this the patient Camron or the one who was *done*?

A bent knee, the world tilted on its axis, her back against the now dew-wet ground, was her answer. But she didn't care about the ground, she only cared that he followed her down onto it.

He laughed low, then groaned in approval as she tugged at his tunic again until it was up and over his head. Ran her hands over the muscles there and smiled in delight at his reaction.

He watched her face, then her hands. 'They're cold.'

'That's not all they are,' she said. They felt... greedy.

She was on the ground, underneath him, everything in her wanting this man whose arms were locked on either side of her head.

His brown hair was tousled from her fingers, a strain was around his eyes, his lips looked swollen, damp from their kisses, his jaw relaxed. But his skin...she wanted to touch all of it.

Half dark from the night, half gleaming from their ride here, from the mist, from the tautness between them. Like he toiled to keep his need in check.

She felt the same. Failing to still her caresses like he had, she said, 'I know there are words involved, but do we have to say them all now?'

A pained smile, a sharp huff of breath. 'No, we'll say the other words later.'

Her eyes tracing her fingertips which traced his collarbone, down the hard middle of his chest, then back and forth in between the lines of his stomach…like the water that had fallen across him that sunny day at the pond weeks ago. And then there was the cave, where he'd been wrapped only in the smallest blanket…

'I can't get that day out of my head.'

'What day?' Adjusting his weight, he began his own slow exploration of her body, but her clothes were still on. Why were her clothes on?

'In the cave when you watched my shadows,' she said with a sigh.

'You stretched for me, didn't you?' His eyes roved along with his hand that went down to her wrist, then back up again.

'I believe so.' She reached around his waist, spanned her hands to feel the firm cords in his back.

'You look surprised by that. Here, let me re-mind you why you might have done it.' Pulling the fabric of her gown so it fell loose about her, he added his kiss to his touch.

He was being so gentle with her, so intent. How could this man be both? How could she have been so cross with him mere moments ago and now couldn't keep her hands off him?

'Tell me this is true,' she blurted.

He jerked up to stare at her. Something more impassioned than lust burned in those eyes now. 'As true as anything I can provide, and farther than any promise.'

Oh.

Sliding her hands back to his front, she placed her hands there. The steady beat of his heart increased, as did his hard breaths. On a groan, his head bowed, and he stroked his nose, his chin, his lips, across every bare inch of her, all the while his hands dug deep in her skirts and dragged them roughly up with one tug, then another.

'Anna.' He said her name as if it contained every letter of the alphabet and was weighted with syllables.

'Tell me you won't throw me in a sack again,' she said, rolling her hips from side to side to help him with the fabric, each time brushing against him in some broken undulated rhythm he began to match with his own.

He kissed up her jaw, nibbled on her ear as she had done. 'But it was so funny when you got cross and chucked all those flowers at me.'

'What?' she said with a pout.

A quick chuckle. 'Did you intend to throw so many fertility blossoms at me?'

'I was mad, and they were there! And they weren't fertility blossoms!' She'd done it because she was trying to get a reaction out of him. She was—

'Lift your hips,' he instructed.

She did and they both looked down at where her legs were wide and his were in between.

'Kiss me,' she said.

'If we do this now, you're mine for ever. Do you understand?'

'No more words Camron.' She wanted this... and this man wanted her. 'Just kisses.'

Grappling at his shoulders, she laid her hand on the back of his neck and pulled him towards her to kiss him.

She'd missed him. Missed this. How could she have missed this?

One night was all they'd had at the water's edge. One night of him looking down at her like she was his world. Why had she ignored the truth all this time?

'I'll give you want you want, what we both need, lass.'

And he did until they were both lost to the pleasure of seeking hands, and ardent kisses capturing needful sounds. Until her hips wouldn't still and her breath wouldn't catch. All of it so slow she ended up begging.

Suddenly he stopped altogether, stopped everything.

Parted lips, ragged breath. 'What now?'

'You said the word.'

What was he talking about? 'No more words. We decided this; you said there would be words later.'

He dropped his head to the crook of her neck, and kissed it. 'You didn't mean what you said.'

She didn't know what she'd said, but he was looking at her so closely, so minutely, she felt compelled to answer. To lay her hand on his cheek and reassure him. 'I didn't mean it. I want this.'

Grabbing her hips, he flipped over onto his back, until she sat on his lap. Looking down at his compelling smile and arched brow, she said, 'What's this?'

'This is us beginning again,' he answered, pulling her down into a kiss.

And they did. Like this she felt part of him and the sky, the meadow surrounding them, and then—Suddenly, all gone again. All movement, all pleasure, all feeling, halted.

Because Camron had grabbed her hips and yanked her up. Held her firmly until she blinked, and fully understood that yes, once again, he'd stopped.

'What are you—'

'You're saying the word again, Anna.' Camron hissed in a breath. 'I promised you I would stop if you said it.'

She wasn't saying words. She'd been babbling, begging him for more, for...

Begging.

Resting her hands on his chest, she leaned over until her face was even with his. 'You wouldn't dare.'

'I gave you a word, Anna, and I mean to keep mine.'

So much pleasure given slowly when she wanted more until she was begging and babbling one word: please. *Please.* And thus in saying it... he'd released her.

'For ever?' Because she couldn't contain what she said while there was so much pleasure being given and received. How could she? This was a trap deeper than a sack of flowers during Beltane's fires. 'This can't be for ever. You did this on purpose?'

'I told you I would.'

She looked between them, but her collapsed skirts covered everything.

'You can't hold me accountable for saying… that. During…that,' she complained.

'I want you to hold me accountable.' He released his hold and she sat back down, feeling him shift underneath her, lacking the connection like before. *Wanting* them to be connected.

'What are you saying?'

'I'm saying I love you. So trust me,' he said.

Her heart flooded, quietened. She believed him. 'I do.'

How could she not when he'd stopped because she'd said a word she was hardly conscious of saying? What had it cost for him to stop them both? Because he'd given her a word to use, and then he'd kept his own?

He sat up, his arms going around her until she was flipped underneath him again, until he joined them. Until he pressed their hands above her head and entwined their fingers. Until he stopped denying them both and made fervent promises as Anna kissed him over and over, muffling any words beneath their pleasure.

Chapter Twenty-Two

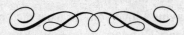

Collapsing beside Anna, Camron took the breaths long denied him, but breathing didn't stop his heart from pounding, or his limbs from shaking. After her fighting him at every step, she was finally his and he was hers utterly.

This time he was certain of her. What more needed to be said? He almost groaned when he remembered. Because it wasn't something, it was *someone*, he didn't want to talk of.

But she believed him now, and it may have had something to do with all their moments they'd shared to get to this point, from shadows in caves, and being naked in ponds and throwing flowers from a sack. But he hadn't seen that wide-eyed open look he knew was in there until he'd given her a word to use against him…and then he'd used it against himself.

To prove she was safe with him, and that he

was honest and true. That she could fully trust him, and she did. Or said she did, and he hoped it was strong enough because he didn't know how else to prove it to her, and he was about to test that trust.

Propping up on one arm, and pulling her skirts back over her legs, he said, 'We're married. Tell me we're married.'

'You dragged me away on Beltane's Night in front of all of Clan Graham, Camron. We're married. Or as good as.'

Not good enough. He wanted the words. She turned to her side, but tucked her arm under her head, and his heart squeezed tight in his chest.

Gentle smile. Soft eyes. Years apart, and this was his reward?

'My hair has grey in it, you know,' she said quietly.

'I do know.' His fingers found one lone strand, pulled it free and gently played with the end.

'When your eyes get all heavy-lidded like that, I don't know how to respond.'

'What are my eyes telling you?' he asked.

She looked between their entwined bodies. Stroked a hand along his thigh, and his body responded. He dropped her lone tress and grabbed that wrist.

She laughed and wriggled out of his hold. 'That this will happen again.'

It was already happening, but not before he had the words that bound her to him. He wouldn't make that mistake again or give her any distance or time to separate them.

'Marry me, Anna.' He said it with a bite. No romance, no softness full of longing. He said it like a command that would determine the rest of their lives.

Her stroking fingertips, trailing dangerously closer to where he was rapidly recovering, and that soft knowing smile, almost had him kissing her, but this time he grabbed her wrist and then entwined their fingers, and he held her hand to his thigh.

When he didn't budge, she gave a perfect pout. 'I've married you in front of all my clan. I, alone, here in this clearing and on Graham land...accept this marriage.'

Unbounded joy encapsulated him, and he squeezed those fingers. Her eyes sheened with tears as his did. But they weren't done yet. Untangling himself from her, he pulled on his tunic. 'Get dressed so we can get the rest out of the way.'

'The rest? We're not leaving, are we?'

The day was about to begin. No more sounds from any celebration were about, but there were people still waiting for sunrise, for the first dew of summer.

He had ridden far enough last night to get away from all of them, but that didn't mean someone who was more sober than the others wouldn't soon be up and about. This woman was his by clan, by word and by heart. He'd told her he loved her and…she hadn't said it back.

'We're about to have our first fight as a married couple and I'd prefer to do it clothed in case you want to put me in a sack and bare my arse in the air.'

Camron's tone was teasing, and there was so much warmth in his eyes it was like feeling sunshine upon her bare skin.

But his words weren't right. They couldn't be right. He'd said he loved her, demanded she admit they were married. All should be right between them.

Anna felt different. Better. As if she'd been one Anna and was now another. Maybe when she was elderly she'd understand how she'd accepted Camron as a husband after he threw her over his shoulder in front of everyone. Until then, she'd blame his kisses, his words. Especially since she now knew his sensitive spots as well, and could explore them all and find even more later.

'We've argued for weeks,' she said.

He jumped up, and held out his hand for her to take, which she did.

Her gown was more off than on, and she stumbled on the voluminous fabric whilst he held her firm until she was steady.

'This isn't about the bet, or your flirting with Hamilton.' He wrapped his braies and snatched up his breeches.

'Hamilton?' She cinched her laces.

Shaking his head, he fastened his breeches. 'If we don't say what we need to now, this'll all come up again.'

'You said you wouldn't make bets with your brother again.'

His mouth curved. Oh, she liked Camron's almost smiles.

'We're done marrying for both of us. And you know full well my brother and I will make bets. But this is about misunderstandings.'

Holding up her arms, she inspected her laces on each side. 'I won't be hiding in orchards or bathing alone in the moonlight again.'

'How about not avoiding me when you're cross with me?' he said pointedly.

Something fluttered in her chest, all the worse because it surprised her, and Camron seemed to know it as his steady brown eyes took in everything.

Why did he look that way, when he'd been so good to her? Did he doubt her acceptance of their marriage?

'I can assure you had I heard the entire conversation about that bet, I likely wouldn't have... done what I did.'

'Are you certain?' He gathered her hair and pulled it out of her dress so it could fall down her back. 'It doesn't do to hold on to anger.'

This was ridiculous. They were married. She was...she was happy. Or at least more so than she'd been before. She definitely wasn't miserable.

Of course, she felt like she should be more happy, but then again, how much time had they spent together like this? Probably not enough, which was a simple explanation for why she might not be bursting with happiness.

Another indication, no doubt, of how cold she had truly become. Yet, shouldn't she be feeling... more free?

When she glanced at Camron, she was surprised by his frown. One she could clearly see. 'The sun's coming out.'

'It's early enough not many should be awake yet,' he said.

'How far away are we?'

He pursed his lips. 'No one will know what we did here.'

Why…why did he say that?

'I went too fast with you.' Stepping up to her, he cupped her jaw. His hand was warm, or maybe she was chilled. When had she become so cold?

'I'm the one who…' She stopped. Could she say this? 'I'm the one who wanted to be with you that night by the river. I told you there were enough words.'

'Not enough,' he said. 'Not enough.'

She sensed some note of scorn in his tone that was aimed at himself that she didn't understand.

'I touch you and that's all I can think of doing, and all I want between us is nothing and no one else.' He rubbed his thumb across her cheek, his expression almost reverent, still full of longing. As if this was the first time he touched her, or rather…as if he still wasn't touching her when she felt his warmth down to the backs of her heels.

He had her, so why this look? What had happened between him holding her, and now?

'A few more words, a bit more understanding. We're almost there,' he said encouragingly. Softly. She wasn't certain he'd said those words for her, or for him. 'And remember, you trust me.'

'We're married,' she reminded him.

'We are, but I won't have you avoiding me, and you will do it again if we don't sort this out.'

She wouldn't. Why would she? Camron was always there, always. She should have known his feelings for her went deeper. That it was about more than him watching her. Because hadn't hers been more than that as well?

She was simply happy, that was all. Happy and not used to it. There wasn't anything to read in his solemn expression. So why did his words feel like a warning, and why did the fluttering in her heart feel cornered again?

Chapter Twenty-Three

'**W**hy would I avoid you?' She wasn't getting it. Fully dressed, still standing close to him he could touch her. But he didn't. He knew what was coming, and she did not. 'We've just talked about that.'

Camron didn't want to lose her, and now that she was trying to trust again, he feared it was too soon, but then, he was done waiting.

'But we didn't talk about the Maclean.'

There was the look he never wanted to see again. Like she'd received a strike that wasn't expected.

Shaking her head, keeping her eyes on him, she walked backwards. One step. Two. 'I don't want to talk of him now.'

'We're talking about him. We need to talk about him because we've ignored this conversation for far too long,' he said. 'But he's the one who always makes you run away from me…avoid me when things go wrong.'

'We ran him off last year. He's gone now.'

He held still, though he wanted to gather her in his arms. This conversation wasn't easy for him either. 'He might as well still be standing right before us. He's been between us ever since he arrived.'

She shook her head, gave a broken smile and then a humourless laugh. 'Jealousy? I didn't expect this now when there's no reason for it. He means nothing.'

Jealous? He was once, until he knew that what Anna and Alan had wasn't true. Not like this was.

'He did once mean something to you. He made you happy.'

She looked around the meadow. 'What?'

'Alan made you happy,' he said. 'Your father knows it too. If he didn't, do you believe either Padrig or myself would have stepped back?'

'You talked to my father about Alan?' She looked behind her. 'I want to return to the clan.'

'You know it's true,' Camron pressed. 'Your father told you of his regrets, too, didn't he?'

She rounded on him. 'And if he did? I was the fool who believed in a false happiness.'

'You were happy. His love was false, that was all.'

'Why do you want to argue about this?'

'Because I don't want you to mistrust every feeling of happiness or love between us. Because those are real. The Maclean was wrong.'

She blinked, looked down and then rubbed her face. There were tears there that quickly dried.

'You were happy and I wanted you to have that happiness.'

'I wasn't happy. I couldn't have been happy.'

Did she doubt all her feelings? 'Then tell me the truth. If I had declared myself in front of you, the clan and Maclean back then, would you have denounced him and gone with me?'

She just stared at him because the truth was, she wouldn't have. Because her feelings for Alan at the time *were* real.

'I am enraged that he hurt you, but I can never regret that Alan made you happy. My only regret is that I did not declare myself before you ever met him, but I was only just eighteen,' he said. 'I can do nothing about the years between us. I can no more change my time of birth than I can change this war that we both know we're on the brink of.'

'Why are you talking of this?'

'Trust.'

'I do trust you,' she said.

'I know you trust me because you didn't say please. I wrapped you up in that sack, but you stayed in there because you knew underneath all that I was good for you. The bet didn't matter; you let me touch you, kiss you, because you trusted me. Now I want you to trust yourself.'

'Myself?' She let out some words he couldn't hear because she was walking further away from him.

If he moved now to hold her still, their words might fail again. He had to hope he'd said enough.

'You need to trust yourself and your feelings for me. It was never about the bet; it was the fact we're happy together and you can't trust yourself with it. So you blamed the bet.'

She looked up at light casting the night from black to grey. She was right there, and yet still seemed so very far away. Could he convince her?

'You said it was enough,' she said quietly. 'You said that if I went part way, you would go the rest.'

That was the night at the river, before she'd avoided him after hearing about the bet, and even then— 'I lied.'

That look. Part hurt, part strength. So brave, her fire wasn't gone. He could convince her.

'I lied,' he repeated. 'I want everything from you. I've always wanted everything. I was willing to coax you for just scraps if that's what it took to get to this point with you.'

'You got more than—'

'Don't,' he said with a vehemence he didn't think he'd ever heard in himself, or that she'd listen to. But she did. She stayed. Her eyes steady. What could she see but a man talking and walking across an empty meadow?

'You've had me most of my life. Even if you only ever held my hand, I could not love you more. You've honoured me with what we've already shared. You placed your trust in me when you barely feel it for yourself. Do you know what a wonder that is?'

Such a pause, with no sounds, only breaths across the mist, and the night fading completely. 'What makes you think, then, that I want any of this,' she whispered.

That was simple. 'You're not running away from me now.'

'Because if I made a dash to the horse, you'd only stop me.'

'Anna—'

She hugged herself and paced. For every step, though, he saw her coming closer.

'There's something inside me that…' she started. 'I wanted to run away. I did ask to leave earlier.'

A few more steps towards him, and he felt himself leaning towards her. 'But you're still here, listening to me. If I could harm the Maclean in any way and know it would make a difference, Anna, I would. But he was in your life for two years, and somehow he's taken up another one as well.'

Anna believed him. Everything he said she could hear in her heart. This was beyond trust if that was even possible. She trusted her family, and her friends, but this was like making a huge leap and knowing he'd catch her.

'He hurt me badly when he broke my trust,' she said. 'He was just so *convincing*.'

'He convinced us all,' he said gently. 'We were all taken in. Seoc, that oak tree of a man, was lied to as well. Should we all doubt ourselves? Or worse, you doubt us?'

She didn't doubt him. And…why did she not think of Seoc, who had been Alan's closest friend? Seoc had believed Alan just as much as she had. He'd apologised to her once and she'd dismissed it because Alan's treachery wasn't his fault.

Yet still she'd held herself accountable. She'd mistrusted herself. This man before her knew it. Was patiently waiting for her to hear it, to listen, to *know*.

What she did know was that if she'd come up with this thought herself, she'd have doubted it. But coming from him? With his goodness, his strength, his honour and kindness? How could she doubt a man who'd so patiently taught her brother to swim?

A few more steps, and she could almost see the emotions in his eyes. What she saw there she could believe. And because she could believe, she truly heard the words he said.

'You can be convincing too.'

He smiled quick. 'And charming? Tell me I'm more charming than he was.'

A startled laugh, and she slapped her palm over her mouth. How could he make her laugh right now?

'How about handsome, then,' he added quickly as if he wanted more of her laughter.

She dropped her hand. 'Your brother is better looking.'

He struck his chest, then made some dismissive sound. 'You make a terrible liar.'

She'd lied to herself pretty convincingly. Her heart beat a little stronger now, though, didn't it? Although still a little sore, there was no longer any fluttering inside for her to run away from or avoid. It didn't mind this pain of remembering the Maclean.

She had been happy. He had been the liar.

And then because she'd mixed up the two, she'd almost ruined her life. It was a revelation. 'You I know I can trust.'

Camron closed his eyes at her words, but then opened them again, and she swore they were a lighter brown so full of light they were. 'Out of all the men in your life, you have known me during all my stages. You know that you can trust what I say.'

So serious when she could tease too. 'No, my trusting you had more to do with one word… *please*. That was a very mean game you played, Camron of Clan Graham.'

'It almost killed me,' he confessed.

'Good. Don't do it again.'

'I just wanted to show you I'm not him. That you can always trust my word.'

'I know.' Two words could not be more truthfully said.

'Do you now?' he said. 'I didn't mean anything by the bet. I'd never play games with you in truth, never play so recklessly with your heart. Not when I need your truth like I need to breathe. Not when I need your heart so that mine beats.'

'I know,' she repeated. What more could she say? He kept looking as if he wanted to convince her of something.

'I'm me, Anna.'

She knew that, and she wanted to prove to him that she understood. Practically running the rest of the way, she pressed against him. His unique scent, his warmth, should have soothed her, but her heart was hammering in her chest, and she couldn't quite catch her breath.

A prickling began on her skin and her palms grew damp. What was this? It was a tiny, almost insignificant sensation, but it hurt. It was the way he was gazing at her, the fact he stood so still, and so strong and certain. A storm could batter the earth, but she knew she'd still be sheltered because Camron wasn't moving.

He wasn't moving. He was still here. With. Her.

Her eyes welled. Was she going to cry? Why? The man she loved was before her, standing tall, baring all of himself to her. Showing her his love.

And that dark splinter, the one that had for years stabbed at her heart, was suddenly yanked out until she felt blessed, stunning relief. A hitch to her breath, one tear down her cheek that he gently brushed away.

'There it goes,' he said softly. As if her finally letting go of her past, her pain, was something awe-inspiring. When it was him who had shown her the way.

His gaze a heavy thing between them, she felt like holding it tighter to her chest.

'You *love* me,' she said.

He cupped her jaw. 'That is what this is.'

'This?'

'What you feel for me too.'

His body pressed back into hers, his calloused thumb gently caressing her skin. She felt…everything. 'I won't avoid you or run away again.'

'I can see that now.' He brushed away the tears trailing down her cheeks. 'I haven't seen your eyes look this bright for far too long. I've missed seeing you like this.'

Because he'd watched her even before Alan had come to Graham land. Watched and waited until he was old enough for her. Then he'd wanted her happy, so he'd stepped back and let her go. Except she was a fool and what she'd thought was love… wasn't. This was love. If all those years ago she had just looked over her shoulder at Camron, she would have seen it.

Or would she have? She didn't know, didn't care. She was seeing it all now. So much of it showed in his eyes, she burst with it. Except he was wrong about her own gaze.

'You've never seen my eyes look this way before,' she said.

His brow drew in, and he rubbed his thumb against her lip as if he asked a question.

'Because these are the eyes of a woman truly in love,' she said with all the certainty in her soul.

Camron dropped his hand so he could wrap his arms around her waist and crush her to him.

His smile was great and wide. A smile he hadn't given when she'd told him she'd marry him. Not even then.

Only now. And she knew, he had had doubts too. Yet, he had taken the chance for them. Risked everything to be here.

She wanted to thank every ray of the moon for all eternity for making him notice her. She placed her hand on his cheek to capture that grin, and he softly closed his eyes, leaned his cheek into her palm.

This was joy, that's what she felt when she was with him. Nothing marred her heart. She was his completely, just as he was hers.

'I'm still older than you are,' she teased.

His eyes snapped open and a challenge began in his gaze.

'These aren't only laugh lines at the corners of my eyes,' she continued.

Then his lips quirked at the corner, and a brow rose.

Oh, she liked this teasing, this holding back with loads of anticipation. But he'd promised her more if they said a few more words, and they'd said them. She wanted it all now, and for some ridiculous reason he liked her talking about her flaws.

'There will only be more grey in my hair tomorrow,' she added.

His fingers were suddenly at her ties, his palms rucking up her dress, as he lifted her. She braced herself on his forearms which bunched underneath her fingertips.

'And I haven't seen your freckles yet.'

He stilled. 'My...what?'

'On your shoulders, you have this smattering of freckles I want to taste, and I can't see them in the dark.'

'It's not dark now.' He rumbled against her throat before he kissed her there, and she shivered.

It was well and proper daytime now. She couldn't see any of the Graham clan, but she could hear people stirring. 'Don't you dare.'

'But you mentioned my body parts, and how am I not to reply?' He lowered his voice even more. 'Don't you need another release, Anna lass?'

Slapping her hand on his mouth, she said the only word she should have told him long ago and would be saying to him for all time.

'Yes.'

Epilogue

Graham land, one week later

'When's the last time he asked you to swing him?' Murdag said.

Anna swivelled her gaze to where Murdag watched Lachie and the other boys play with a ball. Anna didn't understand the objective of the game given someone kicked it to another who picked it up and then pelted someone else with it.

There was yelling, laughter, shouts and screams. It looked painful and she waited, knowing any moment one of them was going to have a broken nose or black eye. But Lachie was there, running with them all.

He was also the worst of them all at pelting someone with the hard sphere.

'For ever ago it seems he was begging to play

with us,' Anna said. 'But recently I think he's caught a few tricks from you.'

'As if you're not competitive!' Murdag scoffed, then grinned. 'Can I say I'm proud of him?'

Anna grinned as well, but she knew her eyes sheened with tears too. Whatever changes Lachie had been through she had Camron to thank for them. Oh, her brother had certainly wanted to learn to swim, but Camron had an encouraging way to teach Lachie to stand on his own two feet, so to speak.

Then Hamilton would knock him down again and they'd all laugh. Oddly, it seemed to work. Lachie was gaining in confidence every day.

'Are you and Seoc going to be that happy soon?' she asked slyly.

'Bite your tongue!' Wide-eyed, Murdag looked around her. 'What if someone hears you?'

'Like Seoc?'

'For the thousandth time, we are not together.'

It certainly seemed that way according to the clan gossip, but Anna couldn't see it. They didn't glance at each other in any specific way... or maybe they were better at covering their attraction. What did she know?

Still, it was fun to poke at her sister. 'You two *are* spending time together.'

'That's only because Beileag and Hamilton are

all...' Murdag made a grumpy face. 'And you and Camron are all...' Murdag made kissing noises.

Laughing, Anna tried to slap her hand over her sister's mouth, but Murdag kept weaving until they were making more noise than the boys.

'What are you on about?' Camron walked up. Hamilton was just behind him.

Murdag's smile disappeared as she straightened with a scowl. 'I'll think I'll go now.'

Camron's brow went up, and Anna shrugged with a *what can you do?*

Hamilton rubbed his hands over his face.

Camron slapped his hand on his brother's shoulder. 'I can't help you with this one.'

'How come you got it so right?' Hamilton said plaintively. 'We're supposed to be twins.'

'I told you I don't feel like a twin,' Camron pointed out.

'Yeah, I know I'm just a brother.' Hamilton frowned. 'But shouldn't brothers share some traits?'

'You look alike to me,' Anna said.

'No, we don't.' Camron put his arm around her waist. Anna leaned into him, her hand on his chest. He did this much and often. 'I always knew what I wanted.'

If there were hours or minutes in the day Camron wasn't reaching for her, she couldn't recall them. Oh, but her heart always matched his.

'You could throw a sack over Beileag, and hoist her over your shoulder,' Camron offered.

Hamilton clapped his hands as if shaking or scaring off that suggestion. 'If I thought it would work I would.'

'Don't you dare,' Anna said. 'Beileag isn't as forgiving as me, and she's stronger than she appears.'

'With knife skills,' Camron added.

Anna was glad Beileag's secret whittling skills weren't so secret any more, and she also wasn't surprised Hamilton was in love with her. She'd always teased Beileag that her skill would captivate someone.

But unlike her torturing Seoc and Murdag, the fun and laughter would have to wait when it came to her friend. She'd thought Camron had secrets, but apparently Hamilton was even worse.

Murdag, who claimed she didn't know, was cross with Hamilton because Beileag was hurt. For all her mischief, her sister was loyal to those she loved.

'Why aren't you walking off in loyalty to Beileag, then?' Hamilton said.

'Oh, don't you think I don't want to,' she said.

'But my husband insists you'll make things right with her.'

'And you believe him?'

'This time around,' she said.

'Always!' Camron smiled.

Hamilton looked to them both. 'At least I can say one good thing came out of that first drunken night we were here.'

'I was always going to win her,' Camron said smugly, and Anna couldn't disagree.

Even without the bet, he was hers and she was his.

Still, it had been a brave or foolish bet between twin brothers to gain a bride by the end of the summer. One brother had got the woman whom he'd always loved, but the other, while pursuing the one he'd thought he wanted, had fallen in love with her best friend instead.

It was like those great tales of lovers…if Hamilton and Beileag would actually talk to each other. Anna wasn't certain of what was happening, and Beileag refused to tell her much. But she couldn't imagine whatever Hamilton did to her was done maliciously. Naive or maybe because she was in love herself, but Anna wished them well.

'There's time,' she said.

'Not when Wallace calls us to war,' Hamilton said. 'It's going to be soon.'

Anna closed her eyes to that, and could feel Camron's grip tighten on her.

'Autumn at the earliest,' Camron said.

'We'll have to prepare before then,' Hamilton said. 'Already there are—'

'I know already,' Anna interrupted, not wanting to hear any more of it.

'Forgive me,' Hamilton said penitently.

'If you're so careless with your words, brother, you won't be able to woo.'

Anna tilted her head up to her husband. 'You were always patient with words, but your deeds...'

Camron laughed, and so did Hamilton.

'Yeah, that sack idea I didn't see coming,' Hamilton said through his laughter.

'Neither did I!' Anna grinned. 'If I were you, I'd become friends with Murdag. Maybe she could help you secure Beileag.'

'She'd rather have my balls,' Hamilton said.

True. 'But she might help you after that.'

Hamilton sobered. 'I hurt her. The kindest, most beautiful woman in all of Clan Graham and I was blind.'

'Say you're sorry.'

'It's not good enough. I'm thinking on leaving early.'

Anna was shocked, but Camron's stance didn't change. Had he already guessed?

'Never thought a challenge would get the best of you,' Camron murmured.

Hamilton's gaze snapped to his brother's. 'The odds were in your favour to win at least once in our lifetime…but especially this time.'

Camron tensed and Anna looked to him and back to his brother.

'What do you mean by that?' she said.

Looking wary, Hamilton licked his lips, but kept quiet.

Camron loosened his arm around her, and Anna stood on her own. The day was warm, the sun was bright, and yet the side of her body pressed close to Camron's was now cold.

She didn't like that one bit.

'It was a lousy bet, but you never had to stick to it,' Camron pointed out. 'I was drunk, and already longing for this woman. It was fine to insist that I kept to the bet when it never truly meant anything to you.'

Hamilton's face flushed and he looked to the side. 'It could have. Murdag's beautiful.'

'Of course she is,' Anna said. She was her sister. 'But two mischief makers were never going to work together.'

Hamilton threw back his head and exhaled roughly.

Camron cursed. 'Apologise to Beileag about the bet, tell her it was all my fault. Tell her it was always her you wanted, and you were just humouring me. Tell her—'

'There was never a bet!' Hamilton dropped his chin.

Anna couldn't possibly have heard correctly. 'What?'

Camron was utterly still.

Hamilton half laughed, half groaned as he stared at his brother. His eyes were beseeching, but there was a curve to his lips as if he shared the jest.

She could guarantee Camron didn't know about this jest.

'This isn't funny,' Anna said.

'There was never a bet,' Hamilton repeated. 'It was to get you to stop waiting to go after Anna, and I—'

'Tricked me,' Camron said.

He didn't sound as cross as she would have been; he didn't sound like anything at all. In fact, everything about him could have simply been as flat as the wall of their home behind him.

'You were drunk and barely able to speak, let alone think of making a challenge between us.'

Some sound came out of her new husband; it was feral and scary. It was also…close to stifled laughter. But that couldn't be right either, could it? She was furious.

Wasn't she?

All the events in the weeks leading up to their marriage happened because of that bet. She'd tortured, denied, refused to have anything to do with Camron because of that game between the twins.

If Camron hadn't stolen her on Beltane, she could still be denying him. Wouldn't she? Camron's beginning expression made her doubt.

'I could always out-drink you,' Hamilton added.

'You could not; it was my suggestion to go for the mead,' Camron said immediately. 'You couldn't even feel your legs the next day.'

'I could always feel my legs,' Hamilton argued.

Camron half growled…if a growl could hold bemusement. 'I could—'

'You could do loads of things to me, but a fact is a fact. You did not make that bet. I was tired of listening to you mope around wanting this woman, who you wouldn't pursue for one reason or another. I realised I'd have to go months listening to it until we were called away again, so I made one more challenge.'

'A false challenge.'

'One you took up as truth, so what makes that false?' Hamilton said archly. 'And I was half in lust with Murdag's new—'

'That's my sister!' Anna said.

'She'd better get rid of that one chemise, then,' Hamilton said.

'You looked!'

Camron rolled his eyes at her. 'Everyone looked.'

Anna cheeks burned on her sister's behalf.

'When you woke the next day, leaning against me and wobbling about like an infant, I knew what to do,' Hamilton said.

'By lying to your brother,' she said. 'About a bet that never happened.'

Hamilton shrugged. 'You have to admit when it comes to strategising and planning, I'm the better twin.'

She would admit to no such thing. Of all the tricks to play! It worked all right in the end, but what if it hadn't? Poor Camron could have suffered if she'd refused him for a bet that never existed!

She wasn't about to blame herself for any of it. She was just as innocent in this as Camron. Hamilton was to blame simply for being so sneaky.

And why was Camron not dragging his brother

off to punch him a couple of times? It's what the brothers always did.

'And now we all know which twin could handle ale and Seoc's mead,' Hamilton laughed bitterly.

Camron stayed quiet as Hamilton's expression never truly changed; it was just his eyes got a little more broken, his victorious expression diminishing.

Oh, this was why her husband wasn't saying anything. His brother was heartbroken, and falling apart before them.

'I was drunk and never made the bet?' Camron said as if he was simply comprehending it just then.

'You can thank me later.' Hamilton rubbed his face and choked on a laugh. 'I did it all for a chance to gloat over my matchmaking skills, and my sweet, knife-wielding lass was the one who got hurt.'

Anna knew how this ended. Hamilton didn't do it for fun, he did it so that his brother kept to the challenge to win…her. Then she was so stubborn the whole courtship became a hardship for everyone.

'Hamilton,' she said, with no clue how to apologise.

Hamilton gave her a weak smile. 'Oh, I loved

how you made my brother earn you. It was I who was too foolish to realise what was happening right before me. To me.'

He looked over his shoulder. 'I believe I'll leave early for Wallace's call. That would be best. Until then...'

'Brother,' Camron said.

'I'm the better brother,' Hamilton interrupted. 'Can we agree I won this one?'

With pressed lips, Camron nodded, and with a wave, Hamilton pivoted down the little path that led to the far outer field.

It was too early to light a fire, but there were others out there, possibly Seoc, who were already on watch. It would be that way for months if not years to come.

Would they be safe? Oh, she couldn't think on that. She also couldn't wrap her head around Hamilton's confession.

'Not a bet?' Anna turned to Camron. 'Is that possible?'

Eyes still dimmed, Camron grinned, then laughed.

'It's not funny,' she said, her mouth curving as well. Because despite all of it, it was.

'At any time he could have said it, and the bastard let me believe I'm the one who made it,' he said. 'He had to know my patience couldn't last.'

She couldn't be cross with his comment. 'It was up to me to fray your patience.'

He grinned down at her. 'And you did it so well.'

'He was probably in too deep with Murdag and Beileag to get out of it.'

'We all may be in too deep, soon.' Camron's smile fell. 'We will be called away. But I'll stay as long as I can.'

'I know,' she said. He had been called away since he came of age. Now was no different... except there was war looming.

So much time she'd wasted fighting him when they could have been lying in more moonlit fields. She may have threatened never to go to the water's edge at night, but Camron always tricked and coaxed her into changing her mind.

'I'll bed you well until then.' He put his arm around her again and pulled her close. 'Love you more than that.'

She loved how he changed the topic. 'Can't I do the same?'

'You did this morning,' he said. 'There I was sleeping all innocently when my wife wakes me.'

'You did not complain,' she said.

'Until I realised how early in the morning it was.'

That was true. Years together in one clan, and

there was much they were discovering about each other.

They both fell silent. Standing at their threshold and gazing around at the clan, Anna leaned into her Camron. Hamilton had already turned behind some homes. Lachie and the boys had completely disappeared. Her father, she could see, was standing next to the widow Una, who had been mourning the loss of her husband for two years now.

'Not a bet,' Camron repeated.

'That was a jest to end all jests,' she said, then had a thought. 'But Beileag, though conflicted on holding the secret, had believed you made it, and thus let you be tortured with my ire because of it.'

Camron tilted his head, his thumb rubbing against her hip. 'True, Beileag was not pleased to know Hamilton lied about all of the bet for him to marry Murdag, and me you, and could have resolved our issues if he had confessed.'

Beileag was a good and loyal friend. 'There were other matters keeping us apart.'

'There could be other reasons keeping them apart as well,' Camron said.

'Knowing your brother, no doubt there are,' she said. 'Her mother being one of them.'

'As if your friend hadn't hidden a few secrets of her own.'

She broke away from him, to face him. If he was going to argue who was better or more loyal, she'd win every time. 'Whittling some pieces of wood—'

'You believe that's all Beileag's been hiding and playing?' Camron asked.

'Of course, what else—' Anna stopped herself. She'd been so preoccupied with Camron she didn't truly know what Beileag was up to. That will have to be remedied later with her friend.

'And here I've been lecturing on protecting her from men,' she chuckled. 'I'm blaming you on my lack of observations.'

'Can we blame the moonlight?'

She could blame the moon.

'And the sack,' he added.

'Please don't mention the sack.'

It didn't take long for the entire clan to know of the sack and their running off. Her father had simply clasped their hands upon their return, and she'd told him she'd agreed to the marriage.

There was much for them to do. But it wasn't laundry day, and the council meetings wouldn't begin for hours yet. It was just them. Together. As it was always supposed to be.

She wondered about the others. Would Hamilton and Beileag have their happily ever after too? And what were Murdag and Seoc up to?

'He'll be back,' Camron said. 'Will she wait for him?'

'I don't believe so,' Anna said, that bit of hope rising in her chest. She almost wanted to laugh because both the twins were blind when it came to love. Something she knew all too much of. At least this time around she could show Camron.

'I. Don't. Think. So,' she said again, this time tapping Camron on the chest none too lightly until he understood too. Beileag had changed. Sweet she may be, but she wasn't waiting any more either.

Camron grinned. She loved that grin. 'Oh, that'll be interesting.'

'It will, won't it?' she agreed. 'Now why are you doing that?'

Turning his gaze from his retreating brother to her, Camron asked, 'What?'

'You're tapping your hand again.'

Camron looked down at his right hand on his thigh, as if he didn't know what he was about.

Then he smiled his half-knowing smile. 'You're not in my arms, Anna.'

What was he talking about? 'That's because we were talking of your hands.'

'We are?'

'Camron!'

'I could tell you one secret.' A light wind tossed

Camron's brown hair over his cheek while the sun lit up his beautiful brown eyes. How could she have ever resisted this man?

'My fingers, my tapping. I know what it is now.'

'What? Because you've been doing it for ever, since you were child. That hand against your thigh…'

'Look a little higher, lass.'

She did, and Camron smirked.

'We need to get inside,' she said quickly.

'Not until you know my secret,' he said too smugly.

'I'm not as patient as you.'

'It's you,' he said bluntly, like he was impatient as well. 'Whenever I look at you, somehow my fingers begin to tap.'

He was speaking far too slowly for what she wanted. Secrets were fine, but when Camron's eyes turned more intent, how was she to care what words he was speaking?

'Why?' she asked with as much teasing as she could. 'Because I make you nervous? Because *calm* Camron becomes a bit agitated?'

His eyes promised retribution. 'No, I was counting. Always counting my breaths…my heartbeats…until I could hold you like this.'

He lunged, but Anna knew what he was about and held still for him.

Swinging her up into his arms, Camron crossed their threshold, and kicked the door until it slammed behind them.

'So, you won't keep tapping now that you have me?' she said.

Shaking his head slowly, Camron walked to their room. 'Oh, no, Anna, my lass. I'll always be counting my moments with you.'

* * * * *

MILLS & BOON ®

Coming next month

LORD MARTIN'S SCANDALOUS BLUESTOCKING
Elizabeth Rolls

He was going to kiss her.

Her pulse kicked up, every nerve dancing under her skin.

Once before, just the once, he had kissed her. In the gig as they drove out to Isleworth on the day he had given her the betrothal ring. Only once, and now he was going to kiss her again.

On the cheek.

She didn't want a chaste peck on the cheek. She couldn't have what she did want – but she could have more than a kiss on the cheek. Even if they were standing on a public street outside a tavern.

With his lips a breath away from her cheek she turned, oh so slightly, and their lips met. Worlds stilled, his mouth on hers unmoving… Time shimmered in stasis – then a sound, half sigh, half groan, broke from him and his lips moved in the sweetest of dances, a large gloved hand cradling her cheek as she caught the rhythm and the kiss deepened. For a heart shaking moment that encompassed an all-too-short eternity every planet, star and moon aligned. Everything danced together for one brief measure. Then, as sweetly and gently as it had begun, it was over.

He stepped back, his hand lingering on her cheek and jaw.

"Kit, I'm sorry. I should not –"

"You didn't."

Slowly she lifted her hand to trace with one gloved finger the edge of his lower lip. "I did. If I can't have what I once wanted, at least I could have that."

Continue reading
LORD MARTIN'S SCANDALOUS BLUESTOCKING
Elizabeth Rolls

Available next month
www.millsandboon.co.uk

MILLS & BOON

THE HEART OF ROMANCE

A ROMANCE FOR EVERY READER

MODERN

Prepare to be swept off your feet by sophisticated, sexy and seductive heroes, in some of the world's most glamourous and romant locations, where power and passion collide.

HISTORICAL

Escape with historical heroes from time gone by. Whether your passion for wicked Regency Rakes, muscled Vikings or rugged Highlanders, aw the romance of the past.

MEDICAL

Set your pulse racing with dedicated, delectable doctors in the high-pre sure world of medicine, where emotions run high and passion, comfort love are the best medicine.

True Love

Celebrate true love with tender stories of heartfelt romance, from the rush of falling in love to the joy a new baby can bring, and a focus on emotional heart of a relationship.

Desire

Indulge in secrets and scandal, intense drama and plenty of sizzling ho action with powerful and passionate heroes who have it all: wealth, stat good looks…everything but the right woman.

HEROES

Experience all the excitement of a gripping thriller, with an intense ro mance at its heart. Resourceful, true-to-life women and strong, fearless face danger and desire - a killer combination!

To see which titles are coming soon, please visit

millsandboon.co.uk/nextmonth